…an combines …
…ophobia and rural gothic with
our contemporary politics of …ollective outrage, call-out culture and
alternative facts … A fast-paced, engaging novel'
*Times Literary Supplement*

'An extraordinary and disquieting work of imagination, and as original as any novel I've read in recent memory … *The Last Good Man* makes visible the dark matter of our troubled zeitgeist, and the cruelty that animates moral community' Rob Doyle

'A clean, crackling novel … McMullan updates Nathaniel Hawthorne's *The Scarlet Letter* to today's sanctimonious climate … An arresting debut about medieval justice that has plenty to say about the dangers of moral puritanism' *Metro*

'An essential and commanding slice of folk horror – a wholly successful exercise in world-building that straddles an uncomfortable line between reality and fantasy' *Lunate*

'A terrific conceit, unsettling and strange' *Locus*

'An earthy, gripping piece … A serious and seriously good book' *NB Magazine*

'McMullan's skill truly lies in his prose…a startling and evocative tale' *Set the Tape*

'An unsettling and startling work of literary imagination … A shocking but compulsive read' *ON Magazine*

'*A Scarlet Letter* for our times ... Zamyatin's *We* meets *Lord of the Flies* meets de Tocqueville meets cancel culture meets spite and malice meets Jesus. Should words be power? Justice or mercy? What price rage?' Margaret Atwood

'A gruesome, disenchanted debut ... McMullen explores the well-worn conceits of provincial claustro[illegible]

'Brilliantly eerie' *Dystopia Junkie*

'Eerie and atmospheric' *Sunday Post*

**THOMAS McMULLAN** is a writer, critic and journalist whose work has appeared in publications including the *Guardian, Observer, Times Literary Supplement, Frieze* and BBC News, and has been published in *3:AM Magazine, Lighthouse and Best British Short Stories*. He has worked with visual artists, game studios and theatre companies in London, Amsterdam, Beijing and Los Angeles. He lives in London.

@thomas_mac

# THE LAST GOOD MAN

THOMAS McMULLAN

BLOOMSBURY PUBLISHING
LONDON • OXFORD • NEW YORK • NEW DELHI • SYDNEY

BLOOMSBURY PUBLISHING
Bloomsbury Publishing Plc
50 Bedford Square, London, WC1B 3DP, UK
29 Earlsfort Terrace, Dublin 2, Ireland

BLOOMSBURY, BLOOMSBURY PUBLISHING and the
Diana logo are trademarks of Bloomsbury Publishing Plc

First published in Great Britain 2020
This edition published 2021

Copyright © Thomas McMullan, 2020

Thomas McMullan has asserted his right under the Copyright, Designs and
Patents Act, 1988, to be identified as Author of this work

All rights reserved. No part of this publication may be reproduced or transmitted
in any form or by any means, electronic or mechanical, including photocopying,
recording, or any information storage or retrieval system, without prior permission in
writing from the publishers

A catalogue record for this book is available from the British Library

ISBN: PB: 978-1-5266-0927-4; EBOOK: 978-1-5266-0926-7

2 4 6 8 10 9 7 5 3 1

Typeset by Integra Software Services, Pvt. Ltd.
Printed and bound in Great Britain by CPI Group (UK) Ltd,
Croydon CR0 4YY

To find out more about our authors and books visit www.bloomsbury.com
and sign up for our newsletters

*For Lydia*

# Prologue

THERE IS GOODNESS AND kindness in the first signs of spring. The moss is merciful. The mushrooms are affectionate. You are unseen, Duncan Peck assures himself. The ground will not give you up. He cocks his revolver and puts his finger on the trigger, aiming through the mist in case the group catches sight of him.

The air is thick enough to turn stones to men and men to stone. Careful not to step on anything that will make a noise, Peck edges towards the sound of heavy breathing, towards a black mark that becomes a body in the bog. It moves like a wounded animal, clawing at the dirt. There is a whistle behind him. Another responds. A man is stuck in the mire, his face bloody, the whites of his eyes overrun. When another whistle sounds, closer than the last, Peck backs away. You are blameless, he tells himself. You are good. He kneels behind a boulder and watches them come.

There are men and women, all in raincoats, black, blue and purple, hoods gleaming. In their wake a figure pushes a wheelbarrow that squeaks across the uneven earth. The half-submerged man is crying for them not to come any closer. He bucks and tries to free himself, pulling his leg with both hands. A group of what must be twenty people surrounds him. In their hands are metal bars and scaffolding poles.

'Geoff Sharpe, you're not to lie there feeling sorry for yourself,' a voice sounds. 'Please don't cause any more trouble than you've already managed.'

Peck knows that voice, just as he knows the head it comes out of. If he is going to stand upright now is the time, but the moment rises and passes. Better to wait until they have a moment to be properly re-acquainted, Peck reasons, watching as the group gags the man's mouth with cloth. Better to wait until we're alone, better to ask then what all of this is about. And so he stays out of view as James Hale pulls the injured man to his feet, freeing his leg from the bog, supporting the man's weight with his own shoulder. His movements are calm and measured. If Peck had only just stumbled on the scene, he would have mistaken it for kindness.

But there is no gratitude in the hunted man's eyes, and no colour in his cheeks as his hands and feet are bound in rope, as he is lifted into the wheelbarrow and carted off at the head of an ordered procession.

# One

PECK HAD HEARD RUMOURS about a village on the moor. A village living in the shadow of an enormous wall. Something that had never been completed. He hadn't believed it. No one had a tidy description and there'd been nothing in what he'd heard to give it substance. No more substance than the dozens of other stories he'd pocketed about clusters of homes spread up the countryside, beyond, where the accounts grew hoary and it felt like lives were knocked loose from the earth. He'd heard about farmhouses populated by bones and communities of agony by the old motorways. There were those who made the journey to see these things for themselves, but they never came back. James Hale had left four years ago and had never come back.

Now that he can see it, the wall is hard to argue against. It is a cleaver in a hill, the only landmark in sight, but its purpose is obscure. There's no sign of anything approaching its size, no castles for it to bridge, no towers for it to encircle. It is the shape of a landscape painting, at least the size of a large barn. Perhaps it is bigger than that. Perhaps it is smaller. Without a point of reference there's little certainty. All he knows is that it looms on the horizon, incongruous in right angles from the moorland dimming around his boots. What restorations were made before the builders abandoned their work? What grand plans for the middle of nowhere? He moves towards it, careful to keep to a faint track worn into the grass. He fears that if he drifts too far from the path he will fall into a bog, but tries not to dwell on the treacherous ground as he moves step by step in the direction of the wall.

Whatever its purpose, Peck feels his shoulders relax. Against the moor, the wall is something to anchor him. A point of focus, not too different from the buildings near his mother's home in the city. Relatable. Man-made. He finds it hard to take his eyes off it as the sun sets. Compared to the woods, the bogland, the brambles that snagged his trousers and nipped his forearms, it is singular. An indisputable sign of human activity, which is a double-edged sword in the wake of what he saw only a few hours before. The man carted off in a wheelbarrow. Strange and violent deeds. Perhaps he should have called out to his cousin when he saw him. What had he to be so scared of? No matter. No mind. He will see him soon, and once more they will be together, in this new place, but with the old jokes and old times that will prop Peck up, stop him falling any farther. In no time at all they will be reunited.

Even from a distance, Peck recognises the shapes of houses and needs to catch his breath at the sight of smoke from their chimneys. The wall is out of place on the moor but the slab is stranger still beside the roofs and the church steeple. It is a backdrop for a play, all so unreal, and for a moment he wonders if the wall and the village are tricks of tiredness. When he wipes his eyes the lids feel puffy. With an effort, Peck follows the line made by the wheelbarrow used to carry the bound man. There are clods of grass like babies' heads, hard to see as the light fades, and if he twists his ankle he will not be able to limp back to the city. The grass is soft, he assures himself. The ground is gracious. But the sun's ringing glow is ringing low, almost gone completely. The track from the wheelbarrow is becoming harder to follow, and Peck is worried if he looks away from the wall he will stray and sink from view.

---

Tim Lawrence wants to get rid of an old ironing board. *The next meeting for the Rosy Singers will take place on Wednesday, not Tuesday.* <u>A pair of glasses have been found outside the church hall, left lens smashed.</u> **Has anyone seen a tabby cat that responds to Pudding?** *If you have a leak in your roof, don't try to fix it yourself. Really. Don't. Contact Peter Morris, as it is his job.* IT IS FRANCIS DOYLE'S BIRTHDAY PARTY ON SUNDAY AND A SMALL DO WILL BE DONE IN THE FAMILY GARDEN.

The notes and missives make Peck stop in his tracks. Instead of heading straight into the village, he has skirted its western side to climb the hill that hosts the wall. In the dark he notices there are tall ladders leaning against its surface and a number of scaffolding platforms stored to one side. There is no sign of any kind of entry into the edifice, which on closer inspection is only a few feet deep. Its foundations must run into the ground for it not to fall to the wind. The thought of steel beneath his feet only makes it bigger in his mind, as if the wall's roots were drawing water from the earth. And for what? There is no indication that it has an interior, or that it was planned as one side of a building. It is too short to be a border. Too flat to be a prison. It has no windows, he notes. Not a single one.

**Sally Lester has a spare wardrobe for collection.** *Sarah Twine will be teaching piano.*

The darkness makes it hard to see everything that has been written, but Peck's torch helps him to illuminate the plastered pieces of paper that cover the surface. He glances behind him to the lights of the houses, imagines the people below, all their lives entangled. They must greet each other by name, he ventures. They must know each other well, to write these messages out in the open. Strange to think of, that familiarity. Not unpleasant. A little daunting. They must say good morning and good evening as they pass each other on the street, he thinks, and feels a weight in his stomach at how unbelievable that seems to him now. One piece of paper advertises an after-school club, which means they must have a school. There is a flyer that mentions a public gathering on the green.

He takes in each message, reads the events, the names, but the sentences drift towards anonymity the higher Peck's gaze travels, the larger the writing grows. The hardest to reach posters, close to the very top of the wall, are painted in almost uniform capital letters, callous and kindred, as if each and every one of them has come from the same brush. He peers from beneath his hood at the words scrawled in red paint.

> GEOFF SHARPE DOESN'T CUT THE MEAT GOOD. I SAW GEOFF SHARPE STEALING SLIVERS. NOBODY LIKES GEOFF SHARPE. I HOPE GEOFF SHARPE DIES.

He feels his throat tighten, considers turning back, or at the very least waiting until daylight before pressing forwards into the village. He looks to the moorland. No point turning back. To what? To a death in the dark. A ditch between stones, somewhere in the woods? No, he decides. It is merciless. Best to keep one foot in front of the other. That's all there is to it. Keep moving forwards, away from the wall and towards the lights of the village.

A lone crow pushes away from the very top of the wall, kicks open its wings, swoops down over the land. Peck catches its black body spark above his head, before it vanishes amongst the gloom. He is not Geoff Sharpe. That much he is sure of. If he were Geoff Sharpe then he'd be changing course without a second thought, but there's nothing of Geoff Sharpe about him. His dirty arms are Peck, his thin legs are Peck, his bony chest Peck and his dirty beard Peck. The man in the bog, that was Geoff Sharpe, and from the looks of things they got him.

---

The tooth in the back of Peck's mouth has grown so loose that he's surprised it's still there at all. If he presses his tongue against the inner side he can push it to what he imagines is forty-five degrees. It has been days since he made the effort to look in a mirror but the tooth was black then and there is no reason it wouldn't be black still. It doesn't hurt. Whatever nerve once inhabited it has given up the ghost. His thoughts towards the dead tooth change all the time. Yesterday it was a mollusc. Earlier it was a stone.

He imagines it is a door knocker as he makes his way past the houses on the south-west edge of the village, onto a tarmac road that takes him farther from the wall, down towards cottages with custard-cream walls. Some of the houses are thatched, some tiled, many look like they belong to a different century entirely. He puts his torch away to keep from attracting unwanted attention. Farther in there are terraced houses with clipped hedges outside their well-ordered porches. Peck spots a football nestled beside a bush, a hopscotch drawn in chalk on the pavement. There is a bicycle leant up against a blue metal gate. All so tranquil, so different from the city. A gust blows and a windchime gossips. A few drops fall on his forehead and he lifts his hood before the rain comes. When it does it comes heavy, pattering over Peck's crown as he treads farther along the road. He is neck-deep in the burly smell of earth. There is a cage made of chicken wire, with a brood of roosters sheltered beneath a wooden roof. A woman and a young girl rush alongside each other on the road, caught out by the sudden downpour.

During his final days in the city, Peck had come to realise that the widening hole would swallow him. It would only be a matter of time before the warehouses ran out completely, and when that happened he would have no choice. In those last weeks he would grip his revolver in his pocket, ears open to the nervous crackle around him. There were more fights, more fires lit. If Hale's letter had come to him a month earlier he might have burnt it. But it came just as the end had become undeniable. He knew it was time for a change. Fresh air. There were well-known reports of settled places farther along the coast, where a few days' walk could take you somewhere with enough empty houses to claim one as your own. Many had gone that way. Perhaps they'd made a life for themselves by the sea. Dartmoor was a different matter. Landlocked and fruitless. The woods were dark, the mires deadly. You did not go walking on moorland without a path to follow. Hale had said as much in his letter. *Beware the bogs that grow deeper in the rain.*

Peck would see men and women come looking for trade, offering wool and honey for boots and pens. Their small processions to the warehouses were proof of life outside, the soil under their fingernails a mark of existences spent close to the ground. It was one of these souls who had given him the letter, pressed into his palm in return for a glass tumbler. The smell on the man's coat had been heavy with rain. Where had he come from? Difficult to say. It was hard to tell one of these people from another. They exited the city with sacks of objects thrown over their shoulders, walked the motorway, but where they went, Peck did not know. The letter was an invitation. An apology for leaving. An explanation that it was nothing personal. Why didn't Peck come and see what Hale had made for himself? He would find a cousin's hospitality if he did.

Along what must be the village's northern limits there is a cluster of detached bungalows, adrift in the deluge, and this is where Peck finds the home he is looking for. Number 29. *As you trek along the hills you will see a grey mark that will not disappear unless you turn away. Do not turn away. There are deep marshes that have grown deeper with the rain. The grass grows over the bog and it is not until your foot falls in the earth that you will realise the danger you are in.*

The bungalow crouches in the dark. The candlelight within is dim. Unblinking.

Before approaching the front door, Peck moves with slow steps around the corner of the building, to a window with its curtain parted enough for him to scope out what awaits. From this angle he can see the other side of the front door, as well as a simple living room. He spies flags tied between wooden rafters, shelves and cupboards, a plant in a pot, a wooden table, and there is the man: James Hale, bent over a plate, picking at a pork chop and a sickly lump of cheese. This man, who had one time been as good as a brother to him.

There is a knock at the door, which is a surprise, seeing as Peck is nowhere near it. Has he been followed on his journey through the village? Through the window Peck sees his cousin with a knife and fork, unmoving. There is another knock. Peck grips the revolver in his pocket and rocks his dead tooth back and forth. Whoever has been knocking turns the handle and pushes the door, which is apparently unlocked. Instead of opening it all the way, the figure squeezes its face through a small gap.

'I don't want to intrude,' a voice tumbles. 'It's just that my shoes are soaked.'

'Where are Charlotte and Maisie?' Hale asks.

'Taking care of the chickens. The rain came through the coop and almost drowned the little ones. I came over to see if he'd arrived today. He hasn't, has he?'

'Have you seen him?'

'No, ha.'

'Then he hasn't come.'

The stranger's laughter is like a pebble in a shoe. 'I thought you might've hidden him away,' he presses, squeezing his face farther through the gap. It is hard for Peck to make out his features, but he seems to be wearing a drenched raincoat. 'I thought you might have kept him from, ha, prying neighbours.'

'Are you prying, Peter?'

'No, no. I didn't mean me. Sarah and Judy. Some of the others. A few have been talking about him, that's all. You know how it is. A natural thing to be curious.'

Hale stands from his table. He is abundant, built like a horse. His shoulders are square but his belly has ideas of its own. He was always big, thinks Peck, but his bulk has grown in the years since Peck last laid eyes on him. 'Curious my arse,' Hale spits. 'Have they been muttering?'

Peter shakes his head against the doorframe. 'They're not making judgements,' he says. 'Just inquisitive, as you'd expect. There's nothing more to it than a few questions. They want to know what he's like, which is understandable. A handsome stranger. I'd be more surprised if they *hadn't* been speaking about him.'

Hale leans on the door, his face bent to the hooded figure. 'Where did you get handsome from?' he mutters and pulls the door fully open, letting Peter spill in with a bucket-worth of water.

Now is the time. Peck pulls himself away from the pebble-dashed wall, rounding the corner of the building towards the front door. As he breaches the threshold he grips his revolver and points it forwards. Peter, coat half off, hoists his hands. His arms are lean. His hair is a shock of red. His moustache is trimmed. His cardigan is pink. The colour in his face has fallen through a sieve. 'Wh … why are you pointing that thing at me?' he trembles.

'You never really know what's on the other side of a door,' Peck replies, and when it becomes clear that there is no one else in the room he lowers the gun. 'Four years,' he states, smiling to his cousin who bounds one step, two step, three to embrace him with such momentum that he is lifted straight into the air. Peck is squeezed tight. It lasts forever, until it is over. 'So, you're looking well,' Peck ventures, slapping Hale's shoulder. 'Still bald.'

'Fatter, though,' his cousin laments, grabbing his gut. 'All this fine country living.'

'Looks like you could do with some of it.' Hale pinches Peck's arm. 'What have you been eating out there, Pecker?'

'Nothing. All the rage.'

There is a loud bark of a laugh at this, and then Hale shuts the door.

'So let's get a proper look at you,' Peck says. He moves a step back and takes in Hale's clothes. There is a white linen shirt and a grey waistcoat, woollen trousers and black boots; a far cry from his own gnarled coat and jumper. The shirt and trousers could be freshly stitched. The rest has most likely been salvaged, as has a thin gold-chain necklace that Peck can see under a loosened collar, settled above a hairy chest. Moving attention to his cousin's head, he notes his neck has grown thicker, the bags under his eyes have sunk deeper, the dome of his bald head seems broader. 'You must get cold out here in the middle of nowhere,' he says, reaching up to pat Hale's skull.

'I have a lovely woolly hat.'

'I bet you do.'

Peter, who has kept his arms raised throughout, finally lets them fall. 'James, listen, he's got a gun. If Judy is looking out her window ... You know what she's like. She'll jump to conclusions.'

'There'll be no conclusions,' says Hale.

'But we don't use guns here.' In front of Peck's eyes, Peter makes a visible effort to calm his demeanour. It is hard, so clearly repulsed is he by the mess of Peck's appearance; the mud on his cheeks and the smell coming from his boots. All the same he holds out his hand for a shake. 'I'm Peter.'

'My neighbour,' Hale clarifies.

Peck shakes the hand. Peter's grip is stiff and seems intent on being the tighter of the two.

'We don't use guns,' the neighbour repeats, subtly wiping his hand on the side of his trousers. 'We just don't believe in them.'

'What's not to believe in?'

'They might be common in the city, but not here, where we don't think only one person has the right to decide on another's, ha, life.' His nose is thrust forward, stance calcified with principle. 'If we see you with one we're supposed to kick you out. But I won't, and I'll do you the favour of not telling anyone I saw you with it, because I'm not that kind of fellow.'

'You don't say,' Peck rolls his eyes to Hale. 'What kind of fellow is he then?'

'I'm a good fellow. A good man.'

Peter is grinning now, and Peck doesn't like the look of his teeth. He fetches the damp letter from his trouser pocket and holds it up. 'There wasn't anything in here about not bringing guns.'

'Just give it to him, you wildman,' Hale snorts. 'You're only going to do yourself some damage if you hold on to it and, to be honest now, Peter's right that we're supposed to kick you out if we see you with it.'

'Chase me with metal pipes? Something like that?'

'What's that?'

'Run me down and tie me up?'

'You saw all that did you?'

'I did.'

'Well you should've come and said hello, Pecker. We could've walked you back here instead of letting you plod through the rain.'

The downpour continues beating, and for a moment it's the only sound to be heard. Peck worries about whether he's shown his hand too early, but now the words are out and there's no way to catch them back. 'Not that I'm judging,' he notes. 'More confused than anything, with that big wall you've got there and that.'

'It's an impressive sight, alright,' Hale beams, and Peck is surprised by the pride. 'We've got to take you there in the daylight. Get you to see it up close. You won't have come across anything like it. It's stunning. That's really the only word I can think of.'

'Oh yes,' Peter chips in. 'Stunning. I'll need that gun now,' he adds.

'But—'

'Just give it to him.' Hale's gone back to his plate, to a wad of pork that's swiftly chewed. 'The city's behind you. You're with us now. There's nothing to fear.'

# Two

Peck leans against a lichen-clad tree, on the edge of a large village green. The sky is milky but the threat of morning rain doesn't stop the men and women pulling their carts into place. The scent of roast chicken animates the air and there is a murmur of excitement in the trail of people making their way south from the square, to where the houses stand thin and the pigs are in their pen.

There is something warm on Peck's right hand and he realises a small boy with a muddy cheek and a blonde bowl cut has knocked a mug against his fingers. Smiling, the boy nudges at his knuckles. 'Hot cocoa,' he shouts, as if Peck is deaf, and as if that wasn't clear enough the boy tilts the mug to show the brown liquid inside. Small clumps of undissolved powder gather around the edges. Peck accepts the gift, and as soon as he does the boy pelts across the grass, back to a group of other small children who are watching the stranger in their midst. Peck looks around, at other mugs being given to other people filtering into the green, and slowly lifts the drink to his face. The steam feels good against his cheeks and he takes a tentative sip, then a gulp that finishes half the concoction; so sweet is the taste, and so distant the memory of hot cocoa that its return overtakes him. Wiping his upper lip, he waves to the children, who scream and scatter.

There are wooden stakes being driven into the ground. A woman is on her knees tying a length of rope to a hook in the grass. Within minutes there are sheets like sails of different colours, caught in the wind before the shopkeepers graft them to the frames. There are flags strung between the stalls, red, white and blue, running the perimeter towards a raised platform. The stage is a metal frame; a proscenium arch draped top and sides with heavy black cloth, its backdrop a white sheet dotted with birds that looks like it could have been taken from someone's bed. The stage is empty except for an assembly of scaffolding, a rack of poles and clasps, held at right angles.

As the villagers fill the green, the pang of food hangs above the heads of men, women and children jostling. The smell of wet earth is masked with the rich scent of pastry and a loaf of barley bread is broken into handfuls, given out in baskets to those that want a taste. Two girls flit away with full cheeks to kick a worn football back and forth, giggling at how far the other has to run. Two buckets have been set behind a rope line for people to test their accuracy with tennis balls. Numbered pieces of paper are being stuck to dented cans of lager and bottles of perfume, for reasons that elude Peck. There are people jumping in old potato sacks and children blowing into small wooden instruments, making sounds like mad birds. The chatter and laughter are overwhelming. He has known nothing like it. The coming together of these people, their curious games and competitions. It is so different from the life he has led. The mug is still warm against his palm, and he cradles its heat for a moment as if it is the only thing anchoring him against the swirl of activity. Warily he places it on a table laden with flasks, stretches his arms and walks farther into the fray, overcome by the sensation of being surrounded by these neighbours, disoriented by their actions and claustrophobic at their glances in his direction, but excited to be amongst it all. He lets himself be taken by the flow.

Away from the throng, a woman with two young sons stands bent forward near a goalpost. There are ropes around her torso that tie a circular wooden table to her back and neck. At first, Peck takes it for another game, but then he notices that the others on the green keep their distance. The legs of the table stick out in the air, and the woman grasps the curved edge behind her hip, lifting it ever so slightly to relieve the pressure. Elsewhere, a lone man close to the pig pen grimaces at the weight of a chest of drawers, tied in firm knots up and around his right shoulder. If he lets the heft carry him too far in its direction, the drawers will shift on their slides, and so he angles himself like a hunchback, furniture elevated above his head. Both of these people cast their eyes downwards, focused on their burden. The woman's sons tug at her trouser hem but she won't be moved.

Peck soon finds himself in front of the stage, still empty but for the assembly of scaffolding. He rubs his cheeks. At sunrise he'd been given the use of Hale's soap and razor, and he enjoys the sensation of his shaven skin. He feels clean, even if his trousers remain bespeckled in mud. Hale had offered him a fresh pair but they were too big, far too big, so he made do with dabbing his own with soapy water before they left. The passage through the main square had been closer to a parade than a morning stroll. Clearly the villagers had not seen a new face for some time and were keen to catch this stranger for themselves. With his cousin beside him, Peck had walked past clusters of interested eyes, tilted contemplation leading them south towards the green. When Hale had told him to wait alone as he attended to business, Peck had worried the public scrutiny would spill over into physical examination. He half expected someone to grab his arm and check his pulse.

Still, the commotion is strangely invigorating. After so many years of withering into invisibility amongst the city streets, the attention the villagers are giving him is almost intoxicating. Just as when he had walked on the moor the night before, his whole reality fixed on not twisting his ankle or sliding into a bog, so too the eyes of others make Peck feel lucid, present in his own body. He is aware of his arms, his legs, his recently scrubbed thumbs that pick against the tips of his fingers, just as he is aware of the wall looming to the west, angled as if it has one eye on the green. Beside him a bearded man is carrying a baby on his shoulders like a sack of potatoes. A group of adolescents slouch by with hands tucked deep in pockets. Two men support the arms of an old woman, helping her with utmost patience as she struggles towards the stage. Someone is whistling. Someone else is cradling a Jack Russell terrier, its rear legs gone completely, right up to the pelvis.

Each of these people gives Peck a look, but his is fixed on a young woman in a worker's apron, frizzy black hair bundled up, sleeves rolled. She catches his eye and walks over. 'You're visiting?' she asks. 'Must be. I heard you were here to see James. There was word that someone was going to be calling on him, so I take it to be you.' She looks down to his boots, lips curling like petals. 'The state of those.'

'Well—' he starts.

'And your coat. The whole thing covered, sleeve to sleeve.'

'Mud.'

'You'd hope, wouldn't you?'

'Is there going to be a play or something?' he asks, changing the subject, pointing to the scaffolding on the stage. 'Is that what's happening here?'

She twitches and stares at the cracks running in branches across the dirt of his boots. There are people around them, the spread of bodies at stalls drawing closer towards the stage. 'Deep down we're fond of one another,' she says, then nods her goodbyes and slips away.

The voices of the crowd are smoothed out as a gagged Geoff Sharpe is escorted by a pair of men, around the edge of the stage to scale a set of wooden stairs, up onto the raised platform where he is all but dragged across the boards to be bound to the scaffolding. He struggles at its clasps but soon wanes when it becomes clear he has nowhere to go. A ripple of applause runs through the crowd, then, as Hale and a group of other men and women march in his wake, wearing raincoats like they are uniforms. They are carrying metal pipes, and with an air of theatrical flair they move to stand equally on either side of the prisoner. Peck recognises the lean figure and red hair of Peter amongst their number, standing on the periphery, his chest puffed like a child's balloon.

Hale steps forward, breaking from the line of raincoats to stand at the very front of the stage, so close to the edge that the tips of his boots overhang its limit. The expression on his face is grave, and he takes his time in surveying the assembled audience before jabbing a finger downwards. 'We're here because we need something to trust in,' he bellows. 'People. Words. If we can't trust in people and words then there's no point living with people and words.'

Peck feels menaced by the sight of his cousin, standing above him as if he could at any second decide to leap. Geoff writhes at the stake, bucking against the poles that support his weight. He grunts and tries to pull down his arms or raise his legs, but the manacles are well made. '*Geoff steals slivers of beef*,' Hale shouts. '*Geoff doesn't cut the beef the way it should be cut.* Fine. The opinions have been expressed, and they've been expressed with unity. We don't write out words lightly. They've been put into action, and here we are to make sure they're satisfied.'

At this, Hale takes a step back, to Peck's relief. He makes his way to the prisoner's side, shoulders stiff with measured strength. 'We need to live by common decency,' he continues when he is ready. 'So we got up and saw all the things written about Geoff here, and there was quite a lot, wasn't there? Serious stuff. More than a simple burdening. It was decided immediately. Not a second thought. Too many sentences for a carry-on. The weight of all those things was too substantial, even for a bed on his back. So our little gang went to knock on his door. Now I don't know if someone tipped him off, but he came out swinging. He knocked one of our lot over and ran. He made his way out of the village. But ...'

Hale pauses for dramatic effect.

'We got him!'

The crowd erupts in applause. Peck doesn't clap his hands, but watches Hale on stage. This is a different man from the one who left him in the city; his hard but quiet cousin. Words are coming out of him so freely now that Peck forgets to catch them, occupied instead by studying their effect on those around, the hands so eager in their clapping, this woman's jaw as tense as balanced plates and this boy's lips squeezed like a fist. As the applause fades he turns to see a young girl at his side, her dark hair parted above a dress dotted with flowers, kept warm with a jacket that looks like it has been stitched from sheepskin. She's looking up at him, but when he waves she doesn't respond. He grins with dirty teeth and she swivels towards her mother, who strokes her hair and regards Peck with eyes that aren't unkind.

On the stage, a woman with a ponytail leans in to take the gag off the captured man's mouth. 'Do you understand why you're here?'

Geoff splutters and calls, 'Where's my brother?'

'What's that he's saying?' Hale asks the woman.

'Something about his brother.'

Geoff is shouting now, 'Gerrard, Gerrard,' over the tops of the audience's heads. Hale gestures for the woman with the ponytail to put the gag back on the man's mouth. Geoff keeps calling the name, but the words are pressed and muffled so they come out as 'Gourd, Gourd, Gourd'.

'You've been accused of stealing food,' Hale informs Geoff, and to this the prisoner violently shakes his head. 'Are you telling me these people are liars?' Hale fans his hand out to the audience. Geoff's calls of 'Liars' are lost through the gag.

'Lure, Lure, Lure.'

Peck watches him shake his arms on the scaffolding and buck his back, but the metal scaffolding doesn't move an inch. Hale opens his arms to the crowd. 'What do you all think? One leg?'

The crowd roars, 'NO.'

Hale asks, 'Two legs?'

The crowd roars, 'YES.'

Hale puts his finger to his lips and thinks it over. 'Two legs is too much,' he pronounces. 'Geoff has done wrong, but we're a good, merciful bunch, aren't we? We're not wolves. We still need to walk with our heads held high, and Geoff here still needs to walk to work.' And with that Hale smashes one of Geoff's legs with the pipe. Geoff screams into the gag; the crowd applauds. Peck feels a surge of nausea, feels himself pale. In spite of this acid tang in his throat at what he has just witnessed, the identity of the executor makes it hard to lay his horror flat. If it wasn't Hale there, he tells himself, if it wasn't his cousin then he would be shaking in his boots at the sight of such applause. But the shape of Hale, whom he'd once known so well, has left him strange.

On stage, there are handshakes and slapped backs. Hale beckons for the row of men and women to step back to make way for a short, stocky man clad in tweed, climbing the steps to the platform. He glides straight past Geoff, who has fallen limp towards the front of the stage.

'I thank you, James Hale,' the middle-aged man calls out to the crowd, his voice reassuring in its stout confidence. 'Good work there from everyone involved.' He claps at the group and the audience follows suit. 'Now,' he punctuates. 'We've got the rest of the day to enjoy. There's tea being handed out at Grace's and I've sweated over a beautiful rack of pies. Come say hello and try some of the shortcrust pastry. Rabbit, ham. We've even got a bit of beef in there. I want you all to have a taste. And, finally, I want to give a warm welcome to someone many of you will have seen already, a relative of our law and order man, James Hale.'

Hale is looking right at him, as is everyone else on the stage. Peck can feel the energy of the crowd shift. His body is inescapable. He turns round and catches sight of the enormous wall over the heads of the people, unmoving to the west.

'Duncan Peck,' the short man calls, letting the name ring out as if he himself has created it. 'Any family of James is family of ours. I hope that you enjoy your stay.'

Peck's face is red, he can feel it. The applause is a shock in the air and it's all he can do to tentatively raise his hand in a gesture of appreciation. After a few moments the crowd begins to move away and Peck takes the opportunity to squeeze upstream, towards the stage. His pulse quickens as he nears, as he climbs the stairs and approaches the unconscious body of Geoff, stopping short when he sees the portly man who closed proceedings hold out his hand to catch Hale's attention. Peter has also lingered and joins the pair uninvited. Peck waits and stands where he can watch without being seen.

'You're quite the speaker,' the short man says to Hale, who smiles but shakes his head.

'That's kind of you to say, Brian, but I'm just laying things out.'

'No need for modesty. People had been unhappy about Geoff for a week or so now. It's good to see it come to a head. Calming. That's what it is.' Turning away from Hale, Brian looks at the crowd, dispersing to the various stalls. 'There's a nice atmosphere, I'd say.'

'Much calmer,' Peter chimes. 'You could set a level on it. You could set a level on the crowd and you'd see that everything was as calm as the calmest, ha, lake.'

Brian looks at Peter as a man would look at a duck. 'Yes, well, anyway, enjoy the day,' he says to Hale. 'Be a good man.'

Peck keeps his head down, watching Brian descend the platform stairs. Here is the heart of it, he thinks, noting the ample waistline and freshly polished shoes, the double chin and rosy cheeks. What a contrast to the bent and broken body in front of him, with its shattered leg, the shard of bone pushed through his trousers. The strength Hale must have to break it in one. Peck rocks the dead tooth in his mouth. He can feel his disgust flourish. All of a sudden he feels unmoored and he can only look at the people behind him as they move from stall to stall. Then there is a whistle. Hale is beckoning with his finger. So he has been spotted, it seems, and Peck tries his hardest to look as if he has been caught unawares by the sight of his cousin. It doesn't work.

'First you wait outside my home like a magpie,' Hale says, playfully poking Peck's chest. 'Now you dawdle around poor Geoff like a vulture.'

'Was he listening to us?' Peter asks, genuine panic crossing his brow.

'I'm sure he was only waiting for the right moment to join in.'

'So, you're the big man around here,' Peck says, keen to change the subject.

'Big enough,' Hale grins, softly patting Peck's cheek. 'Surprised?'

'A little,' Peck admits. 'I don't remember you ever being so …' 'Commanding' is the word he wants to say but he feels reluctant to hand it over. In the city, back when they had been inseparable, Hale had been an extension of his own body, and yet more of an arm than a mouth. They had been a partnership, make no mistake, but when Peck thinks of his cousin he thinks of a man who was happiest standing in the background, waiting to hear someone else's plans. Peck's plans, namely.

'Bold,' he says in the end. 'It's nice to see,' he quickly adds. 'You really held everyone's attention.'

There is a look of unbridled pride on Hale's face and for a few seconds Peck totally forgets the unconscious body of Geoff Sharpe. It is pleasant to think that Hale still cares about his opinion, and that he wants to impress him with his newfound authority. He would do the same, no doubt, if the tables were turned; if it were Hale coming to him, curious to see what a life he has made over the past four years.

'I see someone has gotten rid of the dead cat that had taken residence on their face,' Hale says, patting Peck's cheek again.

'Nothing like fresh country air on bare skin,' Peck quips, reaching up to tap a finger against Hale's broad skull. 'Where's this woolly hat I've heard so much about?'

'Left it at home.'

'You'll catch a cold.'

'Oh no, Pecker. Spring is in the air. Can't you feel it?'

The slumped Geoff Sharpe is in the corner of Peck's eye. 'It's bracing alright.'

The three of them walk down from the stage, Hale and Peter leading and Peck following a step behind as they make their way through the coats and the chatter. When Hale is seen, space is given. There are respectful nods, some of them towards Peck, which he enjoys. As they walk farther from the platform, Hale leans closer towards Peter. He speaks softly but Peck knows the voice too well for his words to be lost. 'All this, so soon after his brother. And all that only a week after the last. Can you ever remember seeing so many burdened? There never used to be so many hard words, I swear.'

They pass the woman with a table tied to her back.

'I hadn't noticed,' says Peter, turning to shoot a look at Peck, then craning his neck to the sky. 'The tease of the firmament,' he says. 'Never quite sure what it wants. There could be some, ha, sun. Fingers crossed.'

'There never was this much of it.'

'Or rain. Hard to tell with these clouds. God, I hope it doesn't pour for a few more hours. I need to fix the shingles on Martin Moar's roof and I don't want to be doing that in bad weather.'

'To be honest now—'

'And we've got the washing out,' Peter interrupts, neck angled skyward, his Adam's apple a foot in a sock.

Movement stops, abruptly enough for Peck to find his face squashed between Hale's shoulder blades. When he steps aside, he sees that in front of them stand a woman and a girl, both with long dark hair; the same pair he found himself next to in the crowd. The woman is tall, wearing black trousers and a woollen coat, with a grey shawl thrown over one shoulder. There is wariness in the way she looks at him, he thinks.

'Tell me straight,' says Peter to the woman. 'Do you think it's going to rain?'

'No,' comes the flat answer.

'Are you absolutely sure?'

'Yes,' she says, irritation whetting the word. 'Maze was asking if she could get some rabbit,' she adds in a softer voice, touching the back of her daughter's head.

At this, Peter bends to stroke the girl's cheek. He pushes a strand of hair behind her ear.

'My little fishie, we're going for tea.'

The girl must be around six or seven, Peck thinks. There are so few children left in the city, or at least so few let out in the open, but here they are everywhere he turns. She seems to ignore her father's words, more interested in the sight of the stranger. 'The rabbit pie is the tastiest,' she explains to Peck, shy about meeting his eye. 'Have you ever eaten a rabbit?'

'Yes,' he tells her. 'But it wasn't wild.'

At this, Peter hurriedly stands back up and gestures to the newcomer. 'Charlotte, this is Duncan Peck. James's guest we've all heard so much about. Duncan, my wife, Charlotte.'

Peck leans across Peter to shake Charlotte's hand. He feels the warmth against his skin. 'I hear you've come from the city,' she says. 'Sometimes we see fires in the distance.'

'Sounds about right.'

'Are things as bad as they say?'

'I don't know what to tell you.'

He looks to Hale, who tenderly squeezes his shoulder. Peter coughs, apparently keen to hurry things along. 'And this is my daughter, Maisie.'

Peck gives her a thumbs up, not knowing what else to do.

'I really want some rabbit pie,' she says to the group.

Hale clears his throat. 'Not to intrude, but I was going to get a bit for myself,' he offers. 'She's welcome to a slice.'

Charlotte's smile is hard to ignore.

---

A crowd has carried Geoff Sharpe from the green, towards a set of wooden stocks that stand in front of a cenotaph. He will be put on show in front of a butcher's, a baker's, a tearoom and a post office that's been converted into a bric-a-brac shop. From the shop's awnings hang ropes in different lengths and colours. There are brown braids the width of an arm, blue sinews that could have fallen from a fisherman's boat. There is rock-climbing rope that swings heavy with pendulum knots. A man with a lazy eye is standing on a stool, face forlorn, as another places a tape measure against his shoulders, his neck, his chest. These measurements cease as the crowd approaches, and the measurer is beckoned to bring a reel of rope from his selection.

Geoff Sharpe, barely conscious, is made to sit on a wooden stool behind the open stocks and extend his legs, the healthy and the broken, over two of the four possible grooves in a plank of wood. This horizontal plank is secured on either side to a heavy stone pillar, together making the shape of a capital H. A man wearing a black hat and carrying a brown leather bag kneels beside the broken leg and, with a single sharp tug, straightens the bone. Geoff's screams last only a second before he faints and collapses on his stool. The doctor digs into his bag, pulling out a thin slat that is pressed against the leg. He motions for the rope to be brought to him, then delicately binds the splint in place. After this is done, he digs into his bag once more, takes out a stethoscope and repositions himself above the body. Happy with what he hears, he stands and dusts off his hands as the upper half of the stocks are brought down to the lower, closed around Geoff's ankles. A young boy, holding a cloth and a bowl of water, darts towards the scene. With the doctor's approval he moves to the pilloried man's side and dabs his forehead with water.

One hand nestled under her chin, Charlotte watches the comings and goings around Geoff Sharpe through the window of the tearoom. Duncan Peck is watching the commotion too, she notices. He is standing in the square, on the edge of the group, looking at the people as they throw a few old apples at Geoff, or at least at his feet. Realising they won't get much response from someone blacked out on the cobbles, they eventually lose interest and wander away, but the newcomer remains, arms folded. He could be dangerous, she considers. It is hard to know what he is liable to do, even though James speaks so fondly of him.

A shard of light breaks through the clouds, splintering through the tearoom windows to scatter across the clinking of cups that surround her, onto the back wall. Behind the counter is a large stack of weather-worn boxes, the word TETLEY emblazoned across their sides. Inside the tearoom customers sit around wooden tables enveloped in bone-white cloth. Plush cushions line elegant chairs, embroidered roses stemming the length of the material. A chandelier grips a handful of candles. A glass cabinet holds a barley and lemon cake. Steam rises from boiled water, from omelettes waiting on the counter. Each customer would swear to a heady fragrance in the air, the sun cracked open in a plume of smoke.

There is nothing more to see outside, so Charlotte pivots her head inwards, to check where Peter has got in queuing for their order. She compares him absent-mindedly to those in front and behind. He isn't an ugly man, she thinks. He was better looking before Maisie was born. She seems to have taken away something that sparked behind his eyes, at least something that sparked when they first met. Not as children. As adults, when he came knocking on her door holding a bouquet of wildflowers and she asked him if he'd spent all day picking them from other people's gardens. She'd never really wanted to get married but hadn't felt strongly enough to stop it from happening. Not that Peter was cruel to her. And with the way things are, children are a priority. Children, that is, not child. They are more than due to try for another. Maisie is already six and enough time has been put between now and the Tragedy for the loss to heal. She counts the time. The Tragedy. Capital T. Thinking of it like that makes it easier to talk about, not that they ever do.

It has been ten months. Not long left to a year. Her body is no longer duped by the swaddled one they'd buried by the Blackbrook.

Sometimes she forgets that Peter's father is gone. How much she had wanted to cause him pain. How clearly she had felt the need to hurt him for what he had done, even if it had been an accident. If it weren't for the fact that those days were the worst of her life, she would like to return to the certainty they had given. The fury. If she could've given it a shape it would've been an arrow, pointing without question to the man who had ruined everything for her. She would like to remember the anger because doubt grows like lichen and she is no longer so sure of things.

Jacob Morris: the law and order she had grown up with. Her mother had always been more excited about the marriage to the son of JM than to Peter himself. It was the protection that came with proximity, no doubt; never said but it was clear enough. She can't blame her mother for that. Charlotte had in many ways felt the same, knowing they would never want, never need to fear about what went on. All the sharper the cut that her mother should die one week after the wedding. Poof. The Sanders name, sanded away. She felt herself a

Morris inescapably, then. Not that it was a bad thing in those days. It used to carry weight.

Peter carries a tray with a teapot and a set of dainty teacups and small plates, squeezing past the queue to reach Charlotte, and on his way he bumps into another customer. One of the plates on the tray slides off and crashes onto the floor, but that is not the end of it. Trying to correct his balance, Peter only succeeds in tipping too far in the other direction, this time sliding the remaining plates, teacups and teapot all clean off the tray and onto the floor with an almighty crash. The room falls silent. Peter's cheeks redden. He turns his head from one customer to another. Charlotte can hear the sound of his name breaking the hush, snipped as soon as it has been uttered, wrapped up and handed from one pair of lips to the next. *Peter Morris, the son of JM.* Soon she has lost track of it, passed from one head to another.

'The floor was getting, ha, thirsty,' he shouts, throwing his hands up. With a cartoonish shrug of the shoulders, he looks around for a merciful laugh, but no one in the room obliges. Charlotte's hand is on her forehead but her husband has not given up yet on his attempt to make light of the scene. He rocks on the balls of his feet with a nervous energy, arms unsure about whether to be by his sides or folded across his chest. He looks at her, but she shifts her gaze to the table.

'At least it'll save on washing up,' he tells the room, voice wavering. With everyone's eyes on him, he makes one final effort to break the attention, chuckling at absolutely nothing. The waitress, Grace Horn, finally comes out from behind the counter to gather up the broken pieces. Mercy. She bends with the dustpan and brush and sweeps the fragments away. To help, Peter picks up a shard, patterned with red flowers, cut from the stem.

'I'm so, so, so sorry,' he tells her. Grace looks up from her work at his outstretched hand and for a moment something seethes within. Without a word, she pinches the shard and lets it drop into the dustpan, stands and walks back to the counter, where she grabs a mop and starts work on the puddle of tea.

'So hard to keep hold of those things,' Peter mumbles once he's seated opposite Charlotte. She holds her hand out and clasps his, rubbing the skin with her thumb. His palms are sweaty. 'Did you see the way she looked at me?' he asks.

'Grace is rushed off her feet,' Charlotte says. 'There's nothing more to it than that.' His hand fidgets, scratching the tip of her finger. It is a little painful. 'These things only blow out of proportion if you let them,' she says. 'And let's not forget she has a bit of a twitch on her.'

'No, you're right. You're right.'

Charlotte looks at Grace, who is wringing the mop above a sink. The row of customers waiting in line are all staring at where they are sitting. Before these people are seen to, Grace throws two teabags in two mugs of hot water and brings them over. Peter starts to apologise but she cuts him off. 'These things happen,' she says, voice crisp, and puts the mugs on the table. It is kind, thinks Charlotte, but it is also humiliating, the grandness with which she makes the whole act. 'Will you be coming back to fix the leak?' Grace asks. 'Only the job you did on the roof doesn't seem to have lasted.'

'Hasn't it?' Peter squirms. He doesn't like confrontation, particularly when it's about his work. He had plenty of that growing up under his father, who was built for roofing like a shovel is for digging. JM was an expert of slate and shingle, knew how to thatch where it was needed, and had made good work until he took on the law and order, a full-time job. His son was left to ply the trade but he didn't have his father's size or skill. Right up until JM was killed he would keep up a few jobs; something he liked to make Peter full aware of. It was undermining, a show of power. He was not a kind father to her husband. He had not deserved Peter's protestations of innocence.

'There's a drip in the kitchen,' Grace says, pointing behind her. 'Do you want me to show you?'

'No, no. I believe you. I – I can come in tomorrow and have a look?'

'That would be appreciated,' she says, then gives Charlotte a quick smile before she turns back to the counter, to the crossed arms of people waiting for their drinks. They used to be friends. Grace is younger than Charlotte but there was a time they would stop and talk almost every day. Conversation was easy. It had been ever since they were children. It was only with the Tragedy that they'd struggled for words. It should've bound them closer, given Grace's experiences, but it made things difficult. Now they hardly speak at all.

'Sorry,' Peter tells the room. A final atonement about the spill that at last seems to do the job, as the customers turn back to chatter and cake.

'How was it yesterday?' Charlotte asks, looking at the oil slick of tea in her mug, which has a picture of a horse on it. 'You never told me about the chase.'

'Geoff? He heard us coming but didn't have time to get ready. Bolted out the gate with one shoe. With all the sharp pebbles I didn't think there was any chance of him reaching the end of his road. He had a pipe in his hands but tripped,' Peter says with a chuckle, verve resumed. 'Dropped it somewhere. But then he did make it out, down by the leat on his way to the reservoir. Didn't get that far, though. Not by a long shot. You should have seen the look on his face at the sight of twenty rampaging chasers. It was so misty he fell in a shallow bog. That's where we, ha, found him.'

Charlotte begins to set out the knives and forks on the table, in front of her, in front of Peter, and in front of the empty seat beside her. 'I don't know why you insist on joining,' she says. 'I stopped going. If you stopped we could spend our mornings with each other instead of running in the cold after our friends and neighbours.'

'You stopped because you had Maisie.'

'*We* had Maisie. And there was never this much of it around before that.'

She looks out of the window, at the square and the stocks where Geoff Sharpe slumps. No one seems to be paying him much attention now, except for a group of adolescents and the wiry shape of Duncan Peck. It is unnerving, the way he is standing there. Charlotte lowers her voice. 'We're hardly up to our knees in good cuts. We won't get meat for a month now.'

'His brother, Gerrard, will help at the shop.'

'He's in no state to do that. Not after last week.'

'I really don't want to talk about this here.'

'Gerrard also made it out to the bogs,' she continues. 'He also slipped away for a day, made it to the Wistman's. And he's had complications, I've heard. I've heard it's not going well. What if he dies?'

'Oh, complications.'

'This is serious,' she scolds.

Peter frowns boyishly and lifts his mug, decorated in polka dots. 'It's a bridge we'll cross if and when we need to.'

'How do we get our meat then?'

'Come on, Charlotte, you know this.'

'Know this? What is it I know?'

'You're fully aware that this is just something we have to deal with as and when it happens,' he mutters, hands cupped to his drink.

Her response is a sharp whisper: 'There's only so many people around here that know how to cut up a pig. And James agrees. Says things have been getting worse.'

'He's been onto you about that as well? Listen. As much as James has done for us, he's not from here. You can't go throwing around opinions like that when you've come from the city.'

'Will you listen to yourself, talking about him like he's just wandered in. Your own neighbour of quite some years. Your own friend in the chasers.'

'Captain, last time I looked.'

'You know what I mean, when you were both under your father.'

He looks away, to the ceiling.

'There have been more punishments lately,' she says. 'I've noticed it. I'm sure everyone else has. The mood is turning sour.'

Peter puts his mug on the table with a loud knock. The word 'sour' lingers like smoke. 'You know this is the way it is,' he says. 'If you don't do the crime you don't get the punishment.'

Charlotte leans in across the table. She looks her husband in the eye. 'And you still trust people to decide that?'

'People are better than a person.'

He doesn't avoid her gaze and it makes her heart sink. The bell draped over the door to the tearoom chimes as it is swung open. Charlotte catches Duncan Peck first, watches him as he looks over a short chalk-board list. Tea. Water. Hot. Cold. Cake. Eggs. A rustle of excitement passes between the tables at the sight of him. The first person to visit in God knows how long. James Hale's cousin. All on his own.

Peck spots the woman he'd met on the green, a coil of hair escaped from the rubber-band bun on her head. She gives him a smile from behind the counter, her hands working with a flask and pot. It is all so different from the city, he thinks. The friendliness he has been shown. The warmth. She slides a tray full of cups towards a customer, beckons for Peck to come closer, where he can talk to her away from the queue of people waiting for tea.

'Deep down we're fond of one another,' Peck echoes, and all she does is roll her eyes. 'You're selling drinks?' he asks.

'Not selling.'

Peck takes in the stream coiling up from the flasks. 'Refreshments at the execution, is that it?'

She looks hurt by this. Peck wonders if she'll walk away. A middle-aged woman to his right, first in line at the queue, is studying his face. There is a perfumed scent of lavender. When he meets her stare she turns to the counter. 'Grace, could you talk to visiting men on your own time?'

Pivoting on her heels, Grace puts a teabag in a pot then pours in the water. 'I wouldn't read too much into it,' she says in a sing-song voice, seemingly to the tea. 'At the end of the day it's not the most important thing, all that nastiness. Not in the slightest.' Her eyes are once again on Peck and there is a sharpness there that pins him in place. 'Deep down we really are fond of each other. It's true. Don't you think, Vic?'

The woman called Vic nods. 'Oh yes, Grace, very much so, especially now that no one is putting on a godawful comedy routine with the crockery.' The women share a look, Vic chuckles then twists and glances across the back of the shop, towards a table occupied by Peter and Charlotte Morris. 'Oh now, don't get me started, Grace. Don't get me started. You'll open the dam and I won't be able to stop.'

'So, do you want a drink or not?' Grace asks Peck, one eyebrow raised across the stream.

'What do you need for it?'

'I told you, we're not selling. It's all for good behaviour.'

Peck looks to the other people in the queue. No one seems to be holding anything in the way of tokens. No food stamps tucked into wallets. *For good behaviour.* He thinks of the city, counting itself down with tins of fruit and grains of rice. What people did for these things could be seen through the window, heard through the walls.

'Do you think I deserve it?'

'You tell me.'

The surrounding conversations seem like they are coming from a dream. Once more Peck feels a surge of emotion. Do the people here realise how rare this is? The laughter and the gossip being shared over cups of tea, the sputter of eggs frying and the people patiently waiting in turn. Maybe this is where the goodness in the world found itself, sat on cushioned seats and held by soft hands that touch each other across clean tables. He looks to the opposite end of the tearoom, where he meets the eye of Charlotte, and she is not turning away. She must be about the same age as him, perhaps a bit older. Her face is long and thin and her attention is unnerving. It is only when a hand grips his shoulder that he turns back to Grace, who is reaching across the counter and pulling him towards her.

'I think you do deserve it,' she says, and Vic is no longer laughing but considering Peck with narrowed eyes. Grace lets go of his shoulder, then tucks a loose strand of hair beneath her rubber band. The right side of her face spasms for a split-second but there is no mention of it. 'Besides,' she adds. 'You're clearly not having a great time in life. What sort of people would we be if we didn't offer a hot drink to those less fortunate than ourselves?'

A bawdy laugh comes from Vic. With a swift movement she picks up the pot from her own tray and pours a portion into a floral teacup. 'Oh here,' she says, pushing the cup towards him. 'Have some of mine. You're family of James Hale, after all.'

As soon as the tea is in Peck's hands she carries her remaining load away from the counter, leaving Grace to serve the next person in line. Peck sips at the brew, weaves past customers, towards the table that had been the source of Vic's ire, to Charlotte, where he directs a glare at her husband. 'I think your man out there is unconscious.' Peck points outside, through the shop window, to the stocks. Geoff is not moving; the group of gangly adolescents are the only ones left to stand and gawk. The very top of the wall is visible above the roofs of the buildings on the opposite side of the square.

'We'll throw some water over him in an hour or two,' Peter says. 'When he's done atoning.'

'I think you might want to get him inside.'

'We'll start with the water.'

Peck sips his tea. 'Strange customs you have here.' Still standing, he looks around the tearoom, at the ruby flowers in the picture frames. He tongues the side of his black tooth and imagines it is a bud on a branch.

'Is Hale's camper bed enough for you?' Charlotte asks.

'It's more than ample, thank you.' Peck takes another sip, enjoying the warmth of the liquid. 'I slept very deeply. It was actually the first time I dreamt in a long time.'

'What did you dream about?'

'Two people talking in the dark.'

---

The afternoon passes without incident. The work in the pastures resumes. Milk is squeezed. A hare is caught in a fit of panic. Clothes are stitched and rainwater is boiled. The lambs in Potter's field are the size of footstools. Close to the road a sheep's skull nestles amongst the bracken, toothy and jawless in immutable stupor. A crow is seen across the bogland.

Peck walks the village with Hale, who is proud to show him every last building. The tearoom he has seen, and there is quick pointing to the butcher's and the bric-a-brac shop. Then there is the church, although it has been without a proper priest for some time. Brian Goss is the closest in that regard, as it is he that volunteers to keep the village records, amongst other things, and that includes keeping stock of weddings and funerals. Hardly a man of the cloth, though. Never says a word about God, for all his love of sermonising. After the church there is the school, for children up to the age of thirteen, at which point they find work with their families. That means toiling in the fields for the most part, although this community has carpenters, builders, foresters, beekeepers, candlestick-makers, washers, scavengers, millers, bakers, cobblers, brewers, chasers, doctors, tailors and teachers. There's always work to do. Things tick over, Peck is told, and the ticking starts in the classroom. The school itself isn't open, given that it is Saturday, although he is shown a wooden box close to its front gate, about the size of a kennel and worse smelling.

'If a child doesn't behave themselves, they have to do their business out here,' Hale explains, lifting the lid to show a dirty cooking pot.

'Jesus.'

'You should have seen it a few weeks ago, when the snow was still around. It's tough, but it gets through to them.'

After studying the look in Peck's face, Hale lets the lid fall down, then pats his cousin's cheek with the palm of his hand. 'Come on, Pecker, it's not that bad. Think about all the mean places we've had to pull down our trousers.'

He laughs at this, despite himself, picturing the pair of them dangling their arses from the edge of a bridge. From the grin on Hale's face he can tell his cousin is thinking the same thing, and the thought that they are sharing a memory without speaking breaks the stoniness in his chest. 'I suppose you're right,' Peck says.

'Teach the little shits some discipline,' Hale says. 'That's what I say.' He claps his hand against Peck's arm, hard enough for it to sting through the coat.

'You give them the law, James.'

'Oh don't.'

'Captain James.'

'It's my name, isn't it?'

'James, we're all so proud of you. James, soul of the village.'

He rubs his head with the palm of his hand and winks. 'I'm still Hale to you, aren't I?'

'That's true. You can run from me, but you can't run from that.'

The smile on Hale's lips wavers. 'You know that wasn't it.'

'I'm playing.'

'I just couldn't be there any longer.'

Peck wants to keep things light-hearted. 'I know. I know,' he says, rapidly nodding. His cousin had wanted to leave the city. The hopeless city. He hadn't. 'I just wish you'd told me when you'd had enough.'

'You wouldn't have listened.' Hale blows hot air out of his nostrils, kicks a pebble into a puddle. 'But I'm sorry. I regret not writing sooner.'

The words needed to be said. Even though his anger had long softened, Peck's sadness about those days is well within reach. 'Captain James, we love you,' he mocks. 'Captain James. Bold as brass.'

Hale chuckles. 'You're just jealous that people care what I have to say now.'

And Peck thinks that Hale is older now, a few lines showing around the corners of his eyes that groan on the grimace. He decides not to pick up the bait. 'The way that Charlotte calls you that. James, Oh James.' At this, Hale stiffens ever so slightly. 'You've got admirers, is all I mean,' Peck adds, and his cousin looks him in the eye.

'Well, I do like it here,' Hale says with a slight smile; a message sent.

After the school they duck inside The Calvary Cross, a pub that seems to Peck like something from a post-card. A large fire lights the low-ceilinged room, casting shadows on shelves of hardbacked books and old glasses. He isn't sure about the drink he's given; nothing like the lager he would sometimes drain from age-old cans. It is sweet and spicy, and he is informed that it is mead, made using fermented honey that's provided by the beekeepers. He relishes it and at his cousin's command is given a second glass.

There are well-wishes aplenty for Hale, who says he is honoured to introduce Peck to each and every person in the room, which he does, with handshakes and nods and more than a few questions, about the times they spent growing up side by side, two boys under the same roof, at first under the watch of Peck's dear mother and then no more. Peck explains why they do not look alike, in that they are not actually related, but have called each other cousin for as long as they can remember. It was his mother's idea. He tells them about how Hale was found, abandoned by his own family, but how tough a young boy he was, even then. He tells them about the fights they'd waged over bottles of water and tins of chopped tomatoes, what a loyal companion he had been as a man, when they had taken turns at sleeping while the other kept watch, and what a companion to share the world with, as they watched the tides come in and out, day after day. He does not mention the complete and utter sadness he felt when Hale left, or that he had thought him dead until the letter arrived at his door.

Tipsy, they drift to the edges of the village, surveying the land that lies beyond the houses, a muddy waste except for apple trees and fields furry with growth.

Vague lines run through a pale green canopy of chest-high grass, blades rounded into thin digits. The crops are barley, Peck is informed. There was a time nothing would grow here, the ground unkind to oats and wheat, but persistence had recovered leats close to the Blackbrook, and meant the village now managed a regular harvest of a few bushels to make bread. Potatoes make up the rest of the bulk, and there are fruit and vegetables grown in greenhouses. Between the cattle, caught rabbits, tinned meats, potatoes and these few loaves, the people are fed. But the people also know there are only so many tins in store, Hale tells him. There were only so many bottles of oil, only so many pigs in the pen, and while the livestock has survived up to now, miraculously so given the state of things, there is no certainty about the next season. New crops have been planted farther down the tributary. So far they have not taken. There is a weight put on these few fields of wisp, and that weight is only going to get heavier. There are mouths to feed. The animals are buckling.

The spring barley had been planted in January and it has not yet grown to its full sandy height. There are signs of gold amongst the green, Peck notices, a glimmer in the wind's ruffles. Beneath the overcast sky it is a hopeful sight. That fitful ripple of gold is not something that exists in the city. It is auspicious, and no matter how hard his cousin tries to taper the enthusiasm, Hale's worries about the future wash off Peck's coat in front of the barley, with its slender fingers reaching upwards.

Alone in the city he had made attempts at subsistence, had sat by the sea with a fishing rod but could not catch a single bite. He was fed and watered by the remnants. With each trip he made to the warehouses he could see the shelves emptying piece by piece. If he could only catch a fish, hit its head against the stone and split it down the middle. When he sat by the sea, looking to the waves, he would chew the canned sardines, imagine the animal; more than a name, a tongue slipped in the water. If he could only catch it, hold it, then the future wouldn't be so undecided. And so the sight of these fields seems a miracle.

On their way home they pass a woman carrying half a skinned pig across her shoulder. The smell of raw meat is strong and space is given for her to walk with purpose to the butcher's. What remains of the animal's head hangs lazily, one pink ear and half a jaw. *The animals are buckling.* This one has buckled in two. Peck has never seen a pig cleaved, and stops in his tracks to watch, beguiled.

'We've already got a lamb in,' Hale shouts at him through hands cupped on the other side of the square. He has wandered to the stall outside the bric-a-brac shop with its tensions of hanging rope, beyond Geoff Sharpe in the stocks, who is now sitting upright on a squat wooden stool, arms folded and hair drenched with cold water. Peck gives his cousin a thumbs up and Hale goes back to browsing the knots, idling around a length of deepest blue.

As evening arrives, candlelight hums, hovering around the edges of Hale's living room. The dinner table is set. Hale drinks a long glass of water. This is only to hydrate, as next he has a glass of something dark and brown, something that smells a lot like whiskey but comes from an unmarked bottle and waits in the bottom of the tumbler. Peck looks to the fruit bowl, empty of fruit but rattled with the bullets from his confiscated revolver. The two lift their glasses, clink and drink.

After enthusing about the apple trees and the barley fields, the school and the pub, there are questions about the wall, the stage and scaffolding in the middle of the green, the furniture carried about. Hale does his best to listen to Peck's misgivings. 'It keeps the peace,' he assures.

'It's strange,' Peck mumbles. The drink has loosened his tongue. 'You have to admit it. The things I read up there about that Geoff Sharpe. Vicious. Don't the writers see each other in the night? What if the person being written about catches them in the act?'

'It's not some ritual of darkness,' Hale laughs. 'We're not whispering prayers under our breath. There are no cloaks or daggers.' A pause. 'Well, there are sometimes hoods,' he admits. 'And the past few months have become a bit more secretive, that's true. Yes, you have a point there.'

Hale straightens his back and squares his shoulders. 'It's not that you can't write on the wall during the daytime,' he continues. 'Plenty of us write things in the daylight. It was only last week that I put up a notice about volunteers for reserve chasers. Practice runs on the moor, finding the right pole for your size and strength. There was no great secret about any of that.'

'Those aren't the messages I'm talking about. You know what I mean. The hard ones. How do those get written?'

Hale shifts his weight on the chair, coughs into his fist. 'To be honest now, people rarely write those all on their own,' he says. 'They tend to do it in a group, where there is already agreement. The bigger the group, the more gets written.'

'And the person they're writing about?'

'There may or may not be something organised, to make sure they are occupied for the night.' He coughs again. 'It's not a case of a few daft cunts going too far with a pot of paint. It's a way of making sure we keep to our responsibilities. Geoff was slacking. Stealing even. There are more than enough rewards for good behaviour around here. There needs to be punishment, atonement, if someone isn't pulling their weight, isn't doing right by us.' He pauses, thinking of how to best put what he wants to say. 'The wall is a final confirmation of something that's already boiled over. That's why it's so important, you see? It isn't where decisions are made. They've already been made. They've come together in people's homes, around the fields, on the streets ... The wall isn't where a judgement is made, only where it's put into action.'

'And you're the action man,' Peck nips.

'This isn't something I dreamt up,' Hale insists. 'I remember being shocked when I first arrived too, honestly now, but I came around. They started me in the fields, strong back and that, but after my first year I ended up working for the captain, the fellow who did what I do now.' Hale frowns at something in his memory. 'Give it some time and you'll see that it's the thread that binds everything together.'

He looks hopeful for a reaction that eludes Peck. Perhaps Hale wants his cousin to nod and smile, or to wink and tell him he understands exactly what he means. Whatever response it is, Peck knows he has not given it, as he watches Hale shuffle in his seat and focus his attention to a corner of the room. 'I didn't mean to but it's becoming clear that I've invited you to our community at a difficult time,' Hale says. 'This was the way of things before I was here, that's true, but I'll be honest with you: the tenor is changing, and there have been more accusations in the past few months than the whole year before. I don't know why. I'm worried it will get worse before it gets better. But listen to me when I say this is not some secret ritual we are performing. There is nothing to be unnecessarily afraid of.'

'Unnecessarily,' Peck echoes the word.

Hale's palm is absent-minded on his bald head. 'The important thing isn't that we do people harm,' he says. 'In an ideal world we wouldn't have to ever do harm but, as it stands, the harm we cause all goes to use.'

'Strange way to talk about breaking a man's leg.'

'You're getting the wrong end of the stick.'

'It's nasty stuff.'

'Ah, quiet now. It keeps our community going. And that's something we need right now in the world, isn't it? A bit of community. A bit of sense.'

Peck flaps his hand to show he doesn't want to fight on this. He's tired and whatever drink he's let pass his lips has made his head light. Who is he to argue about sense? It has been so long since he's had a grip on what is sensible, what is reasonable. Even hearing the word in the air shifts the tone of things, makes it easier for him to feel his hands on the wooden table. Sense. It's hard to disagree that there is a community here. A group of neighbours and friends that he could be part of, feel the support of. There is a schoolhouse and fields of barley; new life that he could spread across the land. There is work for him; there is the pretty face of Grace. Sense. It is the start of a thought he could pull and follow, if it weren't for the scent of cooking coming from the kitchen. Charlotte is in there, working with Peter on a welcome dinner of lamb cutlets and potatoes for the honoured guest. The warm smell of rosemary and garlic makes it hard to think about anything sensible.

Maisie is sat cross-legged on the floor, hunched over an open notebook and holding a pencil. 'What are you writing there?' Peck asks, standing from the table and moving towards the girl.

'My diary,' she says.

'Can I see?'

As Peck approaches, Maisie closes the notebook and runs out of the room. It isn't exactly the reaction he was hoping for, so Peck follows into the kitchen, to see Maisie hugging her mother's legs, peeking at him from behind Charlotte's waist.

'He was trying to look inside my diary,' she accuses.

There is a glint of suspicion in Charlotte's eyes. Her sleeves are rolled to the elbows and there are veins standing out on the backs of her hands. 'Oh was he now?'

Peck feels that the room is waiting for his response, and is suddenly all too aware of how tipsy he is feeling on his feet. 'I was only curious about what she was doing,' he says defensively. 'That's all.'

'You're not allowed to look inside,' Maisie tells him, then sticks out her tongue. It is hard for Peck to tell whether she is playing with him, or genuinely worried that he will read what she had written. Peter has turned from peeling potatoes and is tutting performatively, which makes Peck want to punch him in the face, but he thinks better of it and instead takes a deep breath, calms, then looks to Maisie.

'You're a clever thing, for writing so much.'

The compliment goes down well. 'I do it every day.'

'That's very disciplined.'

'Can you write?' she asks him.

'I'm not good at it.'

'I am,' she states. 'Mrs Twine says I'm the best in the class.'

Charlotte nudges for her to let go of her waist. 'Come on, Maze. Get off me now.'

'I'd hide behind my mother's leg as well,' says Peck. 'If she was still standing.'

'I remember clinging to her like a limpet,' shouts Hale from the living room, apparently privy to the entire conversation. And at this, Maisie releases her mother and runs through the kitchen door.

'Did you two have a nice time today?' Charlotte asks, with what Peck feels is more politeness than interest.

'We made quite a bit of ground.'

'Tiring?'

'I'm light on my feet, and lighter now that your husband has taken my gun.'

'Don't tell her about—' Peter gulps, then turns his attention to the expectant eyes of Charlotte. 'I took it from him as soon as I saw it. There's no need to, ha, tell anyone.'

Why is she married to this man? Peck wonders. There is an edge to her that is nowhere to be seen in the fuzz of Peter's bluster, his barely contained self-doubt. It's obvious that this pale, freckled man lingers around Hale under the impression they are equals but it must be clear to the whole village that he is a joke. Tomorrow,

Peck will tell Peter to give him back his revolver. He'll demand it, he decides. No point making a scene tonight, but in the morning he'll knock on his door and fight him for it if he needs to. He doesn't expect any resistance, at least not from Peter. Charlotte, though … She looks strong and may already know what he is planning. Would she attack him if he beat her husband? Is that what love is? he wonders. Is it killing an intruder at six in the morning?

'I'm sure you and James have a lot to catch up on,' she tells him, apparently keen for him to leave the kitchen.

'A list of the dead,' he punctuates it with an ugly laugh. It's hard for him to keep his attention when the smell wafts, and he lets his eyes close for a moment to focus. The scent of lamb, wrapped around his belly like a frayed rope. Soon there's the sound of lips smacking, conversations interrupted between mouthfuls until there are empty bottles of moonshine on the table. Maisie is sleeping on Charlotte's chest. Talk has turned to memories, as it inevitably does. Peter's memories in particular. Merry on the drink, he gushes about how he too liked to write when he was Maisie's age.

'The alphabet,' he says, beating out the syllables of the word with his finger on the table. 'I adored it. Just couldn't make it all the way through. A. B. C. All that was fine until I'd get to O. Somewhere around there. I'd get, ha, lost. Adrift! The whole thing was a source of great unhappiness. I can laugh about it now but it was upsetting at the time. Alarming! I used to have nightmares about it. I still remember them. Terrible! I was sitting in front of my father, sitting with my legs crossed on the floor, and he would start to recite the alphabet. A. B. C. And I would listen to each of the letters. D. E. F. I wouldn't repeat them, no. I'd just listen to him say them. G. H. I. J. K. L.'

Peter's right hand is toying with the edge of the table, tapping and scratching the wood. 'You see,' he continues. 'It was like each letter was a shape that was going into my head. M. N. I knew each one was taking up room in my skull. And I remember. I remember feeling like my head was filling up. O. P. And I remember thinking: stop it! My head is full and I can't take any more. Q. Stop. Stop. R. Stop. Stop! My head is full up. Stop! I can't take any more.'

His hand is gripping the wood now, fingers pink with the effort. Hale and Charlotte aren't even listening, a different conversation passing between their lips in low voices, but Peck can't pull his attention away. A bead of sweat has emerged from Peter's hairline and is making its way down his forehead. All of a sudden, as if a blockage has been breached, he blurts out 'STUVWXYZ' then giggles maniacally. 'See! No problem.' He sits back with arms crossed, proud, and lets his attention land on Maisie, her head rising and falling with the rhythm of Charlotte's breathing.

'I should, ha, put her down for the night,' he says, suddenly sober and with such surprising tenderness that Peck momentarily forgets his negative opinions of the man. Is that what love is? he wonders. Is it the way Peter Morris looks at his sleeping daughter?

Charlotte's voice is distant. 'I might stay for a bit longer, if that's fine?'

'Oh?'

'It's only next door, Pete. I'm not going to wander off.'

Hale looks into his glass. 'We'll take good care of her,' he assures his neighbour, so Peter gives a shrug and gently wakes Maisie to be led drowsily home.

'My little fishie, come with me.'

Peck circles his black tooth, nudging the tip of his tongue beneath its loose foundations to prod at the gum beneath. He pictures it as a fish, swimming in the sea.

Outside, a pair of bats circle the field. A patch of mushrooms stand patiently on the back of a fallen branch. The eyes of a cow droop into sleep, its jaw settled on a frayed hoof. Beneath the fields, a fox is nestling her young in the dark. A sheep is bleeding out into the Blackbrook. Moths make their way to bedroom lights. There are cries behind walls close to the southern edges of the village. There is paint drying on poster paper. There is movement heard around the western hill.

Soon the candles are out and Peck is lying with eyes closed on the camper that has been set up against the wall, his arms thrown above his head. 'Say it back to me,' he hears Hale whisper.

There's a hushed laugh from Charlotte. 'No.'

'Go on.'

'Why?'

'I want to hear it.'

There's another laugh. 'You're being ridiculous.'

'I'm not.'

'No, that's what you are. Ridiculous. And foolish.'

There's a nervous edge to her voice, and Peck opens one eye enough to squint at what is happening. He sees them talking at the table on the other side of the room.

'Say it back to me,' Hale whispers.

'No,' she insists, harder this time.

'I want to hear you say it.' This is met with stillness, then Charlotte moves a hand from the table and places it against Hale's cheek, only for a moment, though, before she pushes his face away.

'Maisie cries so much,' she tells him. 'All night she cries. I wish she'd shut up sometimes. That's a horrible thing to say, sorry, I shouldn't have said it. I'll go. Goodnight.'

'Do you at least have an umbrella? Let me get you one.' Hale searches a woven basket against the wall, pushing his metal pipe to the side. Peck moves his head an inch to keep things in sight, but the shift creaks the mattress and he is worried they will realise he is awake. His heart jolts when he notices Charlotte is looking straight at him, but she doesn't seem to register his peeking eye in the dark.

'How long is he staying?'

'As long as he wants.' Hale holds out a battered umbrella. 'Say it,' he asks her.

'Why?'

'I want to hear it.'

'I missed this. I missed us.'

'Say it again.'

'I missed us.'

# Three

PETER MORRIS IS A LIAR. HE SHOULD BE BEATEN TO A PULP. PETER MORRIS IS A CHEAT. HE KICKS THE COCKS AND LICKS HIS DAUGHTER'S SLIT. PETER MORRIS SPLIT A ROOSTER'S HEAD.

HALE SLAMS THE DOOR so hard the empty fruit bowl shakes on the table, threatens to fall off, settles. Peck is still sleeping, drool-caked. Pulled out of that slumber by the noise and the curtains flung open to grey daylight, all of a sudden he's looking at the metal bar gripped in his cousin's hands.

'We have to go.'

'What?'

'Put your boots on.'

'Why?'

'Peter's run.'

And with that Peck has a palm to his head, remembering the roots of the pain behind his eyes, shooting a glance at the moonshine on the table, fruit flies flitting around the scene. 'Do you have water?' he asks, soon out of the camper, bleary in the search for a flask, naked except for briefs. There's a metallic taste in his mouth. Hale watches him go, curious to see him struggle but impatient for them to leave. Peck's heart is beating in his ears and it's all he can do to steady himself on the kitchen surface. 'That stuff kicks hard.'

Hale can't contain himself. 'This is serious,' he spills. 'You were sleeping so I went early, to see what people had written. And they'd written about him, about Peter. He ran. I went to his home to find him but he was gone.'

'Wait, what?' asks Peck, rubbing his left eye with his right knuckle. 'Hold on. They wrote what? What did they write?'

'Bad things. About killing roosters. About, well, Maisie.'

'Maisie?'

'Yes.'

'The little girl? His daughter?'

'Yes.'

'Like what?'

Hale doesn't respond, but shifts his heavy weight from one foot to the other. Peck looks for his eye and he finds it full of murky thoughts. 'Ah,' he says. The flask is tipped above a tumbler and a thumb of water hits the bottom with a knock. 'Jesus, if that's the state of things. Who'd write something like that?'

'It doesn't matter. What matters is that it was big enough for everyone to read.'

'To be clear, this is her father they're talking about?' Hydrated, Peck moves from the sink to his camper, to the nest of his shirt and trousers. 'That's sick. Who wrote that? There's not someone coming forward and saying they've seen something? Nothing like that?'

'It's in writing,' Hale answers, growing intolerant at the time it's taking them to move on from these questions. His hands are tight around the pipe. 'It's put there big enough and that's the main thing we have to worry about right now. His name's on the wall and it's on there attached to some nasty sentiments.'

'I'd want to know who wrote that shit,' says Peck, zip and buttons fastened. He considers his surroundings, as if he'd only just arrived. 'And so – what? You're chasing him?'

Hale nods.

'Your friend?'

'My neighbour. He was hiding something, they'll say. And they'll want us to catch him. It's a matter of importance, given his father.'

'And his father was …?'

'A fucker.'

'That a crime now?'

'I'm not getting into it,' Hale grumbles, slapping the air with his hand. 'The important thing is we have to find Peter.'

Sitting on the camper, Peck slides his boots into place. 'To put things straight?' he asks, testing the walls of his cousin's resolve. Hale doesn't answer at first, and the sound of mattress springs as Peck stands is a drawn-out breath.

'Of course. To clear this up.'

'But what if someone wanted to make him look bad?'

'He does look bad. He looks bad to everyone in the village.'

There's a silence then as Peck tries to take this in. In his final few months in the city he had been a pair of eyes and little else, watching the struggles of his few remaining neighbours from behind a window. Now he feels present and, he has to admit, it is bracing. His feet are on the ground. He points to the metal pipe in Hale's grip. 'Do I get something as well?'

'You're keen now?'

'Not on doing damage to the man, necessarily. Although now you mention it I was planning on paying him a visit. Which I won't get into,' he adds when Hale gives him a raised eyebrow. 'We'll just bring him home, so we can get this straightened up. Like you say.'

Hale passes a pole that had been leant up against a broom. It has been cut from a larger length of wrought iron and there is a bulbous knob on the end that reminds Peck of a curtain rail.

'Oh God.'

'What's wrong?'

Peck jabs one finger into his mouth. There is a new bed of flesh and something missing. 'I've lost my tooth.' At this he opens his mouth as wide as it will go and gestures aggressively to his molars. Hale leans in and looks, makes a clicking sound with his tongue.

'It must've come out in the night.' Peck swallows his saliva and feels a twinge of loss. Part of him has fallen away. He looks around his feet, walks back to the camper bed and, placing the pole on the floor, lifts the pillow. He pulls back the blanket and ruffles the sheet. There is no sign of the tooth.

'I don't know, you might've swallowed it,' Hale offers. 'Come on, we need to go.'

The thought of his rotten tooth wedged somewhere in his lower intestine makes Peck gag. On his knees, he has one last scan of the floor beneath the camper bed before standing and slapping the dust from his trousers. Growling, he picks up the metal pole and swipes the air. As if he'd hit the wooden boards himself, there's a knock at the door. He swivels on the heel of his foot, turning to aim at the source of the sound. Hale edges past him to open the door, and there's Charlotte on the porch, her long, dark hair a windbreak, eyes raw but unyielding.

'Can we talk?'

'We're just on our way out.'

'Please,' she insists.

Hale turns his attention from downward to backward, at his cousin and pole both pointed with purpose. 'Do you mind waiting outside?' he asks.

'Fine,' comes the reply. 'But if it starts raining I'm coming back in.' Peck ducks past the pair to join a group of men and women dressed in raincoats outside Hale's home. The door is closed behind him, so he paces towards the small crowd. Conversations are snipped, a few glances find themselves on his shoulders and he does his best to nod from a respectable distance. Grace, dressed in her apron, makes her way towards him, hurrying across the path until her heart-shaped head is in line with his neck.

'Where's James?'

'Hale's inside. Talking to so and so.'

'So and so?'

'Charlotte Morris. I'm still getting used to people's names.'

'Know mine?'

'How could I forget? Grace.'

'Glad you remember the important things,' she teases. 'And so, what's this then? Charlotte's dear Peter has done a runner?'

'That's what I've heard of it.'

'I was just on my way in, you know. I was just heading in to see if the water had been sent, then I see everyone walking in pairs and such, heading up here, going whispery. Peter Morris, Peter Morris, Peter Morris. I thought it might've been about the bad job he did on my roof but I heard he's been up to all sorts.'

'That's the word.'

'What do you make of it?'

'We only met a couple of times.'

'Couple of times. Right.'

'Seems a bit of a prick if I'm honest.'

'Peter Morris. Peter Morris. At the end of the day, it's hard to imagine otherwise. The family he had. The father.' Grace looks off down the street, at the chasers drawn in towards the group, pulled by the commotion. Their faces mean business and some are carrying chains. A man amongst their number is pushing a wheelbarrow.

'What happened to his father? Hale was on about him too.'

'Let's just say there were accusations.'

'What sort?'

'That he killed a little baby,' she whispers. The wheelbarrow moves close to the group. It has clearly been greased since carrying Geoff Sharpe from the moorland. The man who pushes it walks with his back straight, proud at the oiled chirr he brings with him. 'His grandson no less.'

It's a nasty thought and Peck expresses it by blowing the air out of his cheeks. 'God,' he says. 'Horrible.'

'Poor Charlotte.' Grace scratches the skin behind her ear, attention loosely on the line in the dirt drawn by the wheelbarrow. The area around her right eye winces involuntarily. A nervous tic, notes Peck. But who isn't nervous in these trying times? 'I try not to mind myself with others,' she continues. 'But Peter, now. Bad seed. Jesus, the idea of doing something like that. Imagine it was your child. A poor girl like Maisie Morris.' The expression on her face has turned to something altogether harsher and Peck can see the loathing crack its knuckles. 'I try not to get involved but it's disgusting,' she hisses.

'If it's true.'

'No smoke without fire.'

Peck runs his tongue over the space where his tooth used to be. He does not like the gap, too big for his head. 'Do you want me to tell Charlotte you're here?'

She seems taken aback by this. 'No need. I have to head off in a minute and I'm sure she has enough on her plate.'

Peck nods.

'You're looking good with that,' Grace changes the subject, shaking the lingering anger from her cheeks. 'I knew you were a fine person. I could tell you wouldn't be someone to sit back. Plus you've cleaned a bit of the muck from your boots.' Before he has a chance to say anything in return, she snatches the metal pole from Peck's hands and holds it aloft like a lightning conductor. 'I'll tell you what,' she says. 'If you come on later to the tearoom I'll make sure there's something hot waiting. How does that sound?'

'Sounds good to me,' he says, a little intoxicated by the commotion and the attention he is receiving. There's an effort to grab the pole back; he misses having it in his hand, but before he can get close Grace brings the metal swinging down onto the grass, hard, kicking up a clump of dirt. He leaps a good foot backwards, nearly tripping on a stone. When the others turn to see what is happening she laughs and passes the bludgeon back.

'Watch yourself,' she winks, then leaves him for the others.

There's been no word from Hale but Peck is impatient and, embarrassed at his jumpiness, hastens back to the home. He pushes on the front door, unlatched, but stops short when he catches Hale and Charlotte within. His cousin is holding the head of Peter Morris's wife against his chest. So last night wasn't a dream, he thinks, remembering the gift of the umbrella. Hale wants to be careful. Adultery is unlikely to go down well around here, he reckons. After a moment Charlotte pulls away and Peck draws the gap in the doorway tight. They have not seen him and he lingers for a moment to listen.

'Maisie is still asleep. I haven't woken her. I wouldn't know what to say. Where to begin. She— Look— Don't chase him. You can let him go. He'll be back on his own. He's done nothing wrong. He really hasn't.' Peck watches Hale stroke Charlotte's cheek. She cups his finger with the palm of her hand, holds it there, then moves away. 'Someone could see.'

'We're far from the windows.'

'He'll come back on his own,' she says. 'He would never do anything to hurt Maisie. He loves her.'

'It's unfortunate.'

'You're about to hunt down my husband and you say it's unfortunate?'

'It is unfortunate that those words are so strong,' says Hale. 'You've seen them yourself.'

'How can you be so—'

A few people to Peck's back have noticed his hesitation at the doorway, so he knocks on the wood and moves to step through the threshold with a stage cough.

'Yes, well thank you for coming over,' Hale brusquely tells Charlotte. 'We'll get this sorted and I'll let you know what comes of it.'

'There are some people out here looking for you,' Peck ventures.

'Wait here and I'll fetch you in a minute,' Hale orders, as if Peck is an underling, then he's out the door. Peck fidgets, inspecting the end of his pipe while Charlotte looks through the window. A man with a scar on his cheek is pointing at the cow field. Hale nods and points to the field, then to his home, to the window, to her.

*Charlotte Morris has been unfaithful*, Peck thinks. *Charlotte Morris is telling lies.*

'They must've been murmuring about him for a while,' she says, fingers massaging temples. 'I should've listened more carefully. He broke a load of plates in the tearoom yesterday. But they didn't seem to give it a second thought.'

Peck rests the bulbous end of his bludgeon on the floor with a small tap. 'The truth will out.'

'What's that?' asks Charlotte, woken from the window as if a fly had buzzed in her ear.

'The truth will come out.'

'What truth?'

The string running between them tautens.

'Yours, I'd imagine,' he says.

---

Miles to the north-east of the village, past a ruined farmhouse and close to a gathering of gnarled trees, a group of ponies skirt the edge of a sunken ditch. They trudge with hairy heads pointed low, pausing every now and then to bite at blades as the wind rustles their hides. One lags behind the rest, its attention up at the afternoon sky, so overcast that it may as well be twilight. The others are moving down the bank, stringing a line towards a stone cist that stands in the heath. The straggler stays where it is, hair blown over its face and two dark eyes considering the land. The lone animal casts a stumpy sight, as if its four legs are half sunk in the damp ground. Its blood is warm but its body seems petrified, paying no attention to the distance between the group and itself. The breath comes and goes, the heart keeps pumping, but it stands still on the moorland, staring not at the other ponies but at the line of men and women in the distance.

Hale is at the head of the trail, eyes following flattened grass up a hill. Beside him is Peck, taking in the bogland with its auburn skin stretched to breaking, water pooling in the splits, waiting in plain view for anyone stupid enough not to keep to higher ground.

He catches sight of the ponies, at first takes them for horses, tracing a path like ants lost from the nest. All the horses are dead. They can't be horses. Ghosts, he thinks. And if not, they won't last long. The one there on its own, that one is deader than the rest for its slowness or stubbornness, hard to tell which from where he's standing. He looks in the other direction and, yes, just as he suspected, there's not another living thing in sight. Even the birds have stayed away from picking bones-in-waiting. He's surprised anything can live out here. The city is deadly, but at least there are places to hide. Who could hide out here for long, in this empty land?

The giddy spin he'd started out with that morning has weathered. He still feels present, in his boots, in a way he hasn't for years. But the adrenaline has made its way around his veins and left him with uncertainties about what it is they are doing, out on the moor, hunting a man he only met two days ago. He shared a meal with Peter's family, his wife and daughter. If it weren't for the group, he would take Hale aside and ask him, hand on heart, whether this was the best thing they could be doing to help the situation. If people were angry with Peter, whatever the reason, then they could meet all together and air their concerns. There was something irritating about the man, undoubtedly, but wouldn't it be better to let him come back on his own? Until then, they could work on finding evidence for the things he'd been accused of. That would be a level-headed solution, some sense. And yet the flow of the group has kept Peck moving. He thinks about the lone animal, refusing to follow, no doubt dead within a day.

Instead of stopping he studies the chasers in their raincoats. No one has offered Peck one to wear, and although he is fine in his own jacket, perfectly fine, he does feel like an outsider. He is James Hale's guest. Not yet a member of the community. The afternoon is cool but the day's search has gone on long enough for skin to clam, and some of the group have unzipped the top of their coats to let the air touch their neck. When they set out Hale had worn his woolly hat, in part to show it off to him, Peck reckons, but the patterned blue and black fabric, complete with bobble, has been tucked into a pocket. His cousin is right, spring is definitely in the air.

Hale turns to the crowd and points outwards with both hands, towards a pair of granite tors atop swollen ground. At his command the group splits down the middle, half snaking up to one and half to the other. Someone called Martin Moar leads one dissection, Hale and Peck the other, towards a tor that looks much like a council of stones. Soon they're moving upwards, calves shearing with the struggle of the incline. The man pushing the wheelbarrow puffs at the effort. There are grunts and grumbles, but they approach the grand pile of layered rocks without a full-formed word. It is fingers on lips, then, as Hale motions for the remaining chasers to fan out and search for signs of life. Peck scrambles up the side of the tor, looking for boots or blood or fire. He tucks his head into nooks and pokes the end of his pole into crannies, but there's nothing to be found except for bangs and limp echoes. He finds a crevice that could fit a full-grown man. In that space it is difficult to trace the edges of the gloom, but he puts his head into the hole all the same and looks for Peter. There is only the rock, and it's going nowhere.

He climbs upwards, finding holds for his feet in wiry pockets of grass. Within no time at all he's on the tor's highest possible point, the highest on the hill, and from here he looks through the wind, out over the moorland in its sprawl. A vast, empty, darkening place, he thinks. He searches for the ponies but can't find them for the rocks. He looks at the land but can't be sure about what he sees, about what's motionless by choice and what's immovable by design.

The sun is setting. The wind dies down. Peck sits on the edge of a granite outcrop and watches the light bleed out. He can make out their trail, north-east through the valley and dipping into the woods. Once he's spotted the angular jut he's surprised he didn't see it before. The top of the wall, imposing on the landscape with its ruler-straight lines. The village is hidden from view but the wall is unmistakable. Taken against the moorland it looks so unnatural, so much of a statement and yet small compared to the blankness all around. He feels something congeal, suddenly aware of the others below, the threat of their eyes landing on him sat there as they continue their search. 'Peter?' he calls. 'Peter, you may as well come out. We want a word.'

He waits to see if Hale's neighbour appears at the sign of his name and, when he doesn't, Peck unties his boot, shucks it from his foot and rests it beside him. He puts both hands to work in rubbing his sole. 'Are you sure he's here?' he asks, dropping the words down to Hale, who's cupped his hand around his mouth and is giving it all the air he can muster.

'He's here or he's there,' Hale stresses. 'And the other lot are there, so we're here.'

'Still, he might've been in the woods.'

'We looked in the woods. We looked in Bellever and we looked in the Wistman's.'

'And he couldn't have gone to the south instead? Where you caught that Geoff Sharpe? That's where I'd go.'

'There were footprints leading north-east. If he's not in Bellever and he's not in the Wistman's then he's come to hide himself in a tor. Not Beardown. Maybe Crow. Could very well be here in Longaford, fingers crossed. He won't have gone farther. There's not many other places he could get to with only a day to run.'

'Those names mean nothing to me,' Peck mutters.

'We're not going to stop until we've got you,' Hale shouts. 'Come on, neighbour. Let's get you home to your lovely wife and child.'

Everyone around them waits for a response. The words don't even bounce against the rock but sink without a trace somewhere in the mire at the base of the hill. Final effort spent, Hale scrambles up the tor to Peck's vantage point. For a large man he's nippy, and within seconds he's settled beside his cousin, looking out at the red smear dwindle.

'The same boy with his arms wrapped around Mother's legs. Now look at him. So much authority.'

Hale meets Peck's eye but does not keep it. 'Just doing what the people want,' he says.

'They should get you a sheriff badge.' And for a second that image hangs between them, something infinitely more polished than the evening drawing in. 'Remember when we broke into that house on our road and we thought it was going to be empty?'

Hale stares forward blankly.

'And then it wasn't,' Peck nudges.

'I remember.'

'Things change, is all I'm saying. Who would have thought then that you'd grow up to be such a pillar of the community?'

There's a long pause but then a bark of laughter. 'What a crazy night,' Hale crows. 'We really were a pair of wildmen, weren't we?'

The belly laugh is infectious and Peck finds himself joining. 'And you were so scared,' he hoots. 'You were so, so scared.' The laughter continues, and it warms Peck to lose himself for a second, even after Hale stops.

'You were so terrified of them,' he chuckles, correcting some of the imbalance in power he has felt between them since arriving. This is good, he thinks. This is making things better. And they are both picturing the same thing, Peck knows. In both of their minds is the terraced house on the bottom of a road, with its broken windows and overgrown ivy, and the horrors they found within.

'So what are you going to do when you get him?' he asks as his breathing settles.

'I don't know.'

'You seem like you do know. You seem pretty certain of things.'

'I'm not in a position to argue with what people want.'

'What a few nasty sentences want.'

'Nasty sentences people have written in public places.'

'That makes a difference?' Peck presses, as the first raindrops of the evening land on their foreheads. He follows Hale's gaze over the land, to the wall in the distance. There's no chance of reading what's written on it from here, but the shape of it is unmistakable. As if the moorland had sense.

'It's how things work here,' Hale explains, no longer amused. 'It's kept things peaceful.'

'That's a relative term from the looks of it.'

'It's a relative I keep safe and warm,' Hale says, squaring his shoulders. His gold necklace glints around his collar. 'She's old, but I keep her well fed. I keep her in my home where the wind can't chill her bones, and if she coughs I measure out a spoonful of medicine.'

Peck stands, using his pole to help himself up. 'That's not what I meant.' He brushes the dirt from his hands and looks to the others, sat in clumps around the tor. A few have noticed the rainfall and taken to huddling under the overhangs before it comes down heavier. The man with the wheelbarrow has lifted the hood of his raincoat over his head.

'In the cities there is the smell of death,' says Hale, his eyes softer than the sunset.

'Don't get me wrong,' Peck says. 'I'm a guest and God knows I don't want to step on your toes. It just seems like there's a lot of hearsay wafting around.'

He reaches his hand out for his cousin, who grasps hold of it and pulls to stand. 'You can't go throwing words around and not expect anyone to get hurt,' Hale tells him in the tone of a teacher. 'You know it as much as I do. The things you say aren't cotton coated.'

'So you put them on a wall?'

Climbing up was much easier than going back down, and Peck stops to consider where to next put his foot. Hale waits. 'If your words are violent then let's shine a light on them, make people mind the things they say. From up here the wall may seem small but down there it looms. It stays over every man, woman and child and that's the way we want to keep it.'

Peck can see that his cousin's face has lit up at these words. His hairy nostrils flare. His lower lip has snuck beneath his front teeth, pressed against a yellow incisor. By the time they reach the base of the tor his body is a bundle of simmering energy.

'People stand a little straighter when they know they're being watched,' Hale continues, finger pointed right at Peck's face. He's smiling, though, so Peck grimaces back when he asks him his next question.

'You think he actually did it then? That the man living next to you killed some birds and fiddled his daughter?'

Some of the others in the group hear this last part and poke their heads from under the cover of rocks. Hale notices and pulls Peck to the side, out of view. 'You could argue forever about that,' he whispers. 'It's uncertain. What's certain is the way people feel. And from what was on the wall it's certain that they feel he's done wrong. You understand that much, right? One man doesn't have the right to decide another's fate. A community, however ...'

Peck feels patronised, can feel the blood rising behind his face, but before he has a chance to answer Hale puts his hand on his shoulder. It is a gentle movement, and the intimacy of it brings him back to earth.

'Let me take you up the wall after this has all settled,' Hale says softly, one arm around Peck's neck, pulling him close enough to feel the heat of his breath. 'We can climb to the top and I'll show you the view. It's beautiful. Peter's father used to take us up there. You can see the sun rise. It's enough to make you weep.'

'Weep?'

'Cry your eyes out.'

Peck studies his cousin. This is the same boy he knew under his mother's roof, the same man he knew in the city. But he is also different and that difference cracks his heart. Peck had always thought of them on the same line, seeing the world as the right eye and the left. Now there are experiences that separate them. He is not sure what Hale is thinking. Time will correct the balance, he tells himself. They are reunited, finally on the same track in this new life in the country. 'Do you think Peter's father could explain the wall to me?' he asks. 'I'm having trouble.'

'JM doesn't live with us any more,' Hale states, letting his arm fall from Peck's neck. 'His room is free now, in Peter's house, if my camper isn't enough for you.'

'No, no, the camper's fine. I was just wondering.'

'About what?'

'I heard he killed his grandson.'

There is surprise in Hale's expression. 'Where did you hear that?'

Peck isn't sure if he should say. 'Grace, the waitress at the tearoom.'

'Grace,' Hale echoes.

'Is she right?'

'Oh yes.' He scratches the stubble on his cheek. 'But I wouldn't talk about it too much, you understand? Especially not to Charlotte. It was a sad time for us. All of us. The man helped me get my house, made me one of the chasers.' He trails off and a tiredness washes over his eyes. 'Listen, it's getting dark,' he says, looking upwards. 'We should head back.'

'You're letting Peter go?'

'Maybe they've had better luck on the other tor. If not, we'll try again tomorrow. Maybe he did circle back. Maybe he did go home, or farther down. Perhaps south-west to the reservoir. We'll have to see.' With that Hale pats a full stop on Peck's back and waves the seated groups to stand and follow.

As the night settles in, the only lights that remain on the moor are those close to the enormous wall. The rain has found its rhythm. On the north edge of the village things are quiet in the Morris household. A large shape was seen lingering near the back of the bungalow but was gone before an alarm could be raised. There was some noise in the fields but this was taken for nothing. The wind playing tricks.

The fire has not yet been lit. The candles are lonely and shadows are shivering against the walls. There's a cough from the sofa, wrapped in a red blanket. Charlotte is staring at the ceiling, looking at a ring of dampness that runs in a halo above her head. A sign, she thinks. A return. The damp patch had set in after the Tragedy, when Maisie was so full of questions; so many to push Charlotte to the edge and back on a daily basis. They'd told her that Grandfather had gone for a long walk and had never come back, which did little to stop her inquiring about his return so they eventually sat her down and told her that he was very old and he had died. Peter said she could light a candle in his memory, which she did every night for two weeks, placed beside a vigil for her baby brother even though Charlotte did not want it there.

In his father's absence Peter had said he would fix the ceiling, but grief had made him inattentive. He did little but lie and look upwards. And so the damp patch had grown. After around a month of inaction she'd rolled up her sleeves and taken it upon herself. A good thing she did. It was leaves, clogging the pipe and pushing water where it shouldn't, into the attic, where she'd stooped and pressed a cloth against the plaster. If they'd waited any longer she's sure the ceiling would have come crashing down, wood and plaster and all. It would have made short work of their daughter, who loves nothing more than to sit and write on the floor. She'd have been here, and they'd have been at the table and, crash, she would be out of their lives.

Charlotte thinks about it, sometimes, when she needs something immeasurably sad to sink into. If it had happened she does not know what she would have done.

There's a muffled cry. Maisie is pawing vowels against the bedroom wall. For some time her daughter has suffered from nightmares. Charlotte stands from the sofa and listens. Her daughter is moaning now, and it is like she has pressed her mouth against Charlotte's skin, forcing noises against her. Perhaps she should check on her, but she knows she is only sleeping and that soon the bad dreams will weaken to aches. Let her cry a bit, Charlotte thinks. She'll tire herself, like she tends to.

It had been a hard job to keep her away from others all day, which meant staying home from dawn to dusk. Maisie had written in her diary and practised a routine usually danced with school friends, which in their absence Charlotte had been made to take part in. Not that she'd minded. It was distracting to jump and spin for half an hour, forgetting the slander ricocheting beyond the walls of their home. Once, only once, had Charlotte looked at Maisie and considered whether there was truth to it all. Did she truly know what her husband was capable of? Immediately she'd felt ashamed, and wanted to hold her daughter so tightly against her breast, though something had stopped even an arm being raised. Ten minutes in the bathroom, then, to cry into a folded toilet tissue and wish to God that she was somewhere else, anywhere else, and that she was there alone, which only made her feel more guilty as she dabbed her tears and came out of the bathroom to join in with the dancing.

Tomorrow Charlotte will have to explain to her daughter why she isn't going to school, at least for a week or so. She knows exactly what the reaction will be. A brief display of sadness followed by seeming disregard that anything was ever said, then quiet with her pencil and paper before nightmares in bed. She does love it at school, even if she isn't the most popular of children. She is omnivorous, gobbling the maths and the English they give her, and Charlotte has even caught her looking at the books JM left behind, hardback tomes of René Descartes and Bishop Berkeley, although when Charlotte came closer she saw that Maisie was only tracing the indented patterns on the covers.

With a thud Charlotte sits back down and considers once more the ring above her. A stain, she decides. A furry circle. Something like an animal rune. You'd expect it to have been a smudge, where more water has pooled and waited in a splotch, but no, for some unsightly reason it had made an O, a thick O, the ceiling itself saying Oh. Something to do with the order of things above, no doubt. Something in the attic, which water has surrounded, besieged, unable to penetrate. She will have to fix it. She will have to go up there and find out what has made that shape, that letter, that number. A zero. Nought. Oh, Oh, Oh.

There's a knock at the door, harder than it has any right to be at that hour. Charlotte hesitates before standing, to see if the bang brings her daughter scurrying out of her room and into her arms. It'll mean wet sheets to deal with, washed in soapy water and hung out to dry. There's no sound of movement, though, so Charlotte stands and walks to the door. Letting the lock off the latch she opens it to James, his broadness slouched, face a sodden book. She waits for him to start but he doesn't so she takes it upon herself to make things happen. 'I suppose you'll be looking for him in the morning.'

His eyes flick back into the room beyond, towards the warm light. 'How do you know we didn't find him?' There is the twinkle that first drew her to him, the boldness that flashes in spite of the situation, and which has done so well for him here, in a village where most would prefer to keep their heads down.

'You're not coming in, if that's what you're angling for,' she says. 'Honestly, what's gotten into you.'

'I just thought you'd want to know.'

Charlotte reaches for something behind the door, her hands clasping at the neck of a thing long and leaning. Hale keeps his eyes on her, and she keeps them on him. 'Here's your umbrella back,' she says, pushing the folded object towards her neighbour. He has no other option but to take it, and he grabs it by the body as if he's wringing the neck of a bird. After that the door gets slammed shut and Charlotte rests herself against it, breathing.

In the village square Peck struggles to see through the clouded door of the tearoom, dim except for a faint glow in the kitchen. He knocks and, after a few seconds have passed, sees a body shift from the light. The shape of Grace Horn passes out of sight, emerging only inches from him, the space between cut by the single pane. 'Come in,' she calls through the glass.

'Doesn't anyone lock their doors here?' he asks, stepping out of the rain.

'No,' she answers plainly and glides back to her counter, Peck in her wake. 'James Hale was seen coming back empty-handed,' she comments, her voice wearier than when she'd spoken to him that morning. She uses the back of her sleeve to wipe sweat from her brow, pours out a flask into a pre-prepared pot. 'I told you I'd have something hot waiting, didn't I?' And with a smirk she places the lid with a click. Soon they are sitting at a table eating a meal of chicken soup, the pair of them wordless in enjoyment. A salt shaker is passed back and forth across the counter but there is no other interaction until the last bones have been stripped bare. When the meat is gone both of them lean back.

There's an intimacy that hasn't been earnt, Peck considers, but he hasn't made it to his age without taking charity first, pondering implications afterwards. He is a novelty, he decides; a new thing to talk to in this village, which is populated by a down-to-earth sort, more sociable than anyone he ever knew in the city. If she wants to feed him then who is he to push the plate away. Besides, if he's going to be staying here for some time, then it doesn't hurt to get to know his new neighbours.

'I'll need to argue for a bigger portion next time,' Grace says as she scrapes a piece of dried gristle with the edge of her spoon. 'I'll have a quiet word with Geoff.'

Peck is surprised, both at the name and the presumption of a next time. 'Sharpe?' he checks.

Grace waves the name with her hands. Peck pats his lips with a piece of tissue and is surprised by a small burp, which seems to go unnoticed.

'I don't talk politics,' she says. 'So don't bother asking.'

'Am I asking?'

'Atonement,' she pronounces, the weight of the word sagging in the middle. 'Geoff's had his telling-off. That's the state of it as far as I'm concerned.'

Looking out of the window onto the dark square, Peck realises he didn't pass anybody in the stocks on his way here. Presumably the atonement had run its course and Geoff Sharpe has been allowed to go back to his life. It was a grim proceeding but in hindsight it was at least short. 'Law and order and all that,' he says.

Grace's tic makes her right eyelid flutter. Peck tries not to show he has noticed. She gives him a side glance as she finishes her tea, then picks her tooth with the end of a fork. 'If he took a bit more time looking after the pigs and minding the fences then he wouldn't have found himself in such an unpopular position,' she opines. 'I know how it looks when you've got him out there, stuck in God knows what, but it's really very simple. Mind yourself. Don't steal. Don't piss people off.'

She runs her hands up her forehead, into the roots of her scalp. Peck thinks about the barley field, a ripple reaching upwards. 'We all have our responsibilities,' she concludes. 'We all have work to do.'

The rain has stopped and Peck walks by Grace's side after the dishes have been washed. On the road towards her home the wind is the only other presence aside from the clucks of the chicken coop. The pace is relaxed, which is a refreshing change from Hale's march across the moor, and they stop on the wet ground to look at the chickens and roosters sitting in partitioned groups. Grace kneels to touch a feathered head as it sleeps beside the wire mesh, close to a puddle. 'What do you think it's dreaming about?' she whispers.

'Grain,' Peck offers.

'I think it's dreaming about the sea.'

'Doubt it's ever seen the sea.'

Grace looks at him through a squint. 'Just because you've never seen the sea doesn't mean you can't dream about it.'

Waves come to Peck's mind. Tireless, grey and made of glass. 'It'd be hard.'

The chicken opens its eye and there is something petrified about the expression it holds; a fiery ring around a pupil, tightening closer until the black spot could pop. Grace snaps her hand away from the wire with another laugh and the chicken runs into the shelter of the coop. The sight of the animal's fear unsettles Peck. He is reminded of Geoff Sharpe, lying half submerged in the bog. The look on the man's face at the sound of footsteps, his eye shaking in its socket. He spits on the ground and is given a look to make it clear that's not something he should ever think of doing again.

'You saw Charlotte Morris this morning then?' she asks as they walk farther down the path, with a casualness that strikes Peck as intentional. He nods. 'How did she seem?'

'Alarmed.'

In response she makes a humming noise, turns her face away from him, towards the fields with dark hedges disquieted by the wind. But soon the wind dies down and the trees regain their composure. Grace reaches for his hand as they approach her home, a sizeable, thatched-roofed cottage on the periphery of the village. She squeezes his fingers and thanks him for walking with her. Her skin is warm and Peck can't help but be aware of the heat passing beneath his palm. Is this what he needs? Now that her interest is explicit he feels self-conscious, although there's no denying his own heartbeat, thrashing like a rabbit. At that moment a cry is heard, unlike anything Peck has heard before, not even in the longest nights of the city when it could sound like the whole world was wheezing. The cry begins like a howl, breaks into pieces, falls into a low wail. After it has gone the darkness around him seems more evident, as if he could pinch the shade between his thumb and finger and pull it over the both of them. 'Should we see what it is?' he asks.

'A fox,' she assures him. They wait for the cry to happen again but the night is quiet. It's only then that he realises she is still holding his hand, and all at once a sense of paranoia sits on top of him. Where is she leading him? Where is she taking him so assuredly, and why is he letting himself be taken? He slips his hand from hers, stands back to leave.

'Are you feeling alright?' she asks. 'Your face. Looks like the chicken we spooked.'

'It's been a nice walk but I should be going now.'

'Don't you want to come inside?'

The cottage is too big for one person. The windows are covered with thick curtains. He looks for lamplight spilling across the windowsill. As far as he can tell, everything is dark, everything is motionless.

'My cousin's probably wondering where I've got to.'

She looks disappointed, but nods all the same and gives him a weak smile before turning to her door. Before it is shut she flutters her fingers and Peck holds his hand up in return. Left alone, he waits to see what light emerges from Grace's home. He stands there for a minute. There's no sight of a glow, none at all. He lets his tongue fill the fresh gap in his jaw, strokes the exposed gum and pictures fish scales. When the house remains unlit, he decides to walk back through the village, retracing from memory the path they'd taken from the centre.

On the way he looks for the cause of the cry. Look is too strong a word. He waits to see if the cause crosses his path, and he does so by scanning dark draperies between houses. If he finds a body he will make it his responsibility. If there is someone bleeding out he will not let implication get in the way of helping the poor soul. Let the others watch, let them make their assumptions. He is better than that. Peck walks back the way he came, past the chicken coop, the birds all gone from view inside their shelter. He skirts past the path that leads down to the village green, with its empty stage and scaffolding, returning instead to the centre square, its border buildings hemmed around the empty stocks and the worn memorial, a moss-specked cenotaph for some war. To the north is the road to Hale's, to the west is the wall. But he lingers beside the stone pillar, shorn of a head and skinned of its inscriptions. It is there that he hears footsteps, small and dragged, and he listens to them approach with heart racing. If it is someone begging for help he will not give a second thought, but will throw himself into whatever needs to be done. If it is Peter Morris, he will take him home, to talk to his wife and his daughter and to explain in calm words exactly where he has been. If it is someone that has come for him, then he will meet that person there, in the open square. He catches his reflection in the tearoom window, eyeless under overhead light, and stands a little straighter.

Out of the shadows comes a dog, dragging a legless bottom half with its remaining two paws. It is the same animal he saw carried the morning of Geoff Sharpe's punishment; a Jack Russell terrier with both back legs gone. It is breathing heavily and its eyes are bulging, each inch of movement a struggle to force its deformed body a little farther over the cobblestones. Peck watches it move for a few seconds, then coughs. The dog turns its head. As soon as it spots Peck, it stops its crawl. There is no sign of the dog's master, no footsteps following in its tracks. Its coat is wet with the recent rain, muddied from dragging its torso along the ground as if it were a long, white sack. There in the square, Peck and the dog look at each other. A moment passes and, with great effort, the dog turns back the way it came, disappearing from view.

# Four

THOMAS RAMPLE IS THIEVING FISTFULS OF NAILS. *JAMES HALE LET PETER MORRIS GO.* SARAH TWINE IS DRINKING ON THE JOB. THOMAS RAMPLE STOLE MY HAMMER. **ANNA MOAR IS A CHEATING WHORE.**

BELOW THESE SENTENCES SOMEONE has written a message about a hat found by the barley field and if anyone has lost theirs they will find it with Scott Doyle. A home is needed for Ellen Hadfield's five kittens. Brian Goss has written a reminder that it would be helpful if people could clean up their plates next time there is an event on the green.

Peck's eyes linger over the name JAMES HALE. He stands there beside the man with his iron pipe leant against his shoulder. The accusations against Peter have already started to fade, covered in places with the fresh sentences. Peck turns then to his cousin and looks him in the eye with a worry that's hard to contain. Geoff Sharpe was a body far from his own. Peter Morris was closer, still far enough so that the stone thrown into the pond didn't worry him with ripples. James Hale is another matter entirely. It is a name he has known since he was a boy. To see it scrawled there above his head is an intrusion, as if a part of himself had been splashed with something unclean. The wall, in that moment, seems to Peck alive in its malignancy, conscious in its efforts to do them harm, and he would not be surprised to see the lines between slabs open and close with the slight course of breathing.

'We don't do anything if there's only one,' Hale assures, later, when they are sitting opposite each other in the tearoom. 'Or if there are only a couple of bad things written. Normally. More than that and there'll be a burden to carry, but if the name hasn't been written again and again then we leave it.' He rocks a cup back and forth by pressing on its handle with a big finger. They have not been given tea that morning, Peck notices, only a pot of boiled water. 'There needs to be a general agreement. What else would you expect? Go chasing every bad feeling? There'd be nothing to gain. We'd be torn in so many directions and it wouldn't be fair on people. No, we don't do anything if there isn't a sense of consistency. There's no cause for alarm here.'

'Doesn't look good, though, does it?' Peck says, peering out through the glass to the square, with its empty stocks and a few people flitting to and fro along the borders.

'It could look worse, I assure you.'

'You're right,' Peck mutters. 'It could be my name up there. How long until that happens?'

A wounded frown appears on Hale's face, and he gingerly folds one of his hands into the other. Peck regrets exposing his own selfishness. It should be him calming Hale, telling his cousin there's nothing to worry about, that these things surely happen and they should just get on with life. But he is stirred by the sentences. If Hale can have his name plastered there for all to see, what's to stop his own behind being brandished like an order? He can feel the panic rise in his chest. Is he being ungenerous, he wonders? Is this place bringing out the worst in him? A cold sweat covers his face at the realisation that he is tangled up with it, and that he is watched and judged just like everybody else.

'To be honest now, I'd be more worried for Anna Moar,' Hale eventually says, scratching the area of his neck beneath his thin gold chain. 'Infidelity is not taken to kindly around here.'

'Is that so?'

'Gets people upset.'

Peck watches a man and a woman walk across the square, hands held tight and pace kept in perfect step. 'Probably because they're all up to it,' he says.

'I don't know what you mean.'

'Of course you don't.'

Hale is not laughing. 'The fuck are you talking about,' he mutters, careful for others not to hear.

'Mind your language.' Peck nudges his knuckle against his own cup and feels the heat against his skin. Any further reaction from Hale is stifled by a commotion occurring at the shop entrance. A man has stumbled into the tearoom with a nightstand bound to his neck. The weight of it has made his face bright red, and he splutters as he struggles across the threshold. As soon as he is noticed, Grace points at the exit from behind the counter.

'Come on now, Thomas. You know the rules.'

The man is middle-aged and his clothes are too big for him. There is a bruise under one of his eyes and dirt on his knees. He presses his hands together and wheezes the words: 'Please. I've no water at home and the boiler won't let me in until after dark.'

'You'll only be a day or two with it at most,' Grace states, as a parent would to a punished child.

'Please,' he replies.

It's a sad sight, thinks Peck. Pathetic, even. He has a penknife in his pocket. He should stand and cut the man's ropes, free him from his furniture and tell the room that this sort of thing is barbaric. It doesn't need to be like this, when elsewhere there is hope and hard work. There are fields of barley, there are hives of honey, there are classrooms of children. He is sure his cousin would help him, given a choice. If Peck asked Hale, truly asked him, to take a stand, he is convinced their history would outweigh any patterns he has fallen into. They were far from angels in their youth but they were loyal to each other, and Hale would stand beside him if Peck liberated this man from his burden. He knows it. But he does not stand. He does not cut the man's ropes. He does not ask Hale to help him.

'Please,' Thomas begs Grace again. A few people look over. As soon as they see the ropes they turn their attention back to their tables. Grace motions with her hand for the man to be quiet, then walks him as quickly as she can towards the door. He does not resist. She checks no gazes remain, and when none are found she gently repositions the nightstand so that it is better supported on the man's back. Peck catches this small moment of charity and feels foolish for the unease he'd slipped into the night before. Of all the things to be concerned about, of all the uncertainties, why had he been panicked by a walk alone with this woman? 'Go home,' she whispers to Thomas, and leads him outside. On the way back to the counter she catches Peck's eye like a match against the side of a box.

It is not too late for him to leave. If he got himself far enough, maybe he would be out of reach. If he left the moor entirely, made for the coast or headed back to the city, then he'd be out of it. He could run at night, when Hale and the others snored. Give it a few days and he'd be wide clear of the village and its customs, if you could call them that. If you could call mob rule a custom. He'd have to find his gun, of course. His revolver, which he'd almost forgotten about, tucked into Peter Morris's trousers, and the thought of it rushes over his cheeks and he longs to stand up, shake all of this from him. In the city he wouldn't have let himself be dazed, tricked into fascination by communal tearooms and self-sufficiency, built around petty squabbles stamped like commandments. In the city he'd known the exact dimensions between his bed and the window. In a few days he could be back there, with or without his gun, the mattress springs digging into the same places along his spine. If Peck left that night, he'd be careful not to make a peep as he closed the front door, just as Hale had done when he abandoned him years before. In the city he could find a place to hide; somewhere to keep his body unnameable. But how far would he make it before they sent a party to search for him? Why would he run, unless he had done something wrong? And what on earth would he be returning to? To his mother's home, with the hope that the windows remain unbroken? To an emptying stock of tinned sardines? Surely it would be better to stay, where he has a roof over his head and a friend to help him. Better to stay but keep out of trouble. Better that. Better that than a withered retreat. A fading city. A death in between.

'You've nothing to worry about,' Hale soothes. Clearly he has noticed Peck's anxiety. The tension in his voice has disappeared completely. He leans over and lets his hand rest against his cousin's wrist, which surprises Peck with its affection, and he feels a spasm of guilt for considering a hasty departure. For a brief moment he is a boy again, standing side by side with Hale as they burn the body of his mother and her killer. He should not abandon his cousin. Not now they are reunited. They have been through too much together.

'You've done nothing wrong,' says Hale, leaning back again. 'They're angry at me for letting him slip. It makes sense. He's my neighbour. If it escalates and I need to be burdened for a while, then so be it. I can't see it going beyond that. I really can't.'

'I was under the impression you were Mr Popular here.' Hale just shrugs at this. Peck watches him tip his cup towards his mouth. The way his throat shakes as he drinks the hot water reminds Peck of animal entrails throbbing under fur. He rests the empty cup on the table, black grit pooled at the bottom, and raises the pot to refill. 'Who wrote it do you think?'

'It doesn't matter.'

'I'd want to know.'

Hale gives him a sideways glance as he pours more hot water into his cup. Peck hasn't touched his. Hale drinks again, less voracious than before. His lower lip strokes the edge of the cup like a wound sucking a finger.

'Have you had your name up there before this?' Peck asks.

'No.'

'Never?'

'No.'

It speaks volumes, thinks Peck, but Hale doesn't bat an eyelid. He keeps his lips on the cup until it has been drained dry, then rests it on the table.

'We rarely do anything if there's only one mention, or two,' Hale repeats, for his own peace of mind, thinks Peck.

A couple on a table beside them are looking over, their scrutiny sticking like flypaper. A young woman and her mother, the same face but sliced and diced with extra years. They are speaking in low tones, rolling out of reach, but they're looking right at Peck and Hale's table. He meets their eyes but as soon as he does they look away.

*James Hale is losing his touch*, he thinks. *James Hale has let us down.*

---

When they've finished their drinks Hale leads Peck out of the tearoom, across the square where the cenotaph stands. He catches sight of the wall. From here, the biggest words are still visible. It is hard for his eye not to be drawn to them as they make their way towards the shape of a man. He wears a thick brown moustache and a red and white striped apron, sleeves rolled up to expose two muscular forearms, one angled towards his hip and the other wielding a butcher's knife. The fibreglass model looks at Peck through scrunched eyes. He stands with back arched, face shadowed under a straw boater hat. Above him a sign reads BUTCHER'S: A TRADER YOU CAN TRUST. As they enter the shop Peck turns back to the effigy, head unmoved, staring now across the square at people and buildings. A bell attached to the inside of the door rings as they cross the threshold, and Peck is met with the scent of meat.

'Morning Geoff,' Hale says, and a figure emerges from the back room. Peck is surprised. In his mind he'd sectioned this man off as dead, so pale he'd looked in the stocks. Geoff Sharpe hobbles on a pair of crutches towards the glass counter separating the pair from the butcher, the expression on his face souring the instant he realises James Hale is standing in front of him. His curled lips betray his feelings only for a moment, before he manages to pull the muscles into a semblance of pleasantness.

'How's the leg?' asks Peck, genuinely curious, but his question is met with no response. Instead, Geoff keeps his gaze settled on the broad form of Hale, angling his head slightly to show he is waiting for an order. Looking beyond the butcher, Peck notices for the first time another figure behind the counter. Sitting on a wooden chair, set against the wall so neatly that he takes him at first for another statue, is what appears to be a man. He wears the same white overalls as Geoff, the same red and white apron and the same straw boater hat. His face, though, is covered from top to bottom with bandages. The man's hands are clasped at the armrests of his chair. He sits unmoving except for the slightest of ebbs in his bandaged face, wafting inwards and outwards. There is what appears to be a hole, large enough to fit two fingers, placed exactly in the centre of his open mouth. Peck assumes it is open because when he looks at the hole there are no signs of lips or teeth, just blackness. The sight of it against the pure white of the bandages makes Peck shudder. There is no sign of blood, no trace of whatever injury this bandage covers. The terrible invisibility of it, he considers.

'Are we looking bare?' asks Hale, who is peering through the glass counter at the sparse collection spread within. The smell of meat had led Peck to believe that the butcher's shop held a cornucopia of pink, red and white flesh puckered for purchase within glass cabinets, bursting at the seams with fresh cuts. Instead, the plates of meat seen through the counter are notable in their barrenness. Small pools of old blood sit half-caked onto the crockery, but little in the way of actual meat has been placed for show.

'No lamb in the last week,' says Geoff, the words strapped and fed into the air unwillingly.

'And beef?'

'Can't see a cow go right now.'

Hale leans his hands on the counter, palms flat against the glass, his head focused at the sparse collection of sinew as if he is inspecting a collection of butterflies. 'What about chicken?' he asks, pointing to what looks to be a cut of breast. 'That,' he emphasises, the tip of his forefinger making a tap against the glass three times. 'That. One. There.' Geoff considers this, also looking down through the counter at the slice. Peck pulls his attention to the bandaged man, a faint sound of wheezing coming from the hole where his mouth should be. He had been silent before but now his breathing is audibly more of a struggle. Still, he doesn't move his body or his head. Only the ridges of the hole show any sign of movement, bending back and forth with each exchange of breath.

'You've had your portion this week,' Geoff decides. He folds his arms and looks at Hale, right in the eye. When Hale straightens to meet Geoff's stare the butcher weakens, looking down again at the edge of the counter.

'Are we talking portions now?'

Geoff doesn't respond. His eyes stick to the plates inside the counter, but then, confidence collected, he forces his attention back up to Hale. He looks at him and doesn't say a word, and this seems to catch Hale off guard, who blinks and hesitates before rubbing the back of his head. He's not used to such treatment, is all Peck can conclude, a hot wave passing across his shoulders. He recognises the impulse to protect his cousin and is assured by the strength of the feeling, pleased that there is power in the bond they share.

'Good to see Gerrard up,' Hale says, collecting himself, his voice a calm, drawn-out line. 'I heard he wasn't doing well.'

The bandaged man moves his head towards his own name but doesn't speak. He's likely to be a similar build to Geoff, thinks Peck. Although hard to tell his age with the face covered. Geoff continues to focus on Hale, all nervousness pushed out of sight. Peck thinks there's a fire in the way the butcher looks out. The glass counter between them begins to seem brittle. If things got nasty, surely the two of them could overpower the crippled pair and take whatever meat they wanted. A few punches and Geoff would be on the floor, which is unlikely to do much to convince people of their graciousness, but if Hale's position in the town is under threat, would a sign of ferocity be the worst thing? Peck and Hale, surviving side by side.

'Will that be all?' Geoff asks, but before there is time to respond the front door swings open, the bell grounding the room's electricity. In walks the portly man Peck had seen on the stage after Geoff's leg had been shattered. Brian Goss. He walks on polished shoes until he is next to Peck's cousin, his head only going so far as to reach the middle of Hale's torso.

'Morning Geoff,' Brian says with a voice that fills whatever pothole had formed over the last minute. Geoff's countenance changes in front of Peck's eyes. He straightens his back and leads with a smile.

'Brian,' he says. 'Nice to see you. How's things?'

'Haven't complained since I was a boy,' comes the definitive answer. 'I'm not starting now. Things are well. As good as they've ever been. And you? Healing?'

There is a shuffle from Geoff, as he repositions his weight from one crutch to the other. 'Yes, thank you.'

'Good.' Brian smiles as Geoff clears his throat and looks away, like a beaten dog. This submissiveness must have been the treatment Hale had been expecting when they first walked into the butcher's. 'Did you hear all of that about Anna Moar? Cheating on Martin, apparently.'

Geoff tentatively nods. 'Not a nice thing to do, that's for sure.'

'Cruel,' Brian says decidedly, his tone a rubber stamp. 'It's a cruel thing to do. I don't suppose you know who she's been having it off with?'

'I heard it was Scott Doyle,' says Geoff, glancing at Peck.

'Scott? With his daughter's birthday only just been. Tsk tsk.'

'It's what I heard.' Another look to Peck. Why is Geoff looking at him? Is he expecting a reaction? No, thinks Peck. This is the attention of someone who wants to be sure of who is listening. The stranger in the village is becoming a stranger no more. Peck is being taken into confidences, and the idea of this is as gratifying as it is daunting.

*Scott Doyle fucked Anna Moar on his daughter's birthday*, Peck thinks to himself.

'I don't doubt it,' Brian says, face scrunched up as if he's found a bad smell. 'Nothing has been written against him, mind. Only the one thing up there about Anna. I hope it doesn't come to anything. But, if you heard it. And if I've heard it. Well. You never know how these things go. Needs looking into at least. To do something like that. Unimaginable.' There is a mutual shaking of heads in disbelief and a small smile flashes across Geoff's lips. Relief, thinks Peck. Happiness at being allowed back into the fold.

'And of course there's the annoyance of that Peter. I'm sure James has told you all about that.' At this Brian turns his attention to Hale, acknowledging him for the first time since he'd entered the shop. 'Slippery man, was it?'

'He must've set out earlier than we thought,' Hale says, a sheen of defensiveness clear in his voice. 'But don't you worry, we'll look again today. I have a few theories on where he might have got to. There were footprints seen to the south, so he might have circled back somehow.'

'You boys don't want to strain yourselves.' Brian taps to the chicken breast that had, moments before, become a point of contention. Without hesitation Geoff bends over to pick it up, moving to wrap it in paper. 'He hasn't got his father's experience,' Brian continues, his voice aimed at Geoff's back. 'He won't last more than a day out there. Still, it's impressive, no? To get away from our James Hale.'

Brian considers Peck, who straightens from leaning against the white tiled wall. As soon as he does this he feels embarrassed at the reaction, as if he has been caught doing something he shouldn't by the only adult in the room. Brian looks at him only for a second before turning back to the counter. 'I heard you've joined in,' he says. 'With relish.'

It takes Peck a second to realise Brian is talking to him. 'Relish?' he asks.

'That's the word I heard,' Brian says, turning again to face him, his eyes surprisingly warm.

Having been a witness for the past few minutes, Peck now feels himself the centre of attention. Hale is looking at him, as is Geoff behind the counter. Even the black hole in Gerrard's bandages feels like it's aimed at him. His heart is beating faster and he's irritated at his body's betrayal. His face reddens. He wants to laugh it off but can't draw any sounds from his throat. In the end, he just gives a thumbs up.

Geoff leans over the counter to pass the wrapped cut of meat. Brian takes it with a smile, which remains on his face when he turns once more to Hale. 'Tell you what, why don't the both of you have lunch with me?' he asks, his voice a breeze. 'It'd be nice to have the company. What do you say?' He holds up the package, swinging it back and forth. 'I have chicken and you two look hungry.'

---

Brian's home is bigger than most. It stands not far from the western walkway leading up to the wall and to the moor beyond; an enviable position, especially when you take it to be the only house in village to have a balcony. No doubt the cause of some covetousness, Peck thinks, not that Brian looks like he spends many days sunning himself in view of his neighbours. Instead, the balcony is packed from end to end with plant pots. Stout tubs, hanging baskets, clay vats. All of them carrying dirt, dark with the rain. Taken from street level, the balcony is a blend of green, yellow and brown lines, some supple, some brittle, all moving back and forth in the wind. It's an unruly sight and cuts a sharp contrast to the rest of the building. Unlike most facades Peck has seen in the village, Brian's walls are painted neat and clean, no chips and patches worn by the weather. Instead of wearing its scars in view, his house is a brilliant and uniform blue. The same blue as a clear sky, and a reminder of what hangs above the rain. A reminder of what is possible in the best of times, he imagines.

Inside, Brian labours in the kitchen. Peck leans against the doorway sipping a tumbler of water, observing the mess of flour and eggs, the half-empty shells looking like sacked cities, drooling and sobbing onto the chopping boards. There are cut-offs of pastry and metal shapes that have done the sectioning. There are more tools away from the kitchen surface, brushes and rollers, stored in buckets, caked in dry red paint. Whatever sense of time Brian had been keeping comes to an end and he opens the door to the wood oven with a heave. Three pies purr in their new life.

Guided to the main room, Peck and Hale sit side by side at an ornate dining table. The wood has been recently varnished and it feels smooth under the tips of Peck's fingers. On the other side of the room, through an open partition, is a plush sofa and armchair, above which is a large painting of a shipwreck.

'Help yourself,' Brian says, and offers his tray to Hale and Peck in turn, before taking a seat on the other side of the table from the pair. Soon all three men sit in silence with hot pies on porcelain plates, as if conducting some strange séance in pastry. Brian is the first to cut a slice, and he does so in one swift action. For a moment he closes his eyes, drinks the gamey scent, and then lets his teeth sink into the skin. Peck considers the crust of his own pie, a deep brown, blistered black in places.

'How do you find our small pocket of the world?' Brian asks.

Peck pushes the edge of his knife into the pie, releasing a cloud of steam. 'You have an enviable sense of community,' he says.

'Yes, compared to the city I'm sure the lines are easier to make out.' Brian points at himself. 'I am here. You are there.' He takes another bite of his pie, larger than the first. 'Not that there's division,' he insists as he wipes away a speck of gravy from his chin with a napkin. 'Nothing like that. We all pull together. Everyone does their bit.'

'Everyone chips in.'

'You've got a sense of that, have you? Excellent. I'm glad that comes across.'

'I can see everyone pays attention to each other.'

'Very perceptive of you.'

Peck can't help but savour the compliment. 'Keen eyes,' he says, pointing to his own face, to which Hale kicks his ankle under the table and whispers at him to shut up.

'No, he's fine,' Brian offers. 'I'm sure you do. Very good eyes. What makes you think they're keen, as you put it?'

'I can see who gets the best cuts.'

Brian laughs at this. 'Very observant. I'm only a member of the community, though. Just like James here. We have no mayor, no king.'

Hale's head is lowered now, considering the meal on his plate.

'There's not one of us that's lording it over things,' Brian continues, placing a hand on his heart. 'You can think of me as a simple administrator. I keep track of what happens, when it happens, where it happens. Deaths, births, marriages, grain, livestock, weather, building material. It's frightfully boring, to be honest with you, but someone needs to volunteer to keep a record of all the comings and goings. Helps us plan, for sure, and I can't deny there's a part of me that enjoys the thought of future generations looking at what we've lain down.' A sad smile passes across his lips. 'I'm also an enthusiastic cook, as you might have guessed.' He chuckles to himself. 'And I am humoured in my attempts at public speaking.'

'Sounds like a nice way to live.'

'We're only thankful not to be in the city. Such a hellish place, from what I've gathered. It's a living nightmare over there, isn't it?' The question isn't really a question, Peck thinks, watching Brian as he sets his fork on the half-eaten pie, lifting a chunk of chicken from the pooling gravy to his lips. 'All the dirt and the crime,' he goes on unimpeded, a wet speck of pastry flying into the space between them. 'It's a wonder people live there without going mad.' He laps his tongue around teeth and gums. 'But I'm losing myself. I don't need to tell you about how things stand, when you just came from exactly there. You grew up in the city, is that right?' he asks, the edges of his words sanded dull with civility.

'That's right,' Peck says. 'As did Hale.'

'So he did, so he did,' Brian nods. 'I forget sometimes, given he's part of the furniture now. You can tell it every now and then, though; some of the coarse language he uses.' Hale looks up and meets Brian's eye. 'But it's true, it's true, so you'll both know how bad things can be. Every man for himself. It must be a difficult place to keep your thoughts turned upwards, knowing things will run out.' He stretches both hands outwards, beckoning to the room that surrounds them. 'Our walls are still standing,' he proclaims.

'That's very true.' Peck bobs his head. 'One more so than the rest.'

'Strange that we don't have many visitors,' Brian continues. 'It's not that we're averse to them. There's just not many that come. I sometimes wonder why that is. Who wouldn't want to be here?'

Peck looks him in the eye. 'You're not in the most accessible location.'

'Yes, I suppose that's true,' Brian laughs, gesticulating at Peck with his fork. 'I forget that sometimes.' He leans in. 'You made it without a scratch, though. Very impressive.' He leans back. 'You must be something of a survivor.' Peck feels Brian's eyes on him; a paperweight pushing against his face. 'So you're a cousin of James's then?'

'We were boys together, then young men,' Peck explains. He isn't sure how much more to say to this man, who is clearly weighing every word he puts out into the world. 'We were inseparable,' he tells him, which is true for the most part. 'Although he did leave,' he admits, careful not to make eye contact with Hale. 'And then I was alone for some time, until he sent me a letter and, well, I came here.'

'Reunited at last.' Brian claps his hands, then waves to Hale, much like he would a picture on a wall. 'Would you say he's changed?'

Peck sizes his cousin up. 'He's a bit bigger than he used to be.' Hale looks down and, with good humour, pats his belly.

'Fatter, I bet,' Brian agrees. 'Food is the first thing you'll hear us talk about here,' he says, leaning in once again, closer to Peck.

'I think food tends to be the first, second and third point of conversation for most people these days,' Peck replies, leaning in also. He is enjoying the closeness that Brian, who plainly wields power in the community, is inviting of him. Since arriving he'd felt like Hale's guest and little more, but in the past day he has been led, step by step, deeper into the neighbourhood. 'Seems you've got these things taken care of with the barley and the livestock,' he compliments. 'The pigs and sheep are still on their feet.'

'We've been lucky,' grumbles Hale. 'And there have been illnesses. Two lambs gone last week. A pig missing.'

There is no response to this. 'Still,' Peck says. 'You're not starving. There don't seem to be many problems on that front, not in this fine house you have.'

'That's kind of you to say,' Brian beams. 'I try to keep it in shape.'

Hale breathes a hot burst of air out of his nostrils. 'Our cupboards aren't as full as you think. Not for all of us.'

'He can be a real misery, can't he?' Peck smiles. Perhaps his cousin is feeling wounded by his treatment in the butcher's shop. Perhaps he really is concerned about how the village will feed itself should fortunes turn, should their animals die like the others and confirm their worst fears about the future; that things are not in fact climbing upwards and that this pocket of prosperity is nothing more than a snagged sleeve on an outstretched arm. In either case, Peck is strangely enjoying his cousin's newfound surliness. It is giving him an opportunity to position himself as an optimist. Cheerfully, he gestures to what little remains of the pie on his plate. 'This is delicious by the way. It's got a real texture.'

'I'm glad you think so, Duncan. I've got more, if you're good.'

Peck cackles at the word. 'If I'm good?' There's no laughter back. Peck looks to Hale, then back to Brian. 'Do you want me to be good?'

'I do.'

Brian's eyes are on him. Whatever fuzziness lingered around his irises for the past few minutes has dissipated, and he stares with a bucketful of meaning. It's a heavy load. The air is crisp, and Peck shifts uncomfortably against the edge of the table.

'With the world as hard as it is, we must be good men.'

'What are you worried about?' Hale asks, exasperation whetting his words. It's his turn to sit upright now, and he does so after unceremoniously dropping his knife and fork on the table. 'Let's get this over with.'

'Peter Morris is a friend of yours,' Brian states.

'He's my neighbour, is what you mean.'

'And so I want to make sure everyone's going to be well behaved.'

'Is that it?' Hale asks, voice impatient. 'Is that what you're worried about? You think I might've let him get away?'

'It did cross my mind, if we're being blunt.'

There is a loud crack as Hale rolls his shoulders. 'You don't have to worry about us,' he growls. 'I'm reliable, always have been, and I can vouch for Peck. If you're worried then we'll go out tonight. We'll look for lights in the south. Peter is hardly a survivalist, he's not going to have got farther than a day's walk at most. There's no way he'd make his way off the moor, he wouldn't know how. And he's not going to do the same as his father.'

Brian considers all of this for a moment. 'Fine.' Nothing is said then until Peck breaks the silence.

'Did you know his father well?'

The question, asked politely, comes as a surprise. 'JM,' says Brian, letting the letters hang. 'You could say I knew him well, yes. You could say that. Since I was born, really.'

'Seems like he was something of a presence.'

'Literally so. Tall as you like. The law and order man before James here stepped into those particular boots.'

It is as if Peck has picked at something bottled. He can feel Hale stiffen beside him, muscles curdling. Instead of deterring Brian, this body language seems to encourage him. 'Jacob, Jacob, Jacob,' the administrator says with nostalgia on his lips. 'You'd catch him a mile off, with his red hair and a plank of two-by-four on his shoulder. Most people around here will remember him grey, but I'll always remember him with red hair. A roofer, like his father before him. Like his son too, although he very much had the shape for it, quite unlike Peter in that respect.'

The shape of a giant grazes Peck's mind. His tongue passes over the gap in his mouth, running up and down the bare gum as he imagines a footprint in the mud.

With the meal finished, Brian ushers them to sit on the other side of the open partition. He excuses himself for a moment and it is long enough for Peck to stretch his legs and wander around the edges of the room, stopping at a cabinet of small trinkets, a bookcase of old maps and a large chest of drawers, full of files, binders and neatly rolled pieces of paper.

'He has a book on every one of us,' Hale says, watching Peck from his new position on the sofa. 'So I've been led to believe.'

Peck digs his fingers into one of the files at random, prying it open just enough for him to see the handwriting within.

'It won't be those.'

The writing is messy, but there is something about counting grain and sacks. Perhaps it's a list. Whatever the case, it's nothing exciting, so Peck slips his fingers out and tries another page at random. This time there is a hand-drawn diagram of a person lying naked on what looks to be a large wheel. It is quite detailed.

'They're nowhere I've been able to find,' Hale says, in a whisper now, for there are footsteps approaching. Peck lets the page close under the weight of the other files. He quickly neatens the edges before stepping away. When Brian returns he takes the armchair and it is time to join Hale on the sofa, who yanks his jacket when Peck sits on it. Above their host's head is the painting of the shipwreck, and from this distance Peck can make out the detail. The rocks have been at fault. Jagged pillars slashing unceremoniously into the wooden hull, the topsail cracked at an angle, the sun breaking red over the horizon. On the ship, sailors wail at the chaos around. One has wrapped his forearms around a coil of rope and is heaving at nothing in particular. Another is pointing at the foaming water below his position. Everyone is occupied with their own disaster. All except for one man; a lone figure piling bodies into a lifeboat. A sad sight, Peck thinks, wondering why Brian would choose to hang such a tragic scene on his wall. There's little in it to calm the mind.

'Big man, Jacob Morris,' muses Brian, picking up talk as he'd left it. 'He had a reputation for listening to conversations and eating eggs. His dungarees had a pouch that could hold seven. Eggs not conversations,' he adds with a laugh. 'Although it wouldn't surprise me, the way he'd gather chatter. A great big ear. An aerial mast. It wasn't uncommon to see him standing on top of a house, perched on the roof. That's how I remember him, at least.'

'Peeling eggs?' Peck ventures.

'Exactly,' Brian says with a point of his finger. 'On the roof of a house, straddled, enormous, plopping eggs into his maw. And what a mouth it was. Jacob Morris wasn't a talker, not a babbler like his son can be, but when Jacob spoke you knew about it. There was a depth to his voice that was hard to fight. Rarely loud. Low, running underneath whatever else was being said. It nudged at the foundations, you could say. You could have been speaking about the most important thing in the world, the most important thing, then you'd hear Jacob's voice and it would seem as if you were talking about nothing at all.'

'Come on now,' Hale protests, clearly irritated. 'JM spoke just like you or I.'

Train of thought broken, Brian eyes Hale with something approaching disdain. 'One time he fixed my father's roof after a storm,' he says. 'I could hear his footsteps above the rafters. I knew he could hear everything. All the words being said by my family. All the things we were talking about, probably the things only being thought about. That's why the man was invited so often for dinner, you see. All those conversations he was privy to.'

'A bit of a gossip,' says Peck.

'Quite the opposite,' says Brian. 'You didn't feed Jacob Morris to hear what he had heard about others. You fed him because you could never be sure what he had heard about you.' He taps his nose. 'He listened and he remembered.'

'Stockpiled weapons,' mutters Hale.

'He was a man you wanted to keep on your side,' Brian winks. 'Hardly a week would pass before some house or other would ask him inside for a meal. Little Peter on his lap, never going hungry for the warm welcome of others. Of course, that only meant he knew even more about everyone's comings and goings. It made him the perfect person for keeping law and order.'

Hale rearranges his weight on the sofa but doesn't say anything. Brian has leant back into his chair and looks to Peck like a carving cut from wood. How has he ended up in this position of power? Peck wonders. Where does charisma end and meticulous record-keeping begin?

'Big man, Jacob Morris,' Brian repeats. 'There was someone who knew the length and breadth of a sentence. I do miss him sometimes.'

'What happened to him?'

'A pity,' Brian exhales with a shake of the head. 'A real pity. Less than a year ago they found him with his baby grandson's body. It's a terrible thing, to kill a child, especially your own flesh and blood.'

'A terrible thing,' echoes Hale.

There is eye contact, before Brian taps the sides of his armchair. 'Go after Peter tomorrow,' he instructs. 'That's if he hasn't come back on his own by then. You want to let Charlotte get something cooking. When his belly starts rumbling and his mind starts wandering to warmer rooms, you can't blame him for staggering home.'

'And if he doesn't?'

Brian keeps tapping. 'I'm sure you'll do a good job of things.'

Peck contemplates the painting of the shipwreck. A sailor looks up at the broken mast. There is rope around his legs, running along the boards of the ship, curled in heaps and plummeting down into the splintering decks below.

Time is ticking and lambs are bleating. Peck looks at the homes they pass on the walk back from Brian's. The candles have yet to be lit. With the grey sky deepening above, the lines between buildings are growing weak. What goes on beyond the windows seems to blur into the cream painted walls. That same greyness passes into the vines that climb the drainpipes, into the air that sits around. There is the noise of voices from The Calvary Cross and they stop inside for a quick drink. Nothing in the way of money is exchanged, but he is given glasses of mead, drunk swiftly as they stand at the bar. The ceiling is low and the place tastes of firewood. Someone is tapping their foot against a radiator. Words are shared about the weather. A man opposite them blows hard into a hankie, and it is the only time Peck meets the eyes of another. The sun has set and it is getting hard to tell how many people are in the room.

A carpenter, Peck thinks. He had always fancied learning a skill. Something that involved building. He wouldn't know where to start with farming and doesn't think himself much of a teacher, but he has sawn planks of wood and he has hit nails with hammers. It might not be fixing homes but it's a foundation he can work on. After this matter with Peter Morris is squared he will find a carpenter in the village and he will convince them to train him, and if all goes well he will have himself a job. Once he's worked out the fundamentals, he might even build a home for himself. And why not? There's plenty of space to build and it would make sense to have somewhere to call his own. Somewhere close to Hale, so they can both sit outside in the summer evenings and reminisce about the city; the good times and the bad times, his mother with her infinite kindness.

She would be happy to see them pushing things forward, working together like brothers. They are not blood but they are just as good, he thinks. That's a thing to remember. He looks over to Hale who is also in his own head. When he gets out of it he will be told, without argument, that he is loved. The past days have been trouble for him, clearly, but it will pass like all troubles do. What's important is that they are together again, and past mistakes will be forgiven.

When they leave, they see a young man on the pavement, prostrate beneath the weight of a full-length dressing mirror. Peck catches his own reflection, angled against the evening sky. His head is dizzy and the unexpected sight of himself is strange, as if his body belongs to someone else entirely. The man that carries the mirror is sprawled out as if he is sleeping, but his eyes are open and blinking. He has fallen, Peck decides, and moves to help this stranger back onto his feet, but Hale pulls his cousin away by the sleeve. In the mirror Peck spots a cat stalk along a stone wall. A heavy door clunks as it is shut. As they pass one house Peck thinks he can make out the shapes of two people, but it is hard to be sure.

He thinks they might be bent over a table with paint-brushes in their hands.

---

In Hale's home the light wavers in the draught so that Peck's shadow sways amongst the surfaces. The kitchen hasn't been tidied since the dinner party, the night before Peter ran, and the onion skins have hardened into scars. Hale takes it on himself to fill a sink with soapy water and gets to work on scrubbing the pans and crockery clean. Peck watches him put his strength into it, the splay of his broad back bent over plates. The stink of rot passes and the sight becomes almost comforting in its domesticity. Peck can feel a tension loosen across his chest and for a moment he forgets himself completely. He is home and his bones are younger. The feeling washes over him. He needs to steady himself with one hand on the table, wipe his brow with the other.

A bottle of moonshine is soon open, the contents poured into two glasses, picked up and done away with. Now is the time for Peck to open his heart, tell Hale that he has forgiven him for his abandonment and that he is ready to help with what needs doing. Carpentry, is what he has been thinking. Is there someone around that might take him on as an apprentice? But Hale has something he has wanted to say since leaving Brian's home, and before Peck knows it, they are talking once more about Jacob Morris. 'You'd think he was a legend from the way some people gab about him,' his cousin says. 'Brian Goss spouting all that sentimental crap. You should have heard him last year. All this about "big man Jacob Morris, deep voice and clever ears".' He coughs into his fist. 'He had a pair of ears on him, that much is true.'

The comfortable bubble Peck had found himself in pops, and once more he is in the middle of nowhere, under the watch of an enormous wall. What sort of things had JM heard that he shouldn't have? If it had only taken Peck two days to work out what was happening between his cousin and Charlotte Morris, surely this great listener must've known. Surely he had watched her sneak into Hale's bungalow, heard them whispering sweet nothings. 'How did he kill his grandson?' Peck asks, voice leaden.

The directness of the question seems to catch his cousin off guard. 'Suffocation,' he replies, with what Peck thinks is the air of a catechism.

'And why would he do something like that?'

Hale starts to mouth something, stops, starts again. 'It was unintentional.' He makes a faint clicking sound against the roof of his mouth. 'But you should've heard the way he talked to his family after a few glasses, when the same small, mean thoughts wormed their way into his head – God knows why he always circled back on them. The lack of restraint. That was enough to scare Charlotte, I can tell you that, and I'd be lying if I said it didn't scare me too sometimes, when I'd catch him stomping and I'd hear the little baby crying through the walls.' He takes a deep breath and looks for a moment as if tears are about to come to his eyes. 'The man had big hands and was liable to forget their limits. I don't doubt he only meant to hush him. Done without forethought, I'm sure, but Peter could tell you how forceful his father could be.'

'Peter saw this happen?' Peck presses.

'No,' Hale wavers.

*James Hale is telling lies. James Hale has his own ambitions.*

'It was heartbreaking,' his cousin rebounds, emotion creeping farther into his voice. 'I've known the Morrises since I arrived. From day one. I had a lot of respect for the man – but to kill an infant in its crib, even by accident, that's unforgivable.' There is sincere rage in his tone. His hand is clenched and sweaty. Peck questions his first instinct. Perhaps Hale is telling the truth after all.

'And Charlotte?'

Hale picks his words carefully. 'She saw enough.' He rakes two fingers across his cheek. 'Found him with his hands on her son's head the moment he died, what would you make of it?' The question feels like an accusation. Peck pictures a man walking along a darkened hallway, floorboards creaking beneath heavy boots. He doesn't answer.

'She was resolute. No matter his denial, no matter Peter's refusal to believe that he could be capable. She knew how he was. All his control, a hollow likeness of the word. The talk about natural causes was nothing more than an easy fiction.' He scratches his cheek again. It seems to Peck that his cousin has slipped out of the room, into another time and place. His voice is distant and there are long shadows in the gaps between what is said. 'Maybe she's less sure of things now, given time and the mind's rummaging through settled records, but back then she was unwavering and the village was there for her.' He meets Peck's eye and is quiet for a moment. 'When he ran, we tracked him to a farmhouse,' he continues, pulling himself to firmer ground. 'He'd done a good job of hiding his fire but we found him all the same. The building hadn't had a soul in it since people first started moving on. It still had one of those FOR SALE signs out the front. We would've walked straight past if it weren't for the broken window. Only one smashed, right by the front door. Suspicious that.'

Peck tongues the gap at the back of his mouth and imagines a doorway. 'There was fear in that room,' Hale says. 'You could feel it. Here was a man that people used to have a lot of respect for. I count myself in that number.'

The gold necklace has come untucked from Hale's shirt, and is dangling from his neck as he leans forwards. 'He made it to the doorway,' he says, alcohol on his breath. 'In the end, we only had a grip on one of his arms. I remember holding on to that arm like my life depended on it. He was old but the fucker was strong. He would've slipped free if Thomas Rample hadn't slammed the front door on his shoulder. Crunch. Crunch. With five of us on his forearm we pulled. I had a hand on his wrist. Another on his elbow. We pulled. Pulled. Heaved until something broke.'

'His arm?'

Hale pauses, nods. 'Pretty much came right off.'

'I don't believe you,' says Peck.

'You weren't there,' says Hale. 'The children tell stories about it.'

'There's no way in cold hell you pulled an old man's arm off.'

There's a glimmer of pleading in Hale's eyes, as if he is imploring Peck to go along with his tale. 'I'm telling you, it was hanging by a thread.'

'You'd need the strength of a horse,' Peck mumbles.

'There were five of us.'

'Still.'

A pause, then, and the thought of becoming a carpenter's apprentice seems a silly dream. Peck wishes he could tell for certain if his cousin is lying. Has he used a tragedy to his advantage, or does he genuinely believe that Peter Morris's father killed his baby grandson?

'Anyway,' Hale says, looking at the living-room wall. 'He slipped away.'

'Must've bled out,' Peck offers.

Hale rubs his head with the palm of his hand, and without thinking Peck has mimicked the movement.

'All I'm getting at is that you shouldn't pay too much heed to Brian Goss's mythologising of the man,' Hale says, playfully poking Peck's leg. 'JM was big but he wasn't a giant. He wasn't some all-knowing bird or a saintly judge. He was just an old man who did something awful one day.'

As much as Peck wants to let it go, just as Hale clearly does, he can't shake the prickliness that his cousin is spinning stories. 'Was Peter there for all this fighting?' he probes. The question is a puff of air. Hale blinks. Blinks again.

'Yes,' he says. 'He came around in the end. Didn't say a word, though. Just stood there as we fought his father. Stayed in the doorway when we searched for him afterwards.'

This is myth-making in another direction, Peck is sure of it, even though his cousin speaks with such conviction. Truth is a stage in the village green, he considers. 'Hale, I love you. You're like a brother to me. Don't bullshit.'

Hale smacks Peck's leg, playfully but hard. 'I love you too, Pecker. I'm not bullshitting. I'm happy he's dead.' He leans back and for the first time that evening looks relaxed. He blows all the air out of his cheeks. Clearly he has wanted to say his piece about JM, and now it has been covered he is relieved. 'Like a brother, eh?' he teases. 'You remember those two beds we had as kids? How she would come in and give us a kiss goodnight?'

Peck runs his fingers around the rim of his glass and, even though he would rather not, thinks of the bedroom they shared as boys: twin beds, the posters on the wall, the deaths that happened on the floor. That right there is something both of them experienced. No question. He knows Hale is thinking of the same thing, and once more the thought of this being communicated without speech is a source of happiness, despite the grief that starts to rear its face. 'I don't want to think about that,' he says.

'What's-his-name.'

'Don't.'

'Robert Pounds,' Hale chips, before tipping the tumbler towards his mouth.

'I wish you hadn't said that.'

'Why not?'

He can feel his eyes become wet and hates them for betraying him. The last thing he needs to do is remember his mother's killer. Instead, he stands and walks to his camper. He lets his head mush against the mattress, his gaze on the floorboards. The dead can stay where they are. They can stay in the—

'Oh Christ.'

'What?'

Peck leaps up, holding something small, hard and black aloft. 'I've found my tooth!' he exclaims, and it is exactly the thing that is needed to break the spell that has made him melancholy. Hale leaps beside him and inspects the dead tooth between his fingers, then claps

Peck on the back in a gesture of congratulations. They embrace, and all the friction between them is suddenly gone, or at least ignored, until there's a knock at the door that feels as if it comes from inside his skull. The pair exchange glances. After a moment's hesitation, Hale moves to answer. The door is opened, Charlotte enters the kitchen, and straight away Peck's pupils have rolled back. He wipes his eyes, fingers the edge of his tooth.

'Could you give us some privacy?' Hale asks, voice suddenly zipped to the neckline.

In response Peck looks around the room, arms open wide. 'Where exactly would you like me to go?' To which Hale nods at the front door.

'Are you fucking serious?'

'Just for a bit.'

Peck makes a phlegmy grunt, pockets his dead tooth and moves to collect his coat. 'Can't forget this,' he says, reaching back to the table and snatching the moonshine. Hale keeps his countenance firm, so, kit collected, Peck shimmies past Charlotte, brushing against her coat with his arm, and lays eyes on the empty fruit bowl near the door. It takes him a moment to realise what's missing from it; not apples, not pears. Bullets. Not good, he decides. Not good at all. 'The bullets …' he starts, but Hale's eyes burn so he flaps his hand and mumbles some words about saving it for later.

It is raining heavily. Peck pulls his hood over his head. There's a bit of awning so he keeps close to the door, tucking the bottle into his right armpit so he can rub both hands together to kindle a flame. As if it had been watching him, the wind takes a punt and blows spray in his face. Jesus, if that's not the most unpleasant thing in the world. He wonders how long it will be before he can go back inside and, impatient, decides to sneak around the corner of the bungalow to see what is happening through the window. Just as he had done on his first night in the village, he edges towards the glass, careful not to be seen. This time the curtains have been drawn but there is a gap between them that is large enough for him to glimpse the room he just left. He can see Charlotte take off her coat, let it fall on the chair he had been sat on a moment ago. Instead of sitting, she remains standing. The death of her baby, he thinks. And now her husband gone. There must be a weight on her shoulders. He regrets leaving so abruptly and thinks that, if anything, he should have stayed to speak to her.

If everyone in town is to pay attention to each other, he could be the one to spin it in a positive light; the one to bring people together, not pit them as enemies. Not to accuse but to guard. To support. That's the type of man he is, he thinks. Not someone that stirs up hateful thoughts but someone who steps in when others are in need. That's the apple core of it. It is who his mother was when she took in Hale as a boy. It is who he is, in spite of the circumstances, in spite of the life he's spent in ruins. He is holding on to a pip that can grow. Because it is spring. Because there is goodness and there is kindness. Because he is out here, in a real community, with a chance to lead by example.

In the living room, Charlotte takes off her jumper, then her undershirt. Peck's eyes widen at the sight of her naked back, lit only by the candles on the table. He watches transfixed as she reaches out a hand to his cousin. He pulls himself away from the window when Hale takes it. His heart is beating fast. He walks a few feet, determined not to spy on his cousin, but he is drawn back. Too late. Now the room is empty and the door to Hale's bedroom closed. There may be another window to peer through, he thinks, but stops himself from finding it, tearing himself away from the pebble-dashed wall.

Across a fence lies the Morris house, all of its candles blown out. Maisie must be sleeping. The neck of the bottle is against Peck's lips and he tips it up, lets the drink fall out as needles into the back of his throat just as the wind kicks up another spray. It almost blows his hood back but he narrows his eyes and puts one foot in front of the other, moving through the world as if it is all unreal.

The road to the cobbled square is a tarmac stream and Peck is a dreamer amongst the sludge, pulled by the current beyond the butcher's shop. Within a few minutes he has found himself through the village square, then past the chicken coop on the path to Grace Horn's cottage.

His hair is plastered with rain. He looks for signs of life. Light in the gaps. Action decided, he knocks at the door. There is just enough time to consider turning back before it swings open to the face of Grace. She looks both ways before closing it behind him, locking it shut. He notices a pair of men's shoes, black and polished, neatly placed against the wall. She leads him along a darkened corridor, past a staircase, into a kitchen with a single candle on the table. There is an empty pot and an empty glass. They share a few words but do not stay there long before she takes him by the hand again, and he lets himself be led upstairs. There is goodness and there is kindness. On the landing he walks past a child's room, and through the shade he can see a cot and mobile dangling above it; a shoal of blue fish, stuck in formation. Soon he is away from the room and Grace is sitting him on a double bed. She is nervous about him seeing her body, and covers a scar on her belly as she undresses. But he kisses her chest and she exhales softly, rubbing him through his trousers as he slides a hand between her legs.

He is looking at the ceiling, at the half-seen shapes lilting. Peck can feel Grace's hands on his shoulders as she moves against him. His hands are on her breasts, and she is open-mouthed at the feel of her nipples against his palms. The ceiling inhales. For a moment it is Charlotte's naked back, moving in the candlelight towards his cousin's bedroom. His heels are pushing against the bedsheets, his hips arching upwards. Grace's hair is brushing his cheek now and he meets her eye; a bright shape that's dragged away. He is catching her hips and rolling her forward. She is breathing against his neck, shifting herself to grind harder, and harder still. They are gasping together. She is breathing hot against his neck. He catches her eye once more, just as the throb takes its hold and her nails dig against his skin.

# Five

> I KNOW ALL ABOUT ANNA MOAR AND SCOTT DOYLE AND IT IS DISGUSTING WHAT THEY ARE DOING. *SCOTT DOYLE IS A FUCKER.* ANNA MOAR IS A WHORE. **THE DAYS OF JAMES HALE ARE NEARING THEIR END.**

A PAIR OF MAGPIES PERCH like sphinxes on telegraph poles. A lamb is found dead in the river. The sky is roughly threaded and a wren unspools somewhere unseen. Trousers are hung out to dry and laughter is heard close to the green. Charlotte walks back from the wall in time to see James Hale leave his bungalow with Duncan Peck, making their way south. When they eventually find Peter, they will gather him up and take him home unharmed. That much was promised in the arms of her neighbour. She does not regret it, not in the slightest. It was in her power to do and so she did it.

Even if she feels herself distant from him, Peter has been a good husband and an even better father, and it is not right to leave him to his fate. But if he were dead, Hale had whispered last night in her ear, then they could be together. To that, she told him as plain as flour that nothing of the sort would happen. Could he imagine? Surely he could. But he was to get that idea out of his head and go out in the morning to bring her husband back to her.

It is time for a little balance to be restored, if only enough that she can send Maisie back to school and stop her pacing the house like a cooped-up wildcat. It would do James wonders for his own position, given the mutterings. He wants to be careful. If the ire is sticking to him, the last thing either of them want is for it to get stuck on their comings and goings. To that end it may also be worth sending Duncan Peck on his merry way. There's something about him she doesn't trust. She knows he is a dear cousin, of sorts, but the truth is he's not really a blood relative and she has a sneaking suspicion he knows about them. If push came to shove, where would he stand on the matter?

Maisie can't be contained, so she's led by her mother's side to the baker's for them to buy a loaf of bread. The fresh air will do them good, Charlotte reasons, even if she runs the risk of eyes chasing them down. Things turn quick in the village, but not quick enough that the words against Peter will have faded from memory. There will be gossip about her daughter. Perhaps it would have been a better idea to send her to school after all, she wonders. Sarah Twine has been nothing but gold to Maisie. It's not her she's worried about, no. It's the other children. Their mindless parroting of matters they don't understand. Best to wait until Peter is home so they can form a united front. Show this for what it is.

'Can I throw some mud as well?' Maisie asks, tugging at her mother's sleeve and pointing to a man and a woman sat in the stocks. Anna Moar and Scott Doyle. Both are covered from head to toe in smatterings of muck and rotting food. They are upright on two squat stools, legs extended, eyes closed tight. In front of them is a row of various people, a small number carrying bowls of old fruit and vegetables. There's generally very little food that goes to waste in the village, though, so most of the other containers carry a lumpy brown soup that doesn't look like mud to Charlotte.

'Certainly not,' she says, then realises with a surprise that someone is approaching on her other side. It is Grace, smiling, making an effort to catch her attention with a raised hand. As soon as their eyes lock Charlotte feels herself tense. It is as if her footing has been tripped.

'I wanted to see how you're holding up.' The words are kind-hearted, yet Charlotte is panicked by them, the warmth disorientating in its familiarity. She is glad, exposed and apprehensive all at once, uncertain of the dynamic being played out after months of drifting apart. 'We haven't spoken in a while,' Grace adds, acknowledging the strangeness, and it makes Charlotte all the more aware of the distance between them, the closeness they'd had now made to feel like a playground game. It forces Charlotte to consider Grace anew: how she is well liked in the village, treasured even, with her friendly manner and her job serving the little treats that make life worth living; she with her own Tragedy that, unlike Charlotte's, was free from accusations, wrapped in assurances that sickness knows no names, takes who it wishes. She has come over out of the blue, concerned, inquisitive, and isn't that so much like her. There was a time when Charlotte wouldn't have given a second thought to this compassion. Now she feels suspicious and the realisation of it makes her resentful. 'I think you might need a friend,' Grace says. 'Now more than ever.'

Charlotte realises she hasn't responded. She is not sure she can. Not right now. Maisie is still watching the stocks, enthralled by the spectacle of humiliation.

'Sorry, Grace. I can't stop to talk. Maybe another time.' And with a cursory smile Charlotte turns and drags her daughter by the arm towards the baker's, where the smell of bread drowns the stink in the square.

Ever since she was a girl hanging off her own mother's sleeve, the sight of fresh bread has calmed her. This morning is no different, and the loaves make it easy to forget the fears that are rising. She moves her face closer to the generosity of the baker's counter and thinks of the work that has gone into each dusted crust. The barley sheaves that have been harvested, the grains dried and ground. The yeast, the honey and the eggs, each with their own work needed, brought together in the metal oven at the back of the shop. Only a community could make such a thing, and the thought of this is comfort.

If it weren't for the fact she is kept busy helping Peter sort his jobs and supplies, she would love to make bread.

'Mrs Twine taught us how to bake buns,' Maisie tells the baker, Victoria Bray, who is up a ladder placing jars of preserves on a shelf. 'We cooked them in an oven that John Brown needed to chop wood for, and when they came out they were so hot and John Brown tried to eat one too soon and burnt his tongue.'

'Serves John Brown right,' says Vic. 'But can you move your foot from the ladder, dear. I don't want to fall to my death.'

'Sorry, Vic. You know how she likes to tell a story.' Charlotte moves to collect Maisie and brings her back once more to her side. Vic glances down from her position to acknowledge Charlotte's presence but there is neither a smile nor a nod before she returns to the business at hand.

'Have you seen all of that going on out there?' she asks to the shelf.

'With Anna and Scott?'

'Finally out in the open, after we've all known about it for weeks of course.'

Charlotte does not like the path this is leading her down. 'Just one loaf of the barley, please.' And Vic looks at her once more, then makes her way with a huff back down the ladder, basket of jam in hand.

'They came to the stocks themselves, if you can believe it,' she says. 'There's something to be commended in that. Their families will be ashamed, no doubt, but at least the pair owned up to what they were doing. A day in there, followed by a week's burdening, and they'll be on their way.' Vic does not go to the bread counter but takes a step closer to Charlotte, the scent of lavender strong in the air between them. 'And it's a useful thing too that they've taken matters into their own hands, seeing as James Hale is off God-knows-where looking for your beloved.'

'On second thoughts, I'll come back later for the bread,' Charlotte says, not prepared for a confrontation with Maisie standing there listening. She has tried so hard to shield her from the words against her father. She won't have it ruined by Victoria Bray and her wobbly face.

'The bun I made for Mrs Twine was as big as her head,' Maisie gleefully recalls. 'She told the class she could wear it as a hat! That's silly!' At this, the girl breaks into an uncontrollable fit of laughter. 'You don't put the bun on your head, you put it in here.' She lifts the coat and dress she is wearing, exposing her small belly, then laughs some more.

'Maze!' Charlotte leaps to pull her daughter's dress back down. 'What on earth are you doing?' Every time she pulls the dress down, Maisie lifts it back up, finding this the funniest thing in the world. Eventually she is convinced to leave herself be, and is led by the arm towards the shop door. She wriggles free of this grip, though, and for a split-second Charlotte feels her stomach drop. She pivots back, ready to shout at her naughty daughter, but finds Maisie standing motionless beside the baker, who has knelt beside her and is speaking in a hushed voice.

'Did your daddy ever ask you to show your belly like that?' Vic asks, full of sincerity.

The look of confusion this has put on Maisie's face makes Charlotte's blood boil. 'Don't you dare ask my daughter questions like that,' she snaps, feeling her face turn red. With an effort, Vic stands back upright and puts her hands on her hips.

'Sometimes he blows raspberries on it,' Maisie says in a small voice, but both of the women are paying more attention to each other than to her. 'He's on a long walk but he'll be back in a few days.'

'The things they said he did to her,' the baker says. 'It's an outrage. You should be ashamed.'

'Honestly, I don't know what you'd do if there wasn't something to be outraged at.'

'Pardon me?'

There is a pulse in Charlotte's ear. A hot pressure at the back of her head. She looks at the expectant face of Victoria Bray, an eyebrow raised above a wrinkled eye, and slaps her so hard across the head that she falls onto the tiled floor. Maisie's mouth is open, speechless, and Charlotte grabs her by the wrist and yanks her backward. The last thing either of them see before the glass door closes behind them is the baker cradling her jaw, a scream of pain coming from her crumpled clothes, which is lost as they move across the square, past the people pelting Anna Moar and Scott Doyle with shit and apples.

In a wood to the south, two bodies are walking. The dirt grips Hale and Peck as they stalk a gap between the pines. Pipes and poles are back in hand, with Peck's pale fingers around the hilt as breath makes itself known. The cold grazes. Hale is walking a few steps ahead, wearing his woolly hat, and Peck watches it sit on top of his cousin's broad skull like a roof on a house. Few words had been shared since the early morning, when Peck returned from Grace Horn's with a rhythmic rapping at the door, only to be met with a long face and weary eyes. There are hangovers in the air, that's for sure, but some other rot has set in. What has Charlotte Morris told Hale to make him look so dour? What promises have been exchanged?

*Peter Morris is wasting our time. Peter Morris is more trouble than he's worth.*

Peck isn't sure he can remember what Peter looks like. There was a raincoat, a pink cardigan, a moustache, red hair, but beyond that it is all generalities, as if he'd been told a description but never made an image in his own head. He'd like to stamp the length of bones out of him, for making him trudge across the moor. All this trouble he is causing. He feels in his pocket for the dead tooth and holds it between his thumb and forefinger, rolls it in his hand like a stone he might've found on a beach. If they'd caught Peter on the first day then things could have been dealt with. Peck would have felt he'd witnessed a better example of the village in order. How things were supposed to work, out here where everyone knows each other by name. He wants Hale to show him that things could be set straight; that there was a way for people to live truthfully together, to move forwards in their living. The binds that run from house to house needn't cut into the people's wrists. They can be woven together into something unfrayed by bad weather and worse feelings. And yet Peck feels the cord winding around the pair of them, and he can't help but notice it is only the two of them walking in the woods. 'He'll have my revolver,' he says to the ground in front of him. 'Seeing as he took it from me and tucked it into his own belt. The bullets I'd stored in the fruit bowl? They're gone too.'

'Even if he did have it, he wouldn't know how to use it.'

'There's not much out here for him to do but practise.'

Hale tilts his head back at the words but doesn't stop walking. 'Your concern is noted, Pecker.'

'I'm just saying, mind. Not that we need to stop but it's something we should be aware of.'

Someone else could have seen what he'd seen through the window, last night, after Charlotte had stripped herself bare. Another person in the village could have seen what was happening in the candlelight between neighbours. Her naked back was not his business. The moment to knock at the pane had come and gone, and what was there to be achieved by disrupting something that did not involve him.

*Duncan Peck is a useless tourist. James Hale fucked his neighbour's wife.*

Peck feels grotty with the watching of others; a body called into being by the vast wall and suspicious gazes. Their path out of the village had not taken them by the concrete structure, and Hale had not seemed to want to make a detour to check the sentences. Better not to know, perhaps. Better to keep on track with the day's work and let the other chasers pick up any fresh developments. The not knowing makes their position unclear, though, and Peck is aware that no one else has joined them. No raincoats. No wheelbarrow.

*James Hale is a seducer. Duncan Peck is a piece of human waste a piece of shit and God help me if I get my hands on him by God I will wipe the whole of him clean.*

Perhaps it is worse than he thought. Perhaps they are running and this is the pursuit, and at any moment the woods will fill to the brim with the neighbours he's met over the past few days. The thought of this brings Peck's attention down to the ground he's moving across. The earth swells around gullies. The stinking mud heaves. He is sure he's walked this way before, in the opposite direction when he'd first approached the village, but nothing is the same, and all the woods are angled forward, backs bent, hands cupped to ears. Hale seems bigger than ever. Even though the distance between the two of them has grown, his body is gigantic, his palm against a tree as he pushes forwards, his fingers the size of the trunk, his head ducked under the tangle of branches. He's moving forwards, still. Hale's face is turned away, so all he becomes in that moment is a monolith, walking pace by pace on the faint dirt path. He is a dark shape travelling with regularity and Peck is falling farther behind.

'Wait. Slow down a minute.' And his cousin does exactly that, pivoting in the muck to face him.

'What's wrong?' he asks, concerned. 'Have you hurt yourself?'

'I'm just not sure where we're going.' Peck looks deeper into the woods, through the shadows of trees layered on top of each other like strips of blotting paper. There's nothing in the way of movement. Not even a rustle of leaves. 'Did she stay long?' He aims to make the question a good-humoured poke but laces too much acid in it. Hale looks him in the eye, turns away and starts to walk on. 'Did she have much to say?' Peck asks, leaning against a tree for support. 'I suppose there wasn't a lot of talking.'

'Why do you need to know?'

'I don't need to know,' Peck shrugs. 'I want to know.'

At this Hale stops again. The words passed between the two of them colour the edges of silence. 'She told me Peter is a good, honest man,' his cousin starts. 'Everything they said about him was a lie.'

'But here we are.'

'Here we are.' The wind, cut to ribbons by branches, makes its way onto their faces. It builds, whistling above the mud. Hale sets off again, turning away from Peck in a swivel. He walks on several paces then reconsiders, stops altogether and faces back. 'People have written he's done wrong and while that may not mean all that much to you it means a great deal to me,' he growls. 'And it means a great deal to everyone else in our community.' There's a leaden look in his eye. 'In spite of the few hours you spent with him, and in spite of whatever vague impression you may have built up of the man, the fact remains that Peter Morris's full name has been put up on that wall. The truth—'

'Ah, the truth,' Peck interrupts.

His cousin stares at him unblinking. 'I'm not a cold man. I know my neighbour much better than you do. So it comes as a shock. It wasn't me that said such things about him but I'm regrettably in a position where I have to act on them.'

'Why is it regrettable?'

'Do you think I'm soulless?' Hale asks with real anger in his voice. 'He lives beside me. He's been a generous friend for years now. This is shocking to me. It's a jolt. But I cannot let something like it pass. To do that would be to put my fingers in my ears and cry that my own thoughts are more important than those of others. I won't do that. I can't do that. It's not what our lives are built on.'

'If you say so,' Peck replies, heart beating at the confrontation but expression unshaken. 'I wouldn't get too sanctimonious about it, though. People in glass houses and that.'

'What are you getting at?'

'Well, what you were up to last night.'

'What about it?'

Peck can feel the blood behind his face but he tries to remain calm. 'Come on, she's a married woman and all. I get that her husband isn't exactly the most popular face around here, but, I mean, was that wrong? Was what you did last night wrong? When you start talking about the rights and wrongs. Start talking with so much certainty about the whole thing. You're speaking like it's the Holy Scripture. Gut the idiot if that's what you need to do, break his legs or snap his fingers. Just don't act like you're so shiny yourself. Because if we're talking about the rights and wrongs, it seems like you're ready to punish him for things that he might not have done. But you did do something.'

'Did what?'

'Come on. I saw the two of you.'

'It's not in writing.'

'So what?'

'So it's not in writing.'

Hale walks towards Peck, then, squashing the air between them. Peck stands his ground, keeps eye contact with his cousin towering in front of him, but feels his pulse quicken. The pair stare each other down, only the wind between the branches intruding. Hale seems absolutely sincere about this rule of law. It's both alarming and admirable, thinks Peck. In a single movement, he raises his arm and places his hand on Hale's shoulder.

'I'm just trying to understand how things work here,' he smiles. 'That's all. Strange customs, you know?'

There's no more in the way of words as they walk beyond the woods, down into a valley to skirt the edges of a reservoir. His cousin walks a handful of paces ahead as they cross a battered stone bridge. To one side is the water, lulled on top of the land. On the other is a steep drop to grass and stone. Peck leans over the side and looks at what's there: a set of five slopes coming out of arches like tongues licking dirt. He considers the chance of surviving a leap, given the incline.

As he runs to catch up he considers the dry channel; how the water must have found another path, running in passages deep underground, down to the city, out to sea. He climbs, following Hale as he directs their paces towards a monstrous tor, broken through the tip of a hill where it has rubbed and blistered and hardened against the sky. Peck turns around and looks back down to the dam and to the reservoir, a smooth patch running between the forests, clustered in patches of brown on its banks. Hale strides over granite rocks at different degrees of waking from the grassy earth that grips their sides. The farther they move the greater the groupings of stones, breaching the heath in surges, pushing through with ever-amassing population until it comes to the body: a seismic torso stripped of limbs, cracked throughout. 'Sheepstor,' Hale mutters. An act of violence, Peck considers. A crag stabbed, the knife thrown into a bog. Here is a crime scene, and they are looking at the body calcified. The blood all run out, sucked by the ground to run in subterranean channels. The sight of it turns something in Peck, ricocheting into memory. There are ashes in the bracken.

Hale has already begun to push the end of his pipe into the tor's wet gaps. It seems to Peck as if he is checking the wounds, to gauge how long since death has set in. He finds a sitting place towards the tor's base. He should be helping Hale with his hunt, calling out Peter Morris's name and peering into the dark nooks that run across the rock, but his mind is spinning elsewhere, and it's all he can do to sit before he falls. It's there that his eyes come to rest on the remnants of a campfire. There is a patch of ash, black against the auburn ground, tucked beside small stones. Hale has noticed it too, and he motions with a finger against his lips; an order for Peck to keep quiet as he creeps out of view. Peck is alone, then, as he leans forwards and presses his forehead against the tip of his metal pole, staked in the ground like a flag. He holds his temples as he lets his head rest on the cool metal surface, feeling it drain some of his heat. 'I dreamt about Robert Pounds last night,' he says. 'It must've been because we mentioned him. Made it all real again.' He looks up for a reaction from Hale but there's no sight of him. He looks at the laces on his boots. 'You shouldn't have said his name.'

He examines the dirt, drenched in crevasses around his footprint. He remembers a children's bedroom. The room is dark, except for the light that slips in through a crack in the doorway. There are two single beds and a model ship balanced on a bookcase. He is ten and laying in one bed, a nine-year-old James Hale in the other. James is asleep in his snores, somewhere else entirely, but Duncan's eyes are open, out towards the light, towards two figures in the corridor beyond. His mother's hand is resting on her hip, the curve of her elbow observed. Her other hand is thrust forward, pressed against the chest of a man. The conversation rolls out of reach, as his mother speaks in hushed tones at their neighbour Robert Pounds, who has a big brown beard and sometimes waves at Duncan from his window. He lives all alone, since his wife and daughters died. But why is he inside their house? She tries to stifle it, but Duncan's mother lets out a laugh. She whispers into Robert Pounds's ear and he laughs too. What is so funny? Duncan wonders. Are they laughing at him? He sits upright in bed, to get a better glimpse of what is happening, and this movement must have alerted his mother because she turns towards the doorway. Her eyes search the darkness before she draws Robert Pounds out of view.

Peck raises his head from the pole and meets Hale's eyes. 'Are you well?' his cousin asks, a look of concern worn heavy around his eyelids.

'It's fine. I'm fine.' And then Hale does something that makes Peck's heart swell. He kneels beside him, patting a hand against his leg. Here is the man he knows. Here he is to meet him. All is not lost. There is goodness and there is kindness, and there is hope and friendship.

'Peter was here alright,' says Hale. 'But he must have left this morning.'

'Where do we go now?'

'I'll be honest with you, Pecker, I don't know.' Hale stands up again, takes in the land below as it starts to dull, the veiled sun falling low against the horizon. The limits of the reservoir become unclear and everything below them seems to fall together in a shimmer. 'He's much craftier than I gave him credit for,' he admits. 'He could be anywhere. I don't even know if he's set his sights on the city. I wouldn't have thought that he would. Fuck, who knows? Peter never spoke about it before, and it's not like he'd abandon Charlotte, certainly not Maisie.'

The lines around his eyes wilt and Peck feels for the first time fully convinced by his words. This has all come as a shock. He is not making decisions lightly. 'He could be in the bog,' Hale says. 'If he didn't look where he was going. If he fell. The bogs are deeper now, with the rain.'

Peck turns his attention to the tor, to its sliced skin and the dark folds. He looks at a crevice there and thinks he sees the stone moving. Something half-seen is toiling. The granite itself begins to separate. The body falls apart. A black shape detaches from the enormity.

He thinks he sees the cut-off twist in the air but the shape does not return to the rock, and instead begins to come forward, walking one step at a time. Half considering, he reckons it to be a shadow cast by the gloom. The sun is invisible, the shades are getting away from themselves, and this one has grown cockier than the rest. It moves towards where they are sitting, its two arms raised out at them, something glistening in its grip. A mineral. A precious stone held as an offering, he thinks.

Peck stands. Hale turns around to where his cousin is looking. 'Put the pipes on the ground,' Peter orders, his voice a rough surface drenched with rain.

'Peter,' Hale utters, as if naming the shabby figure would anchor it. A black raincoat is wrapped around his neighbour, a hood over its head, but there is enough of Peter's red moustache on show to fasten the name to the spectre. While the hairs around his mouth were clipped a few days ago, now the shrub is unruly.

'Hello there,' Peter says, tightening the strings around his words so they come out polite. 'Please, the both of you, put your pipes down on the ground.'

'We only want a word.'

'I told you he'd have my revolver. And the bullets no doubt.'

'Quiet, Pecker.'

'Pipes. Ground.'

Peck looks to Hale for an action, but the big man lowers his weapon to the soil. Peter's attention jumps then to him, and Peck swears to himself that the eyes harden in their sockets as it does. He hesitates, but in the end lets his bludgeon fall from his fingers and land on the earth with a thud. 'Is it only you two?' Peter hisses. Another hesitation, before Peck and Hale nod in unison.

'You've got to come in.' Hale clears his throat. 'There's no other option. You have to put the gun down, pick up your things and come with us.'

'I'm not doing that.'

Peck, having not moved an inch since dropping his pipe, steps forward. 'Come on now. Give the gun back. You're only going to do yourself some damage.' By way of response Peter cocks the weapon.

'Put it down and we'll have a chat,' Hale intervenes. 'We'll have a nice talk, some water, a bit of sleep in your shelter there. I promise we won't tie the rope too hard around your legs, and then when the sun's up we'll head out and get all this put behind us. How does that sound? Does that sound good to you?'

'It sounds good to me,' Peck offers.

'I broke some plates in the tearoom,' Peter barks across the distance to Hale. 'The tray slipped out of my fingers. It was embarrassing at the time but I didn't think people would— Well, I should have. The way Grace Horn looked at me.'

'Hey now, leave Grace out of this,' Peck shouts, with a fervour he wasn't expecting. 'It's not her fault you're up here.'

'There's no truth in the things they wrote,' Peter continues, directing all of his words to Hale. 'There's no way I would hurt Maisie. You know that, right? She's my daughter. To suggest that I'd— Because I wouldn't. And the, ha, roosters. How ridiculous is that? I've no idea where that came from. Did you see any dead roosters? I didn't.'

'Come on,' Hale says. 'You're getting away from yourself. Let's go somewhere warm and talk.'

'I thought I'd kept on the good side of people. I really didn't see this coming. After my father. After all of that.'

'Now, you know he's got nothing to do with this.'

'I was looking for him,' Peter says. 'I've been searching. I thought I might be able to find his body … Or a skull, or footprints.'

'This isn't because of JM.'

Peter leaps forward and shakes the revolver at Hale. 'You don't know that,' he snarls. 'People haven't stopped whispering. I heard them. I heard what they were saying. They're blaming me for things. They're passing it on to me. It's like a curse, a stain, a— I can feel the weight, and it's not a light load let me tell you that. My family. I love them. I take care of them. I'm decent and, ha, all of the words they've written are nothing more than slander. I know how things work but what went up there was filth – and it's his fault, for them. His name is the one they want up there, not mine. But there's no good in that, is there? There's no good putting his name up because there's no one they can grab and shake about. They can't get him so they've put me up there – and not only me. With my name they put up Charlotte, Maisie, little Maisie, who's never done a thing to anyone. I don't want to see her face when she looks at me in the green. When you hurt me. I don't want to see her there. My little fishie. Her lips wobbling. Her tiny hands. I can't look at that. I'll look away. I'll look up. You can't make me look forward. You wouldn't do that. You can't make me look at her.'

Having worked himself up into a frenzy, Peter breathes deeply. His eyes are bloodshot and Peck thinks him a dangerous bundle of nerves half frayed by the wind.

'Come with us,' says Hale, taking off his woolly hat and rubbing a palm across his sweaty head. 'I'll take care of things. Charlotte wants you home.'

'You've talked to her, have you?'

'We've had words.'

The look in his eye, then. Something flashes, like the moon breaking through storm clouds. 'Oh I bet you've had words,' Peter says. 'I bet you've had a lot of words. Shared a few phrases. I bet you've put a nice, ha, bow on top of the things you said to each other.' Peck watches Hale for a response but his cousin only looks on at the man in silence. 'Don't play dumb,' says Peter. 'Don't play fucking dumb.'

'I honest to God don't know what you're talking about,' Hale replies. 'I'm not the one being accused of things here. So you better think about putting that anger aside and coming along with us.'

'Peter,' starts Peck. 'I don't know you. But Hale here only wants what's best. And what's best for you and your family isn't hiding in' – he gestures to the tor – 'a rock. As nice as it is.' He takes a step forward.

'Don't come closer you – you – fucking intruder,' Peter shakes.

'Look,' Peck counters, unwilling to be intimidated. One hand is raised, fingers pointed forward. 'He gives you his word he'll take care of things.' A nod to Hale. 'You said it yourself. If you can't trust in words, what can you trust in?'

At this, Hale edges towards Peter. 'I promise everything will make sense,' he soothes, arms by his side, and the idea works some type of magic on the man trembling with a gun. The glint in Peter's eyes dulls, his face pales.

'Let me go,' he pleads.

'I'm not going to do that.'

'Let me go, James. You won't see me again. I'll leave. I won't come back. Please.'

'I can't let you go. The writing and the w—'

Hale steps forwards and his skull is uncorked. Blood pours from his scalp, pink matter sprays on the ground. A murmur of birds scatter at the gunshot, twist and coil, but pull together in the end. Hale falls in a heap. The shot rings and Peck's eyes open wide at the sight of the body. He lurches forwards, running to clasp his cousin's shoulders. His heart is in his mouth but, kneeling beside Hale, it becomes clear there is nothing to be done. The back of the skull has broken away. His right eye has burst from the bullet and a pale streak is running down his cheek. Birds fold into shapes that run over the tor and down to the mire. Hale's left boot is desperately tapping the grass and Peck holds him until this jerking stops.

'I meant to shoot him in the arm,' trembles Peter.

'Put the gun down.'

'I've never used one before.'

'Put it down,' Peck shouts. He looks up from the body to Peter, standing in exactly the same position as where he shot Hale, his hands shaking as they hold the weapon away from his chest, as if he wants the revolver as far from him as possible. 'Put it on the ground.'

'I give in. I give myself up.'

He lowers the gun but does not let it fall from his hands.

'Let go of it then,' Peck shouts, his anger getting a foothold. 'Put it down so I can come over there, rip your throat out and feed it to the crows.'

'I'm not putting it down if you're going to do that. You – you can't. You can't kill a man that's given himself in. I have a wife and child. A little child. And – and …' Peck watches Peter, half dazed, walk towards him, towards Hale's body. Peter looks down at his neighbour's corpse, at the pool of blood that has formed around his head.

'I haven't done a thing,' Peter mutters, to Hale, and to Peck. He stoops over the body, over the mess on the ground. He is dazed, and does not flinch when Peck stands, or when he moves to pick up his bludgeon. Peter does not run or cower, but keeps staring at the exploded eye, peering at the murk when Peck approaches from behind and swipes the pipe against his head.

# Six

**JUDY BLOTTER HAS THE HAIR OF A DONKEY.** *JIM DOWRY MEANS NOTHING TO ME.* MAGGIE MIDDLESON FINGERED MY WIFE. HE TALKS A LOT ABOUT PUNCHING PEOPLE BUT I'D LIKE TO PUNCH DOMINIC MARTIN IN THE FACE.

THE PAINT IS STILL wet on the wall; a cardinal dew facing the village as mist hangs over the fields. A sonorous void. The light is new born; it ignites the land in all its contours. A lone cow counts the perimeter of its enclosure. The pigs are burning in their dreams. Peter is in the square with his skull bloodied, legs tight in the stocks. His head is slumped forward, his eyes closed. No one is around, not at this hour.

A grandmother is carrying two full flasks across a courtyard. One has a leak, and leaves a trail of steaming water in her wake; a mark drawn across the flagstones that autographs and disappears. In the tearoom, Peck and a group of men sit around a table. It's too early for the shop to be open, but exceptions have been made and the flasks are passed to Grace, who carries them to the counter where she tips the contents into teapots. There's a groan and a snatch of sound as the cracked vessel splits in two. Hot water spills all over the counter, and she's lucky not to burn her hands. 'Fuck,' she lets slip, attracting the looks of Peck and the men. As soon as she realises she is being watched she hinges on a smile. 'If it's not another thing. That's all we need.'

Peck meets her eye. It is the first time they have been in the same room since he paid her a visit, and she is a ghost of kisses. She wipes her brow with the sleeve of her shirt. He doesn't say a word. She looks down to the broken flask, to the water brooding along the counter. The other men only have time for the body lying on the floor, placed on a sheet of tarpaulin.

Hale's corpse is in poor arrangement, dragged as it has been from the moorland with great effort. It was only after Peck made it to the village with Peter over his shoulder, after knocking on doors in the dead of night, that he'd managed to assemble a party to make the journey back across the moor. Curse the dead horses and all their brittle bones. By the time they'd made it to the tor Hale had swollen, a business of flies on his eye, around the soup that had soaked into the soil. He should have left Peter up there to freeze unconscious, taken his cousin home first, but after all the effort they'd put into finding the runaway he wasn't about to let him go. They'd returned just as dawn was breaking, to this temporary mortuary. Peck looks out of the window, across the square and the stocks where Peter resides unconscious. When Grace brings the tea she touches the side of his hand, and in the view of the others he grazes her fingers. There is a crest of blinks, wren-like in their quickness, impossible to catch.

Later, Peck sits in Hale's living room and looks at a plant on the windowsill. The weight of his revolver is back in his pocket. He inspects the green folds, like so many eyelids waning in the shade. He may as well, he thinks, and picks up the glass of water beside him, walks the length of the space and tips its contents into the plant pot. Better keep a bit of life going. He may as well do that. Because it won't be long until he winds up dead himself, exposed in the village with no one to guard him from their suspicions. Without Hale to deflect the tutting of others, he is sure it will only be a matter of days before they turn on him; an outsider, thieving the home of a respected ex-member of this community.

He hates himself for this self-interest, which buds so effortlessly from the situation he is in. As he considers his cousin's kitchen he calculates the time it would take him to trek back to the city, back to his mother's home. Days of travel. Days for a retreat. His flight would wait until after he'd seen Peter get his due. The red-haired man that had done the killing would be punished, he could trust in the neighbourhood for that. It may be an odious way to do things but writing on the wall had its way of whipping up results. No doubt there would be sentences there about Peter, come tomorrow morning, to add to the accusations already levelled. People act best when they know they are being observed, Hale had said. Well, Duncan Peck is observing Peter Morris, and he will make sure he gets what he deserves.

Peck pulls the black tooth from his trouser pocket and holds it to the light. It is disappointingly real, seen like this. After a moment's consideration, he opens his mouth and feels with his finger for the gap between molars, then presses the tooth back into place. A sting and a taste of blood, before he spits the dead tooth into his palm, wipes it clean and places it in his pocket.

Perhaps he could stay. Instead of leaving the village to carry on as before, he could stay and change things for the better. There is so little he knows about Grace, but she is fond of him. Seems to be. Has shown him kindness. Invited him into her home. He still remembers the shape of her body, her back against his stomach as she slept. When he'd awoken they had switched places. What augurs were in those contortions? he wonders. What could be divined? The leaves of Hale's potted plant quiver in anticipation at the water drunk from the roots. Deep down people are fond of one another, Grace had told him when they'd first met. There's no reason for things to carry on with hate and suspicion. Hale's death wouldn't be for nothing. With a bit of reason, with a bit of time, he could make the village a place where good deeds were rewarded, concerns given air. The enormous wall is not just a canvas for bad blood, he thinks, but a foothold for green shoots, a shore for the seasons to come. He is sure it is what Hale would want and it could be his job to make it happen.

With a flurry Charlotte bursts through the front door, wrapped in a dressing gown, her black hair loose and her right hand gripped around Maisie's wrist. 'Bring him home,' she demands.

'There isn't a lot of knocking around here, is there?'

Her eyes are wild and wide and the look that comes out of them is steel. 'Get him home. Now. Enough harm has been done.'

'You don't say.'

Charlotte ushers Maisie forwards, prodding her body farther into the home. 'Go and read your book,' she says, pointing to the centre of the living room.

'It's a diary.'

'Go and write in your diary then.'

Maisie grants Peck a glance. She looks confused about what is going on, he thinks, but does as she is told and moves to sit. Holding her diary in one hand, a pencil in the other, she flicks through the pages until she finds the place her writing ceases, then goes to work in pushing forward the border between letters and blankness. 'It's clever to keep a diary,' Peck says, hovering closer to the girl on his dead cousin's floor. 'Not enough people do that any more.' He steps closer. 'What's going on in there?' Another step, but as if he crossed some invisible threshold Maisie's attention is provoked and she turns with a swipe of the eyes.

'It's private,' she slices in a small but adamant voice. This stops Peck in his tracks and he looks on, momentarily dazed.

'Good for you,' he settles. 'I mean that. Good for you.'

'Bring him home,' Charlotte demands, snapping her fingers. 'I know. I know. I know James is dead, so don't start at me on that. Pete is my husband and he can be an idiot but he's done nothing wrong. He shouldn't be out there, strapped like a pig in the muck. This has gone on long enough.'

'Done no wrong?' Peck straightens his back as anger clicks into place. 'He shot my cousin, for a start. I loved that man. You're lucky I didn't bash your husband's head in with a rock there and then.' He looks to Maisie, who is occupied with her writing. In hushed tones now, 'You're lucky I didn't kill him myself. God knows why I didn't. He's got a family. You and her, right, but he's done wrong and deserves what's coming to him.'

'You can't say that.' Charlotte squares herself, speaking low enough for Maisie not to hear. 'The word is they don't know who killed James. There's a bit of uncertainty about it.'

'Come off it. I saw him do it with my own eyes.'

'No one else was there, so … you know.'

Peck's mouth opens wide. 'Are you insinuating that I did it? Why would I kill my own cousin?'

'He wasn't really your cousin, though, and why would my Pete kill his own neighbour?' Their bodies angle towards each other. She could hit him, he thinks. 'I blame you,' she says. 'And – and I haven't even seen the body. I haven't even seen what's been done to him.' Her shoulders fall in on themselves but she makes an effort to prop them back up. 'You keep at Pete like he's guilty but you're the one that brought the gun here. Bring my husband home or I'll— You won't want me to. I'll start saying things. About you, and not all of them will be true.'

There's enough rage in her, Peck thinks. He feels the argument slipping out of his hands. 'Listen, would you like a drink?' he offers. 'I've got an old teabag. There's still some hot water in the flask.'

Charlotte thinks this over, looks to Maisie, then takes a seat at the table. 'Tea,' she fires. Peck gets to work in the kitchen, and Charlotte is left with her daughter, writing one word at a time. There is the sound of her pen against the paper, scratching like fingers on wood. Over that comes the sound of water pouring, and the thought of it soothes something in the room.

'You ever wonder what'll happen when we completely run out of teabags?' Peck asks from the kitchen. 'I do, sometimes. Scares the shit out of me.'

'Bring him home,' Charlotte presses. 'At least put a blanket on him.'

'After what's he's done? No. No, I don't think so.' Peck comes out carrying two mugs. 'I'm not one for making people suffer, but he's staying out there until we've got all of this sorted. Hale is dead and that's the state of things.'

Hale is dead. Peck feels his stomach drop. He wants to smash both of the mugs he is carrying on the floor. There are the beginnings of tears in his eyes, he can feel them. Charlotte's eyes are wet as well. The two of them loved Hale most in the world, he thinks. He meant something to the both of them.

'Pete didn't mean to …' she starts.

'So you admit it now?'

'He wouldn't hurt James.'

'Well, he did a lot more than hurt him.'

Charlotte wraps her hand around the mug. 'He's a good person.'

'That's not what it said up on your wall.'

'Don't give me that,' she snaps. 'You don't care about what's up there.'

'Maybe I do,' he says, and it's true. He does care. He knows he will need to care even more if he is to turn things around. 'Regardless,' he adds. 'I care about Hale. Cared,' he corrects himself. 'A great deal. And it seemed to me that it's something you might care about as well.'

Eyes dart up. 'What are you getting at?'

Peck brings his mug to his lips, takes a sip then places it back on the table. He shrugs. Charlotte turns to her daughter on the floor. 'Maisie, put your hands over your ears,' she commands, voice warm and steady.

'But I'm writing. I need my hands.'

'Put them over your ears, dear.'

Maisie makes a loud groan but does as she's told, keeping the pencil tucked between her fingers. Ears covered, she glares obstinately at the wall.

'What are you getting at?' asks Charlotte again, her voice a knife drawn from its sheath.

'To be honest now, I don't blame you,' Peck says. 'If I was living here with all this community spirit I'd start to go a bit last days of Rome as well.'

'You don't know anything about my relationship with James Hale.'

'I have a few ideas,' he says.

To which Charlotte leans across the table to slap him, hard. Her nostrils flare with short breaths. 'James loved me and God help me I knew it,' she says. 'God, if I wasn't aware.' And she is standing over him, the screech of her chair ringing in the air. Her hands are curled into fists but she catches herself before any further blows are made. She considers him intensely, a new binding made between them by her admission. Is this what love is? Peck wonders. Is it a sharp, abrupt pain under the eye?

'I told him once that I wanted to run away,' she confesses, her secret disgorged by grief. 'If we left in the dead of night, what could they do? If we packed our bags and waited for them to sleep. I would bring Maisie. What could they do? But the bogs are deep, he told me. The bogs are deep and if I left I'd be sucked into the ground.' She sits back down, hands shaking but eyes never once leaving Peck. 'I wanted him and I had him.

There's nothing that can take that away. There's nothing to stop that from happening. To have happened.'

'Can I put my hands down now?' Maisie shouts.

Peck rubs his cheek and considers Charlotte in a new light. He doubts she has confessed her affair to another soul. Perhaps she needs someone to tell, now that Hale is dead. Does she regret revealing it to him? Surely others have suspected. She must realise it will come out. Only a matter of time.

'You need to tell them to bring Pete home,' she says, poised but pugnacious. 'I don't like where this is going. I really don't.'

'Do it yourself if you want him home so badly,' he mumbles.

'And ruffle more feathers? Do you think I want my name written up there? No, you're the one people are waiting for on this, as much as it pains me.'

'Can I put my hands down now?' Maisie shouts again.

Charlotte moves from the table. 'We're going,' she commands, before pointing to Peck and telling him it's not a good idea to go around upsetting people. 'It's not a great way to act around here, you understand?'

Maisie is taken up, then, pulled alongside, out of the door before it's slammed. As soon as they're out of earshot, Peck goes for the cupboard, pushing empty pieces of Tupperware aside until he finds a bottle of moonshine. The cork comes out with a plop.

The air outside is crisp. Charlotte can feel her daughter's blood pulse through the veins of her wrist. She makes it a few steps before tears stream down her face. Head held upright, she makes it beyond the patch of grass that separates her neighbour's bungalow from her own, then past the threshold of the doorway. She releases Maisie, who like a wisp floats towards the sofa, opens her diary and continues writing. Not a word passes from Charlotte's lips as she moves into a separate room and sits on a wooden chair. She struggles to compose herself, and with both hands on the table she feels something approaching stability. Why did she tell him? Now Duncan Peck knows, it's a hole she can't repair. Only a matter of time before that pinprick widens, before other people start asking questions and gossiping over fences. It won't be long until she hears her own name whispered in the square.

It would make sense to start packing now. Only a few essentials put in a bag. He died and that is that. What now, with the world vibrating like it is? Maybe it would be simpler for her to leave alone. Then they would be forced to let Peter go, to look after their daughter. It wasn't in them to leave Maisie defenceless, in the village without a soul to care for her. How did they lose their friends? There are those that talk behind her back, she knows, for pointing the finger. Things were better when JM was around, they whisper. She tries not to think about this and searches the cupboard for something to drink.

With a cup of mead in hand she walks back to the living room, to see her daughter on the sofa. Charlotte wipes the area under her eyes and finds a chair to sit in. One in which she can breathe and sit back and gaze up at the ceiling. Her husband is a good man, she tells herself. He deserves better than this. They may not have been together, not truly together, for months, but she likes having him beside her all the same. Is there any truer sign of love, she considers, than to be under sheets, feet skimming. And this will pass. And this is a blessing. James was unsustainable. James was nothing good. She looks up at the shape on the ceiling, the damp O that remains, encircling nothing in particular. Oh, the ceiling says. Oh, he was a charmer, alright. Oh, when he turned up out the blue, Maisie barely two – and the way he looked at her. Oh, it was heady, and, Oh, the secrets and, Oh, the pregnancy.

Charlotte rises from the chair resolute, cup drained. Maisie looks up from her pages. 'I'm going into the attic,' she informs her daughter, and then she's out of the door to find the ladder that will take her through their bungalow ceiling. She fishes it out from a nook, finds the latch, lights a candle and climbs with it into the dark. There in the dust she must duck her head to stop it knocking the rafters. She hobbles to the place she reckons sits directly above the living room. Time to sort this out, once and for all. JM would never have let it get to this. The plumbing on the roof runs somewhere above her head, fixed from clotted leaves, but there is a leak and it must have been dropping on the boxes they use for storage. Looking for damp, she finds a black, circular container in exactly the place she judges the stain to be. An old hat box. She realises what this is and considers turning back, pretending she had never seen it. But she stays, rests the candle on a suitcase, kneels beside the box, and lifts the lid.

Inside is white. White pieces of clothing, small and dainty. The baby's things. Jacob. The name leaps out of the box. There are bonnets and little gloves for the cold. There are bibs and socks and trousers and tops. She digs her hands into the pile and lifts them up. She pushes her fingers down through the soft material, flickering in the light, down through the crepuscular woolliness, reaching for firmness. The tips of her fingers touch the bottom and she retracts. She picks up a sock and considers its smallness. All at once she remembers the weight of him in her arms. Jacob, named after his grandfather. That had been her idea, and not entirely for favour with the giant under her roof. How JM had loved him, as he had loved Maisie. It feels like a defeat to admit it. There are memories of afternoons spent together, her father-in-law yawning with Jacob sleeping soundly against his chest. He was warm to them in a way he was not for Peter, which is agony to know, because it does not fit with what she has told herself; that drink made him thoughtless and thoughtlessness had made him forget his strength.

Studying the sock she hopes for an involuntary pull into the moment, to seek out the certainty once more, but there is nothing she can keep hold of. She wants to smell the top of Jacob's head, hear his gurgling, taste his fingertips with little kisses. The sock had been Maisie's too. Pretty much everything in the box had been, passed down for the new baby. But they are Jacob's things, she thinks. His final things. She had never got to see her son outgrow them. Replacing the sock she contemplates the heap, wishes she could dive into it. With the light throbbing beside her the contents of the box look less like clothing and more like the limbs of some knitted doll. Here is a leg, connected to another, and the bonnet there, sewn onto this bib. What unknowable body lived in these things?

A drop of water lands on the back of her neck. Above her a bulge swells on the rafter, thickening until it too is born and falls. Woken from her thoughts she lifts the container, and in doing so exposes the ring of dampness, formed in a precise circle. Placing the weeping hat box to the side, she inspects the ring with her fingers. It is cold and moist against her skin. Oh, it says. Remember when, it says. But she doesn't want to. She puts her hand in the centre of the circle and pushes down. The surface bends against her effort, as if it too is made of knitted wool. She pushes harder and something beneath her cracks. Oh, the ceiling moans and, although she knows she should stop, Charlotte pushes harder still. She leans her weight against her arm. Oh, the ceiling sighs, as something below gives way. With a loud clap the circle breaks and Charlotte's hand goes through to the living room. The sudden movement unbalances her, and she falls forwards so that her arm disappears up to the shoulder, extended through the hole like a light fitting. Eyes closed, she waits for the floor to fall out from under her. A moment passes and nothing comes, so instead she shucks her arm free and sits upright once more.

'What's happening?' asks Maisie, surprised and staring up from the living room, through the fresh hole, into her mother's eyes.

'I found your brother's clothes,' laughs Charlotte, and at that moment she grasps a handful from the hat box and releases them above the gap in the ceiling. 'Do you remember him?' she asks.

Maisie sits in the middle of a bloom of white. Her face is a mask of horror. 'Will the rain come into our house?'

'No, it won't,' Charlotte tells her. 'Look at the clothes. Aren't they lovely? He was so tiny.' Maisie kicks off a bonnet that lies on her right foot. 'So lovely!' Charlotte shouts. She grasps another handful to rain over the living room. 'Do you remember him?'

'Yes,' her daughter says curtly. 'Baby Jacob died and went to heaven.'

'That's right,' Charlotte replies, feeling herself becoming manic, and so she takes a couple of deep breaths, keeping focus on the baby's clothing and not the hole she has made in the ceiling. 'These were your things too,' she says. 'You won't remember wearing them. You were so tiny.'

Maisie picks up her diary and walks out of the living room.

'So lovely!'

Peter opens his eyes and looks out across the square. No one surrounds him. There's a metallic taste in his mouth and he runs his tongue along the fissures of his bottom lip. He is seated on a small wooden footstool, legs straight in front of him. He tries to move them but they are clasped in place by the stocks. His arms are tied with rope behind his back. His throat is parched, and he swallows his own spit to soothe it. 'Hello,' he calls. 'Is anyone there?'

No one answers. He squints to make out the shapes moving on the opposite side of the square. At first he thinks they are gigantic birds, swaddled in their wings, teetering on stick-thin legs, but as his vision clears he sees them for what they are: the people of the village, walking between buildings, carrying on with their business. 'Help,' he cries. 'Come here. Let me go.' But no one turns their head, and soon Peter loses strength, slumping forwards. 'I've done nothing,' he shouts to the cobbles. 'I've done nothing wrong.'

Peck watches him squirm, but does not approach. If he wanted to throw a cinder block at Peter, he is pretty sure no one would stop him. They might not like it, but they wouldn't stop him. He could pick up a stone from a gutter, stand next to Peter Morris and hit his head until it fell apart. He could even shoot him with the same revolver that killed his cousin, blow his face into bits.

*Duncan Peck is a psychopath. Duncan Peck is a wild dog and needs to be put down.*

But he has already had the chance to kill Peter. Plenty of chances. So there must be something else he wants. A judgement, he thinks. A process. Something befitting the promise of the village, with its school and fields and beekeepers and lovers making new life. Walking in his direction is Grace Horn, wrapped in a trench coat with her frizzy hair tied up in a bun. The moment she sees him she hesitates. He can feel her notice the bottle of moonshine in his hand, and he takes a swig as if to confirm its presence.

'Will you be at the service?' she asks, voice mournful. Peck nods. She takes a step towards him, her mouth close to his ear. 'You don't want to be getting drunk like this,' she whispers. 'Not in the middle of the day. Not when people are watching.'

Stares scatter like sparrows as Peck looks around him. He feels the weight of his revolver in his pocket. In front of them Peter bucks against the stocks but no one is bothering much with him. The sight is absurd; as if a lamb had been tied for a wolf to swallow. But there is no crowd of baying sacrificers, and there is no slavering beast to snatch him in its maws. There are only men and women on the streets, going about their business with the friendly bluster of routine.

'Why don't you come over to mine instead?' Grace asks, a smile on her lips. Uncertainty creeps up on Peck, much like on the night they'd first walked together in the dark. Ever since he arrived in the village, it seems she has known exactly what she wants from him. Yet he knows so little about her. The crib. The man's shoes by the front door. He has seen the ghosts in her home but nothing about them has been said. He points to the butcher's shop. 'I was going to get some meat.'

'Later, then?'

When Peck doesn't answer but sways slightly from side to side, Grace moves a hand to meet his own. It is done candidly, as if she fully intends the others to see. Is it all to protect him? he wonders. Is it to protect her? 'Don't worry,' she says. 'Everything is going to be fine, believe me.'

'Did you write about Peter?'

'What's that?'

His eyes are on her, searching. 'When all of that was put up about Peter, days ago, all about Maisie and the roosters.'

'What about it?'

'He mentioned your name on the moor.'

Her stance shifts. She seems uneasy being asked these questions in public but she keeps a firm hold of his hand. 'Well,' she whispers, 'he did a poor job of fixing the roof in my tearoom, so I was angry at him for that. Then he went and broke a load of my good plates.' He can feel her watching his face for a reaction. 'But no, I didn't write about him,' she concludes. 'No.'

He longs to know what she is thinking. Where does her mind roam? Her thumb strokes the side of his hand. What does it mean to know a person? he wonders, and looks back at the stocks. All this trouble to find Peter Morris and now the man's just sitting there motionless while his cousin lies dead. 'Why isn't anyone doing anything to him?' he asks.

Grace shrugs. 'It's been a busy week. First there was Geoff Sharpe, then there was Peter Morris. There was all that with Anna Moar and Scott Doyle. Now James Hale is, well ...' She squeezes his hand tight enough for it to sting and the area around her right eye spasms. 'Someone needs to take a lead in things.'

She is beautiful, he thinks. What is it about him that interests her? He wants to ask her there and then but before he can say a word she leans to kiss him on the cheek. 'Let's find each other later, yes?' And she's away to the tearoom, where Peck can see her through the glass as she takes off her coat and puts on an apron. He lingers to stare as she ties the laces around her waist, donning the role that will see her through the rest of the day, serving tea and cakes with a pleasant smile. It is only when she has settled into her place behind the counter, ready to attend to the first person in line, that Peck shakes his head clear and passes through the square towards the butcher's shop.

The bell rings as the door opens. It does not have time to close before Peck reaches the glass counter. Geoff watches him, leaning on his crutch, giving a little cough to nudge things forward. His brother Gerrard sits in his chair, face bandaged, but his attention also angled towards the man at the counter. Peck tips the moonshine towards his mouth, puts the bottle down with a chime, then proceeds to look over the meats. 'What can I have?'

'You're to get James Hale's portion,' Geoff explains, then immediately picks up a dishevelled chunk of what Peck guesses is pork.

'Hale died,' Peck says quietly.

'Yes. We heard.'

Despite the crutch, Geoff makes quick work at bagging the meat and plopping it on the counter. 'What's happening about it?' Peck asks.

'What do you mean?'

He grabs the bag and puts it in his coat pocket. 'We need to get people together to discuss what's to be done.'

'About what?'

'About Peter Morris. Him out there in the stocks. And he actually did do this. I saw it with my own eyes.' Peck steadies himself on the counter, having leant precariously to the left.

'What makes you think he didn't do the other stuff?' asks Geoff.

'Come on. I want the man hurt, but let's call a spade a spade. Let's not call it a kiddie fiddler.'

'Don't trust appearances,' Geoff smirks. 'That guy's a nonce. Didn't you see what they said about him?'

Peck looks him in the eye, shrugs, and stands upright. 'If we get people together we can talk about that as well. Then we can draw a line under the whole thing and start being a bit nicer to each other.'

'You want us to be nice?'

'Yes.'

'And you want us to kick Peter's teeth in?'

'Only if we decide together that's the best thing.'

'Sounds like you want your cake. Sounds like you want to eat it too.'

Peck shakes the bottle forward like a finger. 'Nothing more than justice. He shot him, didn't he? He killed Hale.'

'Did he? I hadn't heard that.'

'What are you talking about? He shot him in the head. I dragged his body back with some other men from the village.'

'Not us. We were here. Haven't seen anything.'

'Let me tell you what happened,' Peck says, exasperated. 'James Hale and myself went to take Peter in, quietly. We found him. Hale was shot. Brains blown clean out the back of his skull.'

'That was Peter? Peter did that?'

'Yes it was fucking Peter.' Peck punctuates this with his bottle against the counter. He is losing his patience. 'I want justice. I want a trial. He has a family, I appreciate that, but he's done wrong and needs to pay. Your way of things extends to that much, right?' Geoff does little but look silently back at Peck. Gerrard's mouth hole wafts inwards and outwards to the rhythm of his breathing. Infuriated, Peck bangs his bottle against the counter. 'He shot him,' he barks. 'He shot him. He shot him. He shot him.'

Peck lets the bottle rest against the glass counter, looking to Geoff for a response. Instead, a sound comes from the wall. 'I heard you had something to do with it,' rasps Gerrard. Both Geoff and Peck turn to look at the figure upright on his chair. Where before there was only black, now a pair of pink lips poke through the hole in the bandage. There is a glint of yellow teeth.

'I heard you went with him to the moor, and that you found Peter hiding,' Gerrard continues, his voice a guttural snarl. 'He was weak, is what I heard. As thin as a stick. He had no chance to defend himself. Not that it would cause you any second thoughts. No, I heard that you knocked him out cold and when poor James Hale bent over to pick him up you shot your cousin in the head. Just like that. You put the gun to the back of his skull and without blinking you pulled the trigger. Cold-blooded, is the way I'd put it. But it's not just me saying this. That's what I heard, from several people no less. People who have no reason to lie.'

Gerrard pushes against the sides of his chair, slowly lifting himself up from the seat. He stands upright in his butcher's attire, eyes covered with bandages but lips flapping with spittle through the split in his cloth. His voice is unsanded, coarse with disuse. He coughs and splutters, then continues his volley against Peck.

'I heard that you want his home, because you liked the look of his life. I heard you decided on it for yourself. Like a rat you wanted to come here into our community on James Hale's generosity, then use that kindness against him. What a despicable thing. And what's more, I heard that you want Peter Morris's wife. Beautiful Charlotte. I heard you've already been at each other behind his back, kissing in the shade, where her husband, her neighbour, and her lovely little daughter won't be able to see. That's a despicable way to act. It makes me sick. But the game's up. You've been found out. You've taken it too far.'

Gerrard points his bandaged hand at Peck. The pink tip of his finger juts forth from the white dressing. 'What I've heard from someone else, a reliable person no less, is that you snuck up on James Hale when he was sitting on a rock, looking out at the moor, and you stabbed him in the eye. I heard you set the world to rights, talked about old times, and then you blinded him. I have it on good authority that you took the house key out of his pocket and pissed on what was left of him. Urinated on his body. Disgusting. Absolutely disgusting. And I'm sure that's not all you did. I'm sure if we took a trip to his home now we'd see what a mess you've made of things. Stealing the knives and forks, no doubt, taking the food from his cupboards. Greedy man, aren't you? What a despicable act. What a horrible thing to do.'

---

The evening has come and Peck is left on a ridge to the east, edging the village. A curtain has fallen on his face, inky and grave. If it weren't for the sinews in his heels he would be pushed down by it, the twilight that has roped over him. The land spreads its faintness and Peck looks out beyond the final houses through what might as well be a closed pair of eyes. The funeral is about to begin and he doesn't want to go. He knows there is a body there, within the church walls. When he'd helped pull it on a sheet of tarpaulin along the southern road he'd forgotten what he was heaving. He'd known James Hale since he was a boy, but there was nothing he knew about the corpse. Nothing to know. Where was Hale? The name left somewhere in the wood. Fallen out of a trouser pocket as they'd lugged the corpse through the dark.

The death is breaking his back. Peck feels as if his gut has come loose and is pressed to the sod, the evening shrouded with such weight that it's all he can do to keep his head level and look out at the horizon as it becomes unconvinced. There is something walking there, beyond the stones. If he moves any farther from the village he is sure the ground will fall out from under his feet. The grass will collapse. If he takes one step farther he knows he will fall. If it weren't for the strength in his legs. If it weren't for the bones in his feet. With that, Peck topples onto his knees. The ground is wet and he can feel it soak into his trousers. He feels his body entered by the unsettled land. He sobs for a moment, then wipes at his face. He's made things worse with a smear of dirt, so he spits in his palm and rubs his cheek clean. Peck pushes himself up from the ground, stands, and looks at the receding world.

There is something walking there, beyond the stones. There is something with four legs and a head hung low.

---

The night sits with its knees under its chin. The lambs are circling the splay of an injured magpie downed by wind. In their coop the chickens watch the roosters, their backs against the boards. The clouds are galloping, crazed in the dark, above a church steeple pointed upwards like the nose of a sleeping giant.

Inside, Peck fidgets in the front pew. His bottle is nearly empty, but he holds it against his breathing as he sits and stares at the coffin spread in front of the altar. The idiot sun has long faded behind its coddling, so no light is given to the stained glass except from the candles inside. Gerrard's words linger. The sight of his lips peeking from behind white bandages. *What a despicable act. What a horrible thing to do.*

Already Peck feels the suspicions working on him, the distrust of others a contaminant. The revolver remains in his pocket. Heart racing in his ribcage, he knows that if he doesn't take action soon, the next morning could very well shine on his name. Fixed on the coffin, doused in a smell of incense, Peck tries not to make eye contact with the villagers as they file in to pay their respects. Charlotte and Maisie are amongst the first to take their places, choosing a row two places behind his. Others follow in their wake, and although Peck doesn't turn to see them he can hear the building of voices at his back. He is aware that no one, not even Grace Horn, has decided to share his pew. He listens to the voices stem and sprout. What begins as clear sentences turns into a tangle. An old woman behind him, what sounds like an old woman, sits to talk to her neighbour about the uppity Charlotte Morris striking Victoria Bray, while a man speaks to the person beside him about the finer points of picking carrots. In all cases he listens for his name, a whisper of Duncan Peck under the breath. If he can hear it, he thinks, then he will know they are blaming him. He'll know that he is done for.

*Duncan Peck is a liar. Duncan Peck is scum.*

As more people file into the church, the voices become harder to hold. If he listens out for individual words he can make sense of them, but if he tries to take in the conversation as a whole it is swept up by the rest, carried underground, through channels out to sea.

Staring at the coffin, Peck feels as if he's buoyed on an ocean of incomprehensible chatter; unfathomable, but somehow angled against him. It comes as a relief when the stout figure of Brian Goss strides to the lectern. Hale had said that the portly man was the closest the village had to a priest, and while Brian remains unadorned in anything resembling a ceremonial robe there is nevertheless a ministerial quality to the way he holds himself, one hand clasped by the other. There is a sureness to his movements that settles Peck's panicking mind, and it must be having an effect on the rest of the congregation too as their conversations fade. The quiet Brian has ushered into the church is left on the boil, then, as he surveys first the people and then the coffin, a simple wooden thing made from salvaged timber. The anticipation is convincing, and Peck finds himself eager to hear what the self-appointed administrator has to say.

'James Hale was someone with a lot of law in his head,' Brian finally begins, pausing with the skill of a well-seasoned orator. 'He was, in many ways, the very best of us. A kind man. A fair man. A good man.'

At this point, Brian leans both hands on the lectern, bowing his head as if grappling with dark thoughts. 'But he was taken away from us before his time,' he continues. 'Shot dead. In cold blood. I say that so openly because it is what James Hale would have wanted. He wasn't a man to let niceties get in the way of fact. He was, and always will be in our memories, a staunch defender of truth. He fought for truth. For the truths that we so desperately need in our society.'

Brian stands away from the lectern, walking towards the edge of the stage, looking from one member of the congregation to the next. 'You all know that he would go further than most to defend the people's will. He was a physically capable man, yes, but it was his emotional readiness that made him who he was. It was a belief in the goodness that each of us possesses, in our heart of hearts. And that's the important thing, the crucial thing. James Hale did not think he alone knew what was true and what was false. No. He trusted that all of us, together, could come to a conclusion. He was a protector of our truth. A surveyor of our truth.'

Returning to the lectern, Brian pauses, bows his head as if collecting himself, and then looks up and out at the crowd. 'These years have come with their challenges, yes? Sometimes it can be hard to know up from down. It can be impossible to make out the edges. I know it still sometimes eludes me. But James Hale was a man that made shapes from the dark. He helped to make things clearer for all of us. Separating black from white, bad deeds from good deeds. And now that he is gone, we should remember what he has done for our lives. We are here, in this haven of ours, because of men like James Hale. Let us never forget that, and let us continue to see the world as he saw the world. As a place that can be understood. As a place where we can thrive. Not because of our knowledge or strength or skill, but because we know, deep down, what is right from what is wrong.'

Peck looks behind him to see bowed heads in every row. He turns back and sees Brian, too, with his head stooped low. It is a touching sight and there's nothing he can do to stop the tears when they come. After a moment Brian raises his chin, and looks to Peck with a kind, welcoming smile. 'Of course, we were not the only ones who knew James Hale,' he proclaims. 'We have here with us one of James's oldest, dearest friends. Someone he knew long before finding a life in our community, when he lived in the city with all the poor wretches there.'

There are murmurs then, and Peck angles his head to see where they are coming from. He meets the eyes of Charlotte, who looks at him through frosted windows. 'Duncan Peck, would you like to say a few words about your cousin?' Brian asks, and Peck turns to the altar, the lectern and the wooden coffin. Brian beckons for him to walk forward, and with great concentration Peck puts one foot in front of the other, swinging the near-empty bottle in his right hand with each step. He crosses himself as he breaches the threshold between congregation and apse, and swivels to take in the crowd. Their heads are no longer bowed but attentive to his every move. The expressions are a bundle, a ripple of brows furrowed. He catches Grace, who has decided to sit in the middle of the church, surrounded by others. There must be close to the whole village here. The pews are full, and the back wall is lined with those made to carry their burdens: tables, cabinets, chests of drawers. Of these he recognises a few faces, their attention on him like owls. More than the drink it is these eyes that make him nauseous, and it takes all of his energy not to be sick. If he doesn't do something tonight, he is sure they will come for him.

'I'd known my cousin as a boy,' Peck begins, bending low to bring his hand to his knee. 'From so high. To so high.'

As if he had made an important point, Peck takes a swig of the bottle, before placing it on the surface of the lectern. 'I'm a guest here,' he says. 'Just as Hale was my mother's guest, a long time ago. We took him in then and he took me in now. So I won't overstep myself. I won't get in the way of all the lovely things Brian here had to say. Because they were very lovely, let's not beat around the bush. They were very, very nice words to say and it was a real pleasure to hear them.'

Peck shuffles from the lectern to the coffin, places a hand on it and taps the wood. 'It was clear to me that Hale had grown outwards here, away from the city. And I don't just mean fatter.' There is a flutter of laughter from the congregation, which gives him confidence. 'He's been away from me for a good while and the change seems to have brought out the best in him. Like Brian here said, he touched people.'

A glance is given to Charlotte, sitting with Maisie close to her side. 'My thoughts are with Charlotte Morris in particular. Oh God, you've had a nightmare of it. Your husband is out there, in the stocks, but he's still alive. He's still breathing. There's that, at least. Not in here. In here is death.' Peck burps quietly into his fist before continuing. 'Now I know we shared a few words this morning but I didn't tell you then how glad I am to have met you. There's not another person in this church who knows how I feel in this moment. Not a person except yourself. Because you and Hale were so close. So very close. And I'm sorry that he is dead. I just want to say that to you now. I am sorry.'

There are murmurs from the congregation. Several people sitting around Charlotte turn to stare at her. She looks at Peck as if she could murder him right there and then.

'And little Maisie,' Peck continues. 'Poor Maisie Morris. You don't deserve any of this. You're a lovely child, and it's not a nice thing for you to face. I'm sorry to you as well.'

More murmurs, and Charlotte wraps her fingers around Maisie's hand, smiling politely at those who surround her. Peck can see the attention shifting away from him. Now is the time, he decides, to get them on his side, to bring them to his way of thinking. 'I hope that we can choose to see the best in each other,' he says, raising his voice. 'We can start by being open with each other. Open and honest. There is goodness and there is kindness here. Goodness and kindness. You said that James Hale was a protector of truth? Well, let's continue his legacy by being honest with each other.'

Peck jabs his finger at the coffin. 'The first truth is that Peter Morris killed my cousin.' His voice is a shout, ricocheting across the church walls. 'That is not opinion. It is fact. I saw it! I don't know what else he has done, I can't speak to that, but that murder is something he did for sure. He shot James Hale in the head and I was there to witness it.'

'Rubbish,' shouts a voice at the back of the church. 'I heard you did it.'

Someone else, perhaps it is Grace, makes a shushing sound. Peck squints to see who spoke; someone amongst the burdened, their voice strained by a rope. But he cannot decide which body it was. 'Now, see, that's a lie,' he shouts. 'It's a dog-faced lie. There is no evidence for that. None at all. The truth is I cared deeply for the person in this here wooden box. I loved him like a brother. The man tied up outside, on the other hand … He's the one with this on his shoulders. He's the one carrying it.'

'Why would he do that?' the same voice shouts. 'They were friends.'

This is not going the way he planned, and Peck is feeling dizzy from drunkenness. He will need to paint a picture, to help them understand. 'Can you imagine having a neighbour like James Hale?' he asks. 'Can you dream up the thoughts that would drive you to do something like shoot him? The jealousy. The thought of a man like James Hale; on your floorboards, at your dinner table, in your marriage bed. Imagine such a bright light in your home. Such strong arms around your wife. Can you fathom? Can you grasp it? Such a good man like that. It is crystal clear. Evident. Transparent!'

The congregation erupts into whispers.

'Now calm down,' Peck says with arms spread out. 'I'm trying to help you get into the mind of the man.' He stumbles towards the lectern and grabs the bottle, opens the end and tips the last remaining dregs down his throat. He closes his eyes and listens to the overlapping squabble. He looks at the spray, showering over the edges of the stage, up to his boots. He sees Charlotte glare at him with pure hate, then pull Maisie by the hand. A man blocks their path down the centre aisle but she shoves him out of the way. He catches his ankle on the side of a bench and tumbles to the floor. Others are standing now, but Charlotte forces past, wrenching Maisie along. Grace has both arms stretched outwards, beckoning for Charlotte to come to her, and for a moment she falters in her determination to leave, right up until a woman with a table strapped to her back makes a grab for Maisie's wrist. The woman isn't quick enough but the attempt spurs Charlotte onwards and soon she and her daughter are out of the open church door and into the world, leaving Peck to sway with the waves. He thinks to himself that the coffin would make a seaworthy vessel.

The water is dark, and it flows down to the square, westward past the tearoom, past the chickens and the roosters until it is running across a grass-flayed path, uphill over dust.

Before he knows it, he is at the wall, in the dark with other bodies, toiling without speaking, clinging to the concrete like black insects. Not a word is said aloud. He squints through the dark to see the figures going to work with paint rollers, on the ground, on ladders and raised platforms. He longs to shout his name. He wants them to see him there, proud amongst them in their writing. He is the orchestrator of this. It is he who called for justice against Peter Morris, and he will cast his vote just like the others. The bodies of people, his neighbours, flit around the corners of his vision, some carrying rolled-up posters, some bending over fresh buckets of paint. Snatching a pail and brush, he climbs a stretch of scaffolding, trying not to fall in his dizziness, scaling up towards a wooden platform. The height takes him by surprise, and the drunkenness makes it feel as if he has left the world altogether. With the brush between his teeth and a care not to spill any paint, he makes his way upwards, one rung at a time. The surface of the wall is a rough expanse of bumps and fissures, and it is only at this closeness that he can see the sheer weight of poster paper layered one on top of the other. Remnants of past words peek between strips, contorted at angles like an aerial image of fields and hedgerows. He is floating high above this impenetrable map, with lines that bisect and turn, conscribing and leading nowhere.

Soon he is standing beside Grace Horn, her hair bundled up with a rubber band, specks of red paint dotted across her cheeks. A body amongst a cluster of shades, he goes to work on a plastered patch of paper. He lifts the brush to his nose and takes a whiff, the sharp intoxication of paint filling his head.

PETER

IS AN

OF THE

MORRIS
ENEMY
PEOPLE

## Seven

ROBERT POUNDS SPEAKS TO Duncan's mother as they wait for the food bank to open. He walks straight up to her and asks without introduction why she has not been to see him. He says it with his hands in his pockets and with a smile on his face but the words are covered in nettles and some of the people in the queue turn to look at what's happening. He asks why she's been avoiding him. It seems a strange thing to ask. As far as Duncan's concerned his mother hasn't been avoiding anything. She's done nothing different to her usual routine of going to work and coming back at night, except for the day when people were shouting in the street and school had been closed, when they baked a carrot cake and made a row of houses from empty shoeboxes.

Robert Pounds asks his question again and scratches his beard. Why has she been avoiding him? What for? Duncan's mother says absolutely nothing for what seems like a very long time and then she tells Duncan to go find his cousin. Robert Pounds smiles at this. Go find your cousin, he echoes, and Duncan's mother doesn't like that at all. In a voice she never uses outside the house, she tells their neighbour not to speak to her son. Robert Pounds laughs and asks her why not, but Duncan does not hear the answer, because his mother waits until he is far away before she gives it.

Some older children are kicking a football against the outside of a multistorey car park. Their parents are also waiting for the doors of the food bank to open. Sometimes families will wait for three hours because, even though everyone takes a single box away with them, everyone knows that some of the boxes are better than others. Duncan and James like the boxes with spaghetti hoops. The older children are taking turns to kick the ball as it bounces back. Each time it hits the wall it makes a loud thwack. When Duncan asks if they've seen his cousin a couple of the older children look at each other, then say that James is in the car park. There are no lights inside the building but Duncan does not want the older children to know he is scared so he walks straight past the barrier without stopping. The ground inside is covered with broken glass and something with four legs and a tail is swaying from a piece of wire that has been tied to the ceiling. Duncan hears the older children laugh and realises they are watching him from the entrance, but he does not move towards the thing hanging by its neck, nor to the pieces of wood that have been abandoned on the ground below it. Instead, he follows the ramp that leads from one level to the next.

On the top floor he finds James, sitting on the bonnet of a red car that has had all its windows smashed. Duncan asks him what he is doing and James doesn't say anything, just picks at the laces of one of his shoes. Duncan knows his cousin sometimes gets sad. He also knows James isn't really his cousin, and that he's actually a boy his mother found on the same day his father died, when lots of other people died too. That was something they never spoke about, but there were times when James remembered it was where he came from, and that was when he got sad. When James goes quiet like this, Duncan knows it's best to be quiet too. He only needs to be nearby, his mother says. It is enough to be nearby. So Duncan does not ask James to come down, or to explain why he had walked so far from the food bank. Instead, he makes sure James can see that he is there and then he looks over the railing to the street below.

There he sees the older children kicking the ball and he sees his mother and their neighbour Robert Pounds. They are talking to each other farther down the road, away from the food bank, away from the queue, which means James and Duncan won't be getting spaghetti hoops for dinner. Robert Pounds is pacing with both of his hands on the back of his head. Even from this height Duncan can see that their neighbour has been crying. It is strange to see him cry. Duncan can't hear what he is saying but suddenly Robert Pounds stops pacing and tries to move his arms around Duncan's mother's hips. She pushes him away. Then he turns around and kicks a metal bin. The other people on the street are watching this happen. The older children have stopped playing with their football. Robert Pounds looks around, then puts his hands in the air and walks away, around a corner and out of sight. Duncan watches his mother stand with her arms folded, alone, looking down at the pavement. Then she turns around and joins the back of the queue.

Later, at night, when James is fast asleep, Duncan can hear footsteps on the landing. Quietly, he gets out of his bed and edges his small head around the doorway to peek at who is there. And it is Robert Pounds, walking in the dark. Duncan does not say a thing but watches as his neighbour steps towards his mother's door, and he listens as Robert knocks his hairy knuckles on it and whispers something in a voice that sounds like he is talking to a cat. Duncan's mother opens her bedroom door and turns on the hallway light. Duncan ducks his head back into the bedroom when she shouts, and he runs back into his bed when there is a crash and Robert Pounds runs down the landing, clutching his face as blood dribbles down his cheek. Duncan meets his cousin's eye when Robert shouts from the stairs, and when his mother screams back, and it is only when everything has gone completely quiet that they walk downstairs to find her sweeping glass from a broken window.

For a moment, Peck forgets where he is. He lifts his head from Hale's bed, mouth caked in hardened drool. Face down, lying on his stomach, he shifts his weight to right the room around him, dislodging a bottle from where it lies between his legs. It makes it to the edge of the bed, teeters and falls onto the floor with a smash. With a heavy sigh Peck swings himself upright, sitting on the edge of the bed, considering the broken glass and his own tenderness, as well as the dried paint on his fingertips. The sound of the smashed bottle has woken Grace, who is staring up through a single eye that loosens its sureness in front of him. There is still red paint on her cheeks, and there is smudged lipstick on her lips. She too wipes drool from her chin and sits up beside him.

'When my son was alive we'd go looking for horses,' she croaks, speaking as if she has started a conversation in a dream. 'I'd carry him on my back for the most part. He was happy to grab my hair like a pair of reins. I knew all the real horses were dead but there were enough ponies to convince me that there might be some hope. I mean, what keeps ponies alive that doesn't keep a horse on its feet?'

Does she want an answer? Peck isn't sure. In the end he just rubs his palm against his stubble and shrugs. She picks at the spots of paint on her face, chipping them off with her nail one at a time. 'They say there are fewer and fewer ponies,' she continues. 'So maybe they'll be the next to go, then the cows, then the pigs, then the sheep, then the dogs, then the cats, then the birds, then the mice, then the worms. I don't know where we fit in all that.' A splotch of paint on the skin under her left eye is proving difficult to remove, and Peck watches her dig a nail beneath its edges. When it eventually breaks from her cheek there is a scratch mark left behind.

'He'd just begun to talk and could sort of say "pony", although it was only really clear to me and his father. Punny. Punny. Like that. Punny. I think that's why I started looking for horses, so that he could see a real one, and I could point to it and say the word "horse". Then he could point to it and say "horse", and then everything would be alright because the horse would have its name.' She turns to Peck, wide pupils tightening in their irises. 'What happens to the animals when we forget their names?' she asks with genuine disquiet. He doesn't have an answer. He wraps his fingers around her hand and gives it a squeeze. 'We never found anything,' she continues. 'Not in all the times we went out for our walks. I used to look so hard. The rocks would seem like horse heads. The birds in the sky were horses galloping. It got to the point where I'd see so many horses that I'd question what they even really looked like. After enough walks, I started to find it hard to remember if I'd ever seen one myself or if I'd just misremembered it from a picture book. You understand? It's like forgetting the face of someone you used to love.'

'I remember horses,' Peck assures her, although he can't be certain of the last time he saw one of the animals breathing. 'I even remember an elephant.' He pictures a raincloud, drinking from a pond in a bare enclosure, all the other cages at the zoo empty and his mother refusing to leave. 'I do.' It's intended as a comfort, but Grace looks at him with glass in her eyes.

'Maybe things are winding down,' she says wearily. 'If that's the way it's going we need to make sure we're looking after ourselves, protecting what we have, because God knows a strong gust of wind could blow it away.'

Peck strokes her cheek with the back of his fingers; there is dry paint on his skin and flecks fall as he soothes the scratch beneath her left eye. 'Everyone in the village needs to help each other, so we don't go the way of the horses,' he assures.

She bats his hand away. 'I'm not saying that at all. What I'm saying is we need to look out for each other; the people under the same roof. You and me.' Her tone is serious. He feels told off, but also brought further into an intimacy that is not really his, built around another. 'We need to protect ourselves, keep each other safe. Do you understand? If I'm nice to people, it's only because I need them to be nice to me. If I'm cruel, it's—' She furrows her brow. 'You're not even listening.'

'I am, I am.' He grabs her hand and presses it hard against his lips. 'I hear what you're saying.'

She looks suspicious and for a moment like she could pull away, but then she kisses him on the cheek. 'At the end of the day, the most important thing is that we keep our heads above water.'

He studies her fingertips, the nails cut short. 'Do you feel like you know me?' he asks.

It is a stone in a pond. She looks at him anew, as if aware she has been speaking to someone else; a different body from the shadow in her mind. A sadness passes across her eyes like an animal in the dark and then it is gone. 'I think we work well together,' she says, not answering his question.

As Grace rests for a little longer, Peck picks himself up, avoiding the smashed glass of the fallen bottle, and makes his way in search of a dustpan and brush. Grabbing hold of the kitchen counter he looks out at the scene around him. Like a bell remembering past strikes, the veins in his head throb at the thought of the previous night, and all together and all of a sudden the word 'Death' makes itself known. He decides that nothing will be the same, not now that his oldest friend has left him alone in the world.

His eyes latch on to Hale's potted plant. The leaves are green and motionless, and don't offer a word of thanks when he pours the very end of the water flask into its soil. Unlike the rest of the room, the plant looks identical to when Hale was alive. Tentatively, Peck strokes the leaves, and for a moment he isn't sure if the texture against his fingertips is living or plastic.

There is a knock at the door, cracking any conclusion.

**CHARLOTTE MORRIS FUCKED HER NEIGHBOUR.** THE MORRIS FAMILY ARE SCUM. *I NEVER TRUSTED CHARLOTTE MORRIS AND IT LOOKS LIKE I WAS RIGHT NOT TO.* I HOPE CHARLOTTE MORRIS LEARNS A FEW HARD LESSONS. MAISIE MORRIS IS A CHEATER'S BITCH. *CHARLOTTE MORRIS IS A SLUT.* **DUNCAN PECK KILLED JAMES HALE.** LONG LIVE JM. DUNCAN PECK IS A LIAR AND A DRUNK. I'D LIKE TO CUT THE TITS OFF CHARLOTTE MORRIS. **PETER MORRIS IS AN ENEMY OF THE PEOPLE.** I WOULD LIKE TO GRAB CHARLOTTE MORRIS BY THE NECK AND TELL HER A FEW THINGS ABOUT WHAT IS RIGHT AND WHAT IS WRONG.

In front of all this Brian Goss stands beside Peck, who examines the words with open mouth and eyes. Last night, in the dark, he had seen the name Morris. He remembers that. But he did not see these sentences. At least, he doesn't think he did. Perhaps he had heard Charlotte's name mentioned once or twice, perhaps he had seen her name plastered in paint. The whole thing was a blur. He wrote about Peter, that is for certain, but the next thing he can recall is Grace leading him by the hand back to Hale's bungalow.

Before he can talk, Brian motions for Peck to follow and the pair trace their way east from the wall, through the silent and sleepy village to Brian's home. Once there, the record keeper tells Peck to take a seat on the sofa while he prepares some tea, and it is all Peck can do to look at the painting of the shipwreck on the wall. The boards are split and the sailors heave at severed ropes. 'She ran in the night,' Brian explains, his voice tranquil. He is sitting in his armchair with a cup of tea resting on his lap. With one finger he strokes the porcelain handle.

'I wanted Peter's name,' says Peck. 'Just his name up there. I thought people would— I didn't mean for Charlotte to—'

Brian fans his hand downwards, to indicate that all is well and everything is alright, but Peck carries on speaking with rabid urgency. 'He killed Hale. That's what I talked about at the funeral. That's the case I presented. You got that? I thought they got that.'

'That wasn't what they took away from it,' Brian notes, bringing the decorative teacup to his lower lip.

Peck holds his head in his hands. 'Why did you let me talk?' The words he's read cling to him. He eyes Brian with a new sense of uncertainty. Was he there beside him? Are they brothers in their scrawlings now?

'Don't beat yourself up about it.' Brian hovers the teacup close to his mouth. 'The Morrises haven't done themselves any favours lately,' he says, dolefully, as if it is the regrettable explanation for everything that has happened. He sips the tea and pauses, thinking something over. 'Quite a few people came to me afterwards saying they were impressed by the way you spoke,' he continues. 'Confident. Maybe a little loose, but confident.' He blows at the surface of the tea before taking another sip.

'Charlotte is a good woman,' Peck insists. 'She's nothing at all like the picture that's been painted of her. And Maisie, that little girl. She's going to be scared to death by all this.'

Brian makes a face and places his teacup into its saucer with a clink. 'Under normal circumstances we'd consider choosing you a piece of furniture to carry.'

'What's that?'

'Your name was also up there. Twice, in fact.'

Peck has not thought properly of his own name. But Brian is right. It was there amongst the sentences. The portly man is looking at him like a buzzard. The table and the sofa become threatening. 'Consider it a caution,' Brian eventually says. 'Do you have your own rope, though? If not, it may be worth talking to old Patrick Hardy in the bric-a-brac for a fitting. It'll be more comfortable that way, should it have to happen.'

Brian fits his seat as if it had been assembled around his body. He fills the room as if it had all been built precisely for him. No mayor, no king. Only Brian Goss and his judicious direction. With a groan the administrator gets up from his armchair and busies himself with a cardboard box propped up against the wallpaper.

'Are you speaking from experience?' Peck asks.

Brian lets out a short, stinging laugh. 'No,' he says, amused. 'No, I am not.' He turns around and is holding something in his hands: a black raincoat. 'So, will you be joining?'

The chasers trail through the forest, carrying pipes and metal bars, held in hands, slung on shoulders. Down by the river a man pushes a wheelbarrow over roots and uneven ground. Peck's cheeks are sullen and his eyes look out at the rocks and trees like sewn-on buttons. Something has retreated in him since he set off, he knows this; if he could he would dive into his heart to fish it out, grab the edges of it and pull it back, heave it out, then arrange it as before.

He looks out at oak trees, bowed between boulders, each and every one coated in a layer of green moss; not objects, he thinks, but momentary imprints, legs kicked up under blankets. He clambers onto the rocks, cautious that the granite will collapse into feather-stuffed flatness. And if it does he could lie there, facing upwards to watch the branches jut against the grey sky. He would stay there, the ground beneath his hair, and drift into sleep. It is not too late for him to refuse, to return to the village, but he is a part of things now. He wears a raincoat like the rest of them. The dry paint remains under his fingernails. And to think he planned to turn it all around. He wanted to inspire confidence in people; convince them to help their neighbours instead of hounding them for every slight and sin. There is part of him that is ashamed for the anger he felt towards Peter Morris – still feels – but there needs to be some justice in the world. A line could be drawn between truth and lie. A line on the ground like the wall itself, keeping one from the other. But which side is which, and where is he now, as he ducks under branches, half dazed, longing for sleep? Perhaps Grace is right. Perhaps all he can do is keep his head above water. But he will not hurt Charlotte, he tells himself, he won't harm her.

'Where are we?' he asks a woman pacing beside him.

'Wistman's Wood,' is the answer. The air whistles between her teeth as she says it, and Peck thinks of dew under smoke. All is ancient, green and downwards reaching. The rain falls in plump drops through the branches, caking the woods, and the diced wind rises above the trudging group, scattered around limbs that need stooping to traverse.

There are two bodies huddled nearby, behind a body of stone. Charlotte watches the group make its way forwards, up the densely wooded hill. She holds Maisie tight around the waist, pushing her close to the moss-topped rock. Her other arm is over Maisie's head, hand covering her mouth. The girl doesn't struggle but closes her eyes as the granite touches her cheek.

When they ran from the church the night before, Charlotte knew which way things were moving. That drunk idiot Duncan Peck and his idiot mouth. Never before had she wanted so badly to cause a person pain. And to think she had confided in him, in a moment of weakness, a torment, a flash, the agony uncontainable and there he had sat, listening to it all. His is a leaky ship, not to be trusted. It is his fault James Hale is dead. His fault her husband sits hungry and humiliated. How hard it had been to shield Maisie from all of that; the sight of her father in the square. She should have taken her to see him, but she had put it off. Give it a day, she'd told herself. Give it a day to see if things sort themselves. No point causing stress. Nothing to be gained from standing there in front of him, legs in the stocks, violence in the air and tears streaming down her dear daughter's cheeks. She would protect her from that, from all the mess that was Duncan Peck's doing.

After the funeral there was no hope of pretending everything was normal, not that it had stopped Charlotte from trying. She'd fed Maisie dinner and read her a story, and only when her daughter fell asleep had she stuffed a few crusts, a wedge of cheese, a flask of water, fresh clothes for Maisie and five days of knickers for herself into a backpack. She'd tucked a kitchen knife into her belt and had sat by the window waiting for the lights to go out in the other houses, and after midnight had come and gone she'd pulled Maisie awake. Sweet girl, she hadn't complained once. Her only request was that she could carry her diary in her hand, the spine of it nestled against her palm.

Charlotte had explained that they were going on an adventure. It was accepted. If her daughter realised they were running away, she wasn't going to say a thing. And so they played along, going on an adventure as the sun rose behind the clouds. For an hour or so it seemed they might be safe. But with Maisie's little legs progress had been slow, and it wasn't long before they heard the sound of whistles behind them.

Charlotte looks over the top of the boulder, careful not to make any sudden movements as she tracks the path of the group, stalking close to where she and Maisie hide. She calms her breathing. The chasers will move by without seeing, she tells herself. In a few minutes they will have cleared the woods and taken their search north. Then the two of them can push on eastwards, beyond the moor into whatever it is they find outside its borders. She does not yet have a plan but she thinks there is seawater to the east, just as there is to the south. If it is only ruins they discover then it is ruins they will contend with, but if they reach the coast and find a boat, then the world will open up. And Peter? She does not have an answer for that. Not yet. For now they only need to keep still and wait for the chasers to pass.

Mouth covered, Maisie looks up at her mother. She moves to speak through the fingers on her lips, but is stopped. 'Be quiet,' Charlotte whispers. 'Keep still.'

Things are not right. The group is not moving farther away. Whoever is leading has decided to change direction, and the men and women now begin to move directly towards Charlotte's boulder. In a few seconds they will reach her. If they happen to break cover she will surely be discovered, dragged kicking and screaming to the village green. She will be beaten, she considers. Maybe worse, as there is no James Hale to keep them in check. A decision needs to be made and, taking hold of Maisie's wrist, Charlotte pulls away from the mossy stone. There is the swoosh of waterproof sleeves; the sound of the group grows louder, but Charlotte does not turn to look at their position as she creeps away. They will make it, she assures herself, and within a day they'll be on their own, having to deal with a whole other set of circumstances. Food. Shelter. How happy it will be, then, to remember the time when it was only their neighbours they feared! Charlotte almost laughs for reassurance but concentrates instead on not crushing the rotted wood as she directs her feet across the earth.

'My diary,' Maisie pronounces, and wriggles free from her mother.

Charlotte grabs her by the hem of her coat, finger and thumb squeezing the material with all the strength she can muster. 'No. Maze. Stay here.'

'My diary,' Maisie declares again, and manages to slip away from Charlotte. And then she's apart, split, bounding back towards the boulder they had hidden behind, towards the notebook she must have dropped in the moss. Charlotte is after her, clambering as fast as she can to scoop Maisie in her arms, bury her deep. She reaches out, extends her fingers, but Maisie does not take her hand. Charlotte urges her daughter but she does not move. It is too late. The pursuit has cracked wood, and the sound spreads its wings like an ugly bird.

There is the sound of someone moving. Peck points his bludgeon in the direction of the noise. At his command the group fans out, hammering boots over the stones. The sounds come thick and fast, crashing over wet leaves and broken sticks, and within seconds they have circled the boulder. The rush of movement fades. Peck breaches the barrier to find Maisie kneeling on the ground, cradling her diary.

He searches for signs of Charlotte, but she is not there. The girl in front of him looks downwards, eyes cast away from the people around her. She trembles, so small on the ground. She looks to have fallen from the nest and without hesitation he bends to gather her up in his arms, unmoored, unmothered.

---

As the sun sets, Peter bucks at the stocks. There are heavy bags beneath his eyes. Peck and his gang of raincoats are moving along the edges of the square, filing in a line like a returning battalion. 'Is that my daughter? Is that Maisie?' Peter shouts, and when he does Maisie squirms against Peck's shoulder, so violently that he is forced to put her down before she falls. She runs straight to her father, to hug him tightly, and the tenderness of it makes Peck feel sick, as if he is the one responsible for the situation they are in. There is movement amongst the group to separate the daughter, but Peck calls for them to stop and they do as he says, which delivers him a jolt of satisfaction.

'And I don't know where Mother has gone,' he hears Maisie say between sobs.

'I'll be home soon,' Peter tells her, his hands still bound behind his back. 'We'll find her together.' He looks beyond his daughter to the men and women surrounding him, their metal poles and chains. 'Go with them now, Maze. Don't worry. I'll be home soon, I promise.' He tries a smile and she gives him one last hug before walking back across the square.

She is terrified, Peck thinks to himself. But what can he do? He could demand that Peter is released. Send him home to be with his daughter. That would be the kindest thing, no doubt. But the impulse comes and goes without making a dent. Peter has crimes to face. If he weren't in the stocks he would only try to escape, just as Charlotte has. No, the best he can do is keep Maisie safe until this has settled. It's ugly but for the best. And there she is, standing in front of him, eyes on the ground. He does not try to pick her up again, but kneels on the cobblestones. 'I know this must be scary,' he says in the gentlest voice he can muster. 'But your daddy has done something bad.'

Her regard comes up from the ground, questioning. 'What did he do?'

'He was silly and someone got hurt, and it made me and your mummy very sad.'

Instead of asking any more questions, Maisie wipes the sleeve of her jumper against her eyes.

'What are you saying to her?' Peter shouts. 'Maisie, don't listen to him.' He tries to kick his legs from the stocks but only succeeds in tiring himself out, and is left sapped, head bowed, a faint whimper coming from his lips. His distress is making her upset again, Peck notices, and he moves to pat the girl's arm. It is clear that she doesn't know what to do; to run back to Peter, or run away, or stay where she is, and she can only sniff and shiver as she is picked up once more, held against Peck's shoulder. She buries her head against his neck, all so she doesn't have to look at her father, he thinks.

'I've seen things from the other side,' Peter cries, voice threadbare. 'And let me tell you now: it's a pack of, ha, lies. People are fond of my family. I am an upstanding member of this community, as is my wife. We've done nothing wrong.'

The voice fades as they get farther from the square, the chasers whittling away as people depart for their own homes. Peck looks through the windows of his neighbours as he passes their houses, catching the reflection of Maisie's head on his shoulder. Through a glass pane he sees a woman carrying a wooden table, kneeling beside two boys, and he stops for a second to watch as the rope is cut from her back with a bread knife. The wooden table falls and lands on its feet. There are hugs, and there are tears. Massaging the lines on the back of her neck, she walks to the window and pulls the curtains closed.

---

In Hale's home the light is dim, anaesthetised by the sound of peaceful breathing. On the camper is Maisie, dreaming where she lies. Her head is angled to one side, her body facing upright, hands wrapped around her diary. Peck stands above her and watches the rise and fall of her chest. He holds a cup, and he idly swishes the dregs in a circle. There is wind on the window. Peck remembers a story he heard as a boy, about ghosts pushed this way and that by the wind. Spirits did not decide their own direction, his mother had told him. They were led by gusts. The dead were a lot less stationary than you might think, brought into towns, wafting across shutters and knocking hats off heads. His mother said their memories came in as cold fronts, loved ones lifted up by the wind, blown over the living. You may feel that the past has settled, that you can move on with things, but then the wind comes, blowing ghosts on your face.

What was being carried then by the gale against James Hale's window but the man himself? All his weight pressing against the walls of his home. The thought of it strikes Peck's nerves. He wonders if he should open the door, to let his cousin in, to let in the rest, piled in the village over the years, blown about like flotsam on tides. No, the door will remain shut, not because of Hale's ghost, but because at the head of that haunting is one face he can't bear to see, one memory he does not want to remember. His mother.

He thinks about the wall, how still and calm it had been, without the sounds of the moorland, without the wind. As he'd stood shoulder to shoulder with his new neighbours, painting in red, he had felt lucid, feet fixed in the ground. It keeps the peace, Hale had told him. It keeps the community going. And that's something we need right now in the world, isn't it? A bit of community. A bit of sense.

The wind blows against the window. What does Maisie dream of? Peck wonders. Is she somewhere else? She turns onto her side, and the diary falls from her fingers onto the floor. Peck stoops to pick it up. There's nothing in the way of a lock, although a clasp shaped like a tiny belt stops it from falling open. He would have to feed the leather tongue through the buckle if he wanted to spread the pages, and he touches the end of it with his forefinger. He looks to Maisie, her hands pressed together as if she is praying. Lying on her side, her head teeters over the edge of the camper. A few inches farther and she could fall onto the floor. He teases the end of the clasp, flicking it with his fingernail. For a small book, it feels heavy in his hand. It's private, she'd told him, and remembering this, respecting this, he places it gently beside her hands. Like an anemone her fingers coil to clutch it without waking, retracting inwards.

He bends over the camper and scoops Maisie up in his arms. She does not stir, and rests her head against his shoulder as he carries her through the living room, past the threshold into Hale's bedroom. There he lays her on the bed, and when she is in place he lifts the sheets over her body and over her diary, then tucks the edge around her neck. Happy that she is comfortable, Peck sits on the edge of the bed and watches her eyes twitch under their lids.

The rain is on everything. The lambs are waterlogged. The edges of pig bellies are obscured with muck. The Blackbrook has broken its banks. Miles to the east, the rain falls on the ground and flows in shapes that aren't its own, none of its own; a flicker of contours that vanish into dimples and pool into ditches. Its patterns are wordless and gone too quickly to name. Charlotte raises her face, pausing for a moment in the deluge before pressing forwards, upwards, to a hill she does not recognise and its alien heap of granite. Her trousers are ripped, her legs bleeding and muddy, and as she reaches the summit she half collapses on a stone. Breathing armfuls, she considers her place in the world.

There are no lights on the horizon. She can see no sight of the village or of the wall. She has walked all day and does not know where she is. This is the farthest she thinks she has ever been from her home. It is dark, darker than she is used to, and the moorland is dizzying in its indirection. There is only the ground beneath her, prickled and frayed. This is the limbo-land, she decides. If she were to die here, no one would find her. It would be as if she had fallen into the sea. The ground has already ripped at her shins, she thinks. What will it do when she can't keep her eyes open any longer? The mires here are yawning, broad enough to eat her up. She'll be picked clean and left unfound. The rain slows, and Charlotte imagines her bones disremembered.

With her heartbeat slowing, the shame comes to shore. All she can think about then is her daughter's hand, refusing to reach out when she tried to grasp it in the woods. She should have stayed with her there, but she ran, and each and every opportunity she'd had since that moment to turn around had flown past like a bird. She had known that every step was farther from Maisie, but she could not stop, had not stopped, has only stopped now, on this rock, when the day is done. For the first time since she was born, her daughter is truly away from her, and it is all her doing. She has abandoned her. The rain stops. Charlotte heaves. Her stomach wrings itself dry at the thought of Maisie's hand. The fingers that wouldn't reach out to touch her own. She shivers, stillness bringing with it pinpricks on grazed legs.

But she isn't about to die, she decides and, collecting herself, Charlotte works her way back down from the hill, towards a lone tree, bent sideways from the wind. It is the anatomy of a deformed hand, sprung from the soil; the only thing of substance that she can see. The clouds have wrung themselves dry but the wood remains damp, glistening black. There are no leaves on its warped branches. The more she looks at it the more monstrous it becomes, so far from the woodland and contorted in its wilderness. One of its fingers points towards her. She grabs hold. Her leg goes up on the bark, two arms on the dead digit, and she pulls with all her weight, swinging back and forth on the branch until it dislocates with a wet pop. Not caring how much noise she makes, she pins one end of the branch to the ground underfoot, howls, and twists it beneath her.

Soon she has split the stick into forearms, and carries these back under the silent watch of the tor. There, squatting beside a boulder, she piles them into a small pyramid. Fishing in her backpack, she finds a box of matches, plucks one from the mound and, cupping her other hand, strikes the match against the side of the box. The flame sputters and dies before she has time to hold it against the wood, so she tries again. That match doesn't even ignite, so she throws it behind her. The third match burns bright enough for her to bring it to the side of the heap, but the wood sits passive beside the flame. Flinging the match into a puddle, she rests the back of her hand against the outermost stick. It is drenched, too wet to burn. She brings her arms down on the pile and sends it scattering.

The boulder beside her moves. Charlotte swings around, grabbing hold of the kitchen knife in her bag, wielding it towards the rock. In front of her the mottled surface folds and collapses in on itself. A fissure that runs its length grows and deepens, then ruptures. The outcrop arches backwards on itself, splits in half, exposing a gaunt human face, soon rising above her head. The skin is furrowed into field rows. The expression is charcoal. The old man in front of her is a giant, swaddled in a blanket of animal furs. 'I thought you were a ghost,' he says.

---

In his cave JM kneels, working at a fire while Charlotte sits wrapped. She looks at the objects stored around her. Empty dog-food tins, chopped wood and piles of animal bones. She watches her father-in-law carefully choose which sticks to move to the flames, his body contorted to fit in this primitive shelter. With an effort he ties his long limbs into a knot to sit next to her, then contemplates what he has created, crackling by their feet into woollen smoke that passes out through a cavity. The fire warms, but the air is wounded with a draught.

JM is dead. At least, that is what she believed. The sight of him breathing dislodges her, as if she has slipped into the past, and although there is anger and shame for now they swirl beneath her, under older associations of home. There was a time when it made her feel safe to know she was under his roof. Safe but uneasy, given his place in the village, and privy as she was to the way he could be from time to time. That is the feeling which is on her, the fear and the comfort braided together. In the firelight, she can study his face. Peter's essence is there, somewhere, but hard to pin amongst the age and hardness, which seems harder now. There is a sinewy strength in his neck that reminds Charlotte of a skinned hare. She considers his shoulders, intact. 'You still have your arm,' she says.

'Why wouldn't I?' His voice is cobwebbed.

'James Hale ripped it off, is what I heard.'

'Is that so?'

'They let you bleed to death.'

He laughs; a violent clap. 'No such thing. They never found me, and James Hale certainly never laid a finger on my arm.' As he laughs again, the strings tighten in his neck. 'He spun a good story, I bet. All the better to step into my shoes. All the better for James Hale and his quiet ambitions.'

Her mouth is dry but she swallows. They have yet to say a thing about what happened between them. 'How are you still alive?' she asks.

'There's rabbits and ponies left, no matter what you've heard.'

She begins to measure how much time has passed since he was ousted but realises she has done it before, when she sat in the tearoom and counted the distance from her baby's death. 'Ten months.'

'I couldn't tell you,' he says with a flick of his wrist. 'I keep my calendar by sunrise and sunset.'

Charlotte looks to the bones on the floor of the cave. A fuzz of gristle clings to the ends, flecked and purple, as if they have been chewed by a pack of dogs. JM reaches out with an enormous hand to stroke her cheek and, surprising herself, Charlotte allows his rough fingers to make their way from the corner of her eye to the corner of her lip. When he is done his face folds like paper into a smile.

'So it's really you,' he says, and motions for her to embrace him. As if the choice is not hers to make, she leans in. He is huge, but thinner than she remembers. Under his weather-beaten jumper she can feel ribs sticking out like wooden boards in sand. The rage rises up in her, then. She pulls back, abruptly stands and steps back, knows that she has to get away. But he is standing too, and he follows her as quick as a wolf to the mouth of the cave. 'They wrote about you?' he asks, his tone demanding an answer.

The moor is a footstep away. The light from the fire does not stretch far, and everything beyond its limits is dark.

'What did they say?'

James was always convinced that JM knew about their affair. He would tell her that her father-in-law made it his business to listen to everything that went on. Sometimes JM would give her a look, as if he was aware of everything, but Charlotte had always believed he would come to her if he knew. Or tell Peter, as much as he scorned him. 'Nothing good,' she mutters.

Stooped against the stone JM inspects her expression but does not ask any further questions. 'You must be angry,' he sympathises. 'You must be furious, no doubt, to be caught in the end.' A large stick falls with a crack into the fire behind them. 'I was always worried you were too reckless,' he says. 'Too wrapped up in yourself.'

She spits in his face. The saliva speckles across his nose and cheeks. It has been a long time coming, but as soon as it has landed she feels a wave of regret, barbed and bristling in the back of her head. He wipes it away with the back of his forearm. If he is going to have his revenge for being cast out, let it happen now. Her pulse is drumming and she readies herself for the retaliation. They must be miles from another human being. If she screams, there will be no one else to hear it. JM is unflinching in his eye contact. It is the same stare he gave across the doorway, as the cockerels were crowing themselves hoarse. That was the last time she had seen him alive, or so she had thought.

'I'll say the same thing.' His voice is screwed on tight. 'I put my hand on his head, to see why he was crying so strangely. Nothing more.'

'I know it was an accident— ' she starts, but he interrupts.

'No. It wasn't. He just died.' He loosens in front of her. 'You mistook me. Not that I've let myself be encumbered by your delirium. I've made a new territory for myself and I am happy here.'

It is too much. She cannot keep his stare. She turns to the entrance of the cave. Her baby was so full of life, bursting with the stuff. Laugh like a hiccup. Little Jacob and all the love he soaked up. A happy baby, pleased with the world. She does not want to think any more about that night. She does not want to picture the little body being carried away from her. For a while she is silent, looking out at nothing in particular.

'You won't get far on your own. Stay. If only for tonight.' JM has returned to his position by the fire, sitting with his legs crossed. He dabs the last flecks of spittle from his face with a blue handkerchief pulled from his pocket. She wishes she had the certainty she had the last time they were together. It would be enough to push her from the shelter, into the night where she could be buoyed above the bogland.

'Why are you here?' she asks.

'Where else would you like me to be?'

'Why haven't you gone to the city, or the coast? Why haven't you come back?'

'Ah.' JM pokes the burning wood. 'Well.'

'Why are you still here?'

'At first I was waiting,' he says. He stretches his right leg, groaning as the limb extends across the floor. The left leg is next, and with a crack the bone settles. There's a whisper of relief as he rubs the muscles around his kneecaps; a movement that is frail and aching and reminds Charlotte that he is, despite his size, an old man.

'What were you waiting for?'

'Regime change,' he laughs; another violent clap, ricocheting amongst the animal bones. 'A more sympathetic moment, when your ambitious lover wouldn't leverage a personal tragedy to break every bone in my body,' he scoffs. 'But now I've settled into a new pace of life. There is food for me to eat. There is water for me to drink. I sleep deeply and the wrongs I've suffered are far from my mind.' He shoots her a look.

With a deep breath she rejoins him by the fire, to the shapes dancing as if they are blindfolded. There are those that would welcome his return, she suspects, because there are those that have come to hold a grudge against her for pointing the finger. She has heard his name whispered in the tearoom, and Maisie has said more than once that there are stories told about him at school. A quiver of wind passes over Charlotte's head, and she thinks of the night-time. 'This is no way to go on,' she says.

'Is that so?' He seems amused, as if she is a child frustrated about the weather, and it's enough to curdle her grief back into anger.

'Yes,' she states. 'Do you think this is a way to live? Do you think I'm happy about being hounded out of my home, scared to death about what my neighbours are doing to my daughter? Do you think that's something I'm content with?' There's a silence then, filled with her heartbeat.

'What do you want to happen?' JM asks, and he is testing her, she realises. She thinks about the stocks in the square, the stage in the green, the faces of her friends and neighbours, of her husband, of sweet Maisie.

'I want to hurt the man whose fault it is that I'm out here. I want to hurt him and then I want to blow down the wall, smash it down, tip it over, flatten it so I don't ever have to look at its ugly face again.' Her tone is earnest but she knows that it is only her exasperation speaking. There is no possible way for her to get rid of the wall and, even if she did, they would only find something else to plaster with paint.

JM tuts at what she says. She wants to scream, and is about to stand up again and do so but he motions his heavy hand downwards and, even without contact, she feels herself pressed towards the ground. 'Everyone has a right to the wall,' he says. 'We've both had the sharp end of it, but it's a beautiful thing.' His voice is soft and sincere, and under the frustration it hurts all the more for Charlotte to hear him speak like this, after everything that has happened. Pity sits on her, followed by sadness. 'It's what we've contributed,' he declares. 'It's what we've managed out here.'

He continues to massage his legs, folding them at the knee so he can reach his long calf muscles. It is clear that he has not had someone to speak to for some time, and Charlotte wonders what he has uttered alone in this cave. What curses against her has he said in the dark, and what has he heard echoed back? He sits upright to poke the fire with a twig and the dancers splinter into sparks. They wait for a split-second, unsure of themselves, before realigning their feet on the smouldering log, clasping hands and shaking bodies.

'Everyone can write there,' he continues. 'Anyone who lives in our community. All you need is a bucket of paint. If someone is beating up their apprentice, or if they are hoarding food, or debasing their position, you can broadcast it. You can tell the people, and the people can do something about it. It gives a voice, you see. A voice to people who might otherwise not have one.'

She recalls similar speeches to the village, about voices given, responsibilities and justice. It was JM, after all, who had encouraged the people to write as they felt. This was the man, she considers, who had been the body of law and order since she was a little girl. All of it before the Tragedy, all before the words turned on him, her words, and brave James Hale had led the search to find the monster hiding on the moor. How strange it must have felt for him, how humiliating, to have his name painted for all to see.

'When I was your age there'd be things up there that would surprise you,' he reminisces. 'Sometimes you'd wake up and there were love letters. Poems. Marriage proposals.' The end of JM's twig goes once more into the fire. He prods the wood with it a couple of times, then throws it into the flames. She can see the skin around his neck, as thin as parchment but riddled with veins. The tension across her back eases, and a desire to hold him, to wrap him in blankets, rises somewhere inside of her. He is an old man who does not know where he should be.

'We still have your room,' she notes, stating a fact. 'No one has touched it.'

'James Hale wouldn't be too happy about me sleeping in my own bed.'

'James is dead.'

In an instant, the cave takes on new focus, all the surfaces become sharper. JM has not moved, yet his huge body seems to angle towards her, listening carefully to everything she has to say next. 'What's that?' he asks.

'Someone brought a gun into the village and, well, there was a fuss.' She doesn't want to tell him about Peter, or the things they said he'd done to Maisie, or the sadness that has grown inside her since she heard her neighbour was no more. She never considered what they had to be love, not properly, but perhaps it had been. 'He was shot,' she says.

'By whom?'

'Duncan Peck.' She says it without thinking. 'His cousin.' His attention is back on the fire, and she can see him processing what she has said. 'I thought you were dead,' she murmurs. 'I thought you were bones in a ditch.' She straightens her back and, reaching out, rubs the knuckles of his left hand with her thumb. 'Do you see what this is, Jacob? This is a chance for you to make amends.' Caught in ambush by the emotion, she grips his hand a little tighter. 'Come back with me. This is what you were waiting for. We can go back together. You can atone for what you did.'

He meets her eye and she thinks he might protest, but all he does is scratch his inner thigh with his free hand. 'Do the people still talk about me?'

It is hard to know how to respond. 'Yes,' she says. 'They haven't forgotten you. Some of them even miss you, I think.'

He slips his hand out of Charlotte's grip, bringing it to rest in his lap. He looks to the logs at the base of the fire, at the fissures glowing red. 'And fat Brian Goss, is he still alive?'

'As far as I know.'

This answer brings only a slight nod.

'Maisie will be so happy to have her grandfather back,' Charlotte insists. 'Pete will be over the moon. I know he will. He always resented me for how it happened.' She tries to smile, make light of it, but cannot. 'After you atone we can go back to how things used to be.'

JM does not look at her. 'I have nothing to atone for, my dear. And I am quite happy in my new kingdom.'

There is a throb in her neck. 'You don't understand,' she says, voice trembling. 'I've left my little girl.'

The expression that covers him in that moment is nothing she can hold on to. He opens his blanket of furs and makes a space next to him. 'Come here,' he tells her.

# Eight

Robert Pounds watches them walk down the street. Duncan's mother steps a little quicker as they pass his house. Even though he leans in his doorway with a mug in his hand, she does not stop to say hello. Duncan and James have been told not to talk to him. Not under any circumstances. But Duncan can't stop himself from looking at Robert Pounds; at his sad eyes and hairy face, at the cut on his cheek that Duncan's mother has made. Their neighbour does not wave or move from his doorway, but watches as they hold hands and make their way along the pavement. Work and school are closed again. They have played cards and they have made lemonade to drink in the garden. They also broke a clock on the mantelpiece when Duncan threw a cushion from the sofa at James, so Duncan's mother told them with a hand on her head that they were going for a walk. After they tied the laces on their shoes she waited by the window for a long time before opening the front door, and it is only once Robert Pounds is behind them that she says anything: that now the clock is broken they will have to make their own time. Neither Duncan nor James understands the joke, but Duncan's mother laughs so they laugh too.

They decide to walk to the harbour. On their way they hardly see another soul. There are metal barriers that they have to navigate around. There are smashed windows and they have to be careful not to step on the glass. At one point James and Duncan jump on black bags of rubbish piled high on a street corner, but Duncan's mother shouts at them to stop. A church that had been set on fire the night before is still burning. A man walking a dog tells Duncan's mother she shouldn't be outside alone. She tells him she isn't alone. She is with her children. When they get to the harbour the boats are broken and bunched together and the sight of it seems to make Duncan's mother sad as she sits on a bollard with her arms folded. James follows Duncan as he makes a game of scaring the seagulls that are gathered near an upturned bin. James is unsure at first, but he too spreads his arms and makes a roar as the birds shriek and fly away. James follows Duncan when he makes a game of balancing on a chain that runs between two posts, and he follows Duncan when he stands on a wall and looks out at the sea. There is something there, face down in the water. Neither of the boys can tell what it is, but Duncan's mother has seen it too and she stands and takes them by their hands and walks them home, past the smouldering church and the piles of black bags, past the broken windows and metal barriers, onto their street and past Robert Pounds, who is still leant against his doorway with a mug in his hands.

Later, that night, Duncan stares from his bed through the half-open door at a shape on the landing. Robert Pounds walks in the dark, edging towards his mother's bedroom. It is happening again, the same as before, but this time something glints in the neighbour's hand: a knife taken from a block in the kitchen. Duncan gets out of his bed, walks towards the threshold, where he sees Robert Pounds softly tap at his mother's door, holding the blade behind his back. Before the man can whisper any words Duncan screams as loud as he is able.

The eyes of Robert Pounds turn on him, wild and white, and he rounds on the boy standing there in his pyjamas, pushing him back into his bedroom. Death isn't something Duncan can get his fingers around, so he kicks and grabs at the intruder as James wakes and screams. The noise is enough to wake Duncan's mother, and she runs from the corridor to find her neighbour wielding a carving knife above her son's head. She doesn't say a word as she wrestles Robert Pounds, not a pinch of speech passes between her lips. Only heavy sacks of breath land on the carpet, only panicked animal noises as she grips the man's wrist and tries to push it away from her son, away from her own face. The angle he's at between the floor and the wall has his arm crooked, and Duncan's mother sticks her fingers into his ribs, unbalances him and bends his hand back. He does not let go, and so she pushes his hand farther, forcing Robert Pounds's grip and the knife against him, into his cheek and straight through to the back of his throat. There is an awful retch before Duncan's mother jettisons herself backwards. Her neighbour is left to flail at the hilt of the knife but only manages a few weak claws before he collapses into his own blood.

James's screams stop as Duncan's mother kneels in front of the twin beds. Her face and neck are speckled in red, and she looks to her son with love in her eyes. Duncan sits upright and stares at his mother's face. Her eyes are green. Her pupils widen.

There's a wet slap. Her jaw hangs loose.

Robert Pounds has crawled from where he fell, pulled the knife from his face, and has pushed it into Duncan's mother. Immediately, James leaps from his bed and jumps on the man, slamming the heel of his bare foot against him as if squashing an insect, stamping on his neck, already punctured, over and over until it breaks apart, buckles into pieces. Even though he is only nine, he does not wince. The sounds that come out of Robert Pounds are unlike anything that's walked the earth, but Duncan is transfixed by his mother's face. He does not look to the man dead on his carpet. He reaches out to touch his mother's cheek. He wraps his small arms around her head and pulls it close to him.

Peck wakes on the camper bed to see Maisie standing above him. 'You were snoring,' she declares, hands on hips, as if this is something that should be said as honestly as possible. He moves to sit upright, digging his elbows into the mattress and fingernails into the corner of his eyes.

'You'd snore too if you had as much sleep in you as I do,' he tells her, and looks at the mess around him. Maisie doesn't move or respond to his words, but remains standing with hands on hips, looking at him with a vague sense of disapproval. 'What is it you want?' he asks.

'I'm hungry.'

And so he lifts himself from the camper bed and lumbers into the kitchen. He searches for food, pushes boxes to the side, opens dust-set Tupperware. Maisie watches, perched on a stool, observing his struggles. Eventually scraps are found, shoes put on, hot water collected from the boilerman, a quick shave with Hale's razor and within an hour the pair sit opposite one another at the dinner table, a bowl laid out for each of them. Maisie dips a spoon deep into the grey soup, unearthing chicken bones. Peck watches her scoop the water, press her lips against the metal and portion the broth into mouthfuls. As she finishes the meal, Maisie picks the small bones up between her fingers. She turns them one way and the other, then arranges them into a small pile, to one side, beside her sleeve. Her hands are caked in dirt, Peck thinks. He hasn't thought to show her the sink until now. There are dark splotches down the length of her arms, as if she hasn't washed for days.

Peck chews on his bones, sucking the ends, but Maisie keeps hers apart.

'When is my mother coming home?' she asks.

'I don't know,' he admits, and when her lip starts to tremble he adds, 'I'm sure she'll be back soon. She's just gone for a walk. She wanted to take you but she was so excited to keep going that she, well, she just needed to go on her own.'

When the chasers got back from the search, there had been disagreement about what was to be done next. Some had said Charlotte would die out there on her own. Others had said she'd come back of her own volition. Peck had argued they should look again. A few people were with him, but it was felt that too much had happened in the past week to risk anyone else getting hurt. If Peck wanted to help, he could mind the girl. Fine, he would, but it seemed to him that the village was feeling the gulf left by James Hale. No one has yet stepped into his boots. They seem to be avoiding them if anything and it was creating an air of stagnancy. He could smell it.

'I know you're lying,' Maisie tells him. 'I know she wanted to run away.' The girl is staring him down, eyes sharp, bordered by straight black hair. He is impressed, a little intimidated, unsure what to say in return.

'Are those for the birds?' he asks, pointing a finger to the pile of bones on the table.

Later that morning she carries the chicken bones with her as they approach the village square. She cups them in her hands as she walks beside Peck, outside the tearoom, up to the stocks beside the cenotaph.

Peck's hand slaps Peter Morris across the face, sending a line of saliva away from his chin onto the earth. 'Wake up,' he orders, and Peter opens his eyes, caked in brittle scales. The smell on him is pungent. There are remnants of thrown vegetables at his feet. Peck stands aside. Maisie approaches her father, the bones offered up in her hands. It takes Peter a moment to make sense of the shape standing in front of him, as if he is searching through memories, sifting through cards to find a name to put to a body.

'Hello Maze, hello sweet fishie, what's that you have for me?'

There is something in the heaviness of his eyes, trying their hardest to open wide, that sends a jolt through Peck's heart. He looks behind him, to the people moving on the path around the square. There is a group of young men idling on the corner, laughing at a middle-aged man struggling against the weight of an empty bookcase. Deciding the group isn't paying the three of them the slightest bit of attention, he stands aside to let Maisie get closer to Peter.

'I have something for you to eat,' she says. Eye-level with her father, Maisie selects with great care a bone from her palm. She holds it up, towards his face. Carefully, she puts it between his lips, where he lets it sit for a beat before sucking it into his mouth. Without speaking, he chews, and with a loud crunch the bone splinters against his teeth. The moment he swallows it, Maisie is ready with another bone, which she again places between his lips, before sliding another, then another, into his mouth. He chews and swallows them all, until the only thing left in her palm is grease. It's a tender thing, Peck thinks. To feed her poor father like this. Perhaps he has been cruel in keeping her away from her own flesh and blood. Has Hale's murderer suffered enough, kept outside for days on end? Is it his own spite, not the village's, that is keeping him here? Certainly, it wouldn't take much for him to raise the wood around Peter's ankles, to let him return home and keep his daughter safe in Charlotte's absence. But he can't bring himself to do it. He can't find it in him to let the red-haired man go, despite the pain written across his face. Beneath it all, there is something about him that Peck dislikes, hates even. He walks away from the stocks and beckons for Maisie to do the same.

'Wait,' Peter calls, his voice cut to shreds. 'Don't go. Where's my wife? Please. Where is she? Have they found her? No one has told me anything. Is she well? Is she safe? Maisie. Maze. Don't go. Come back. Your mother. Where is your mother? Where is she? Don't leave me. Don't leave me. Please, don't leave me.'

Despite the steeliness she'd set out with that morning, Maisie dissolves at the sound of her father's cries.

'You've been bad,' she yells at him, then looks at the cobblestones and bawls, attracting the gazes of everyone else in the square. Peck can feel them waiting for him to do something, so he kneels down beside the girl and gives her a hug.

*Duncan Peck is a kind and thoughtful man.*

'Get your hands off my daughter,' Peter shouts, and bucks so hard against the stocks that he falls from his stool onto his back. From the writhing body on the cobbles, screams sound across the square: 'Get off her. Get off her. Get off her.'

Whispering for Maisie to stay where she is, Peck stands and walks back towards Peter. A globule of spit comes from the bound man's lips and lands directly on Peck's cheek. There are eyes on him, he can feel it. The top of the wall is visible above the roofs of the buildings. He bends and grabs Peter by his arm, twisting him so his face is squashed into the brown pulp that covers the ground. He digs into his own pocket and pulls out a penknife. He can hear Maisie shrieking over Peter's muffled wails, and with a few quick movements he cuts the rope that ties the man's hands behind his back. This is of great surprise to Peter, who lies stunned for a few seconds on the cobbles before stretching his arms out on the ground.

When Peck stands again, he sees that everyone in the square is watching him. He lifts up the cut rope and, all at once, they clap.

*Duncan Peck is merciful. Duncan Peck is compassionate.*

The applause lasts for a few seconds, then ends as people go on with their business. Peter's legs are still in the stocks but his newfound freedom allows him to lift his body back onto the stool. And so he sits once more with his legs out in front of him, but now with arms folded across his chest. 'Wait,' he cries as Peck turns to go, and as Maisie waves goodbye. 'Wait. Don't go. Don't leave me, ha, alone. Don't leave me here in the cold. I've done nothing wrong. Don't leave me here. Don't leave me here. Don't leave me here. Don't leave me. Don't.'

Peter's words echo in Peck's ears as he leads Maisie away from the square, anywhere but there, and before he knows it they've walked along the south road where the houses open up around the green. The place is empty except for a few pigs in their pen and a pair of children playing penalties with the goalposts. The stage remains, framing the scaffolding of manacles as if those metal shapes are a performance in themselves. Maisie's movement on the grass disturbs a congregation of small birds, which dart into the air and skit beneath the sky in the direction of the wall. He can take a moment to breathe, he thinks, a chance to work his thoughts into a sensible shape.

He considers his young charge as she runs from him, skipping across the grass to the other children. It is as if she has come straight from school, not her father's humiliation. Where is the sadness that filled her only minutes ago? He wonders if all this is normal to her.

Or is she stronger than him, waiting for the right time to fight back? She has no reason to. He's not keeping her prisoner, only making sure she's fed and watered until the impasse is over. It's not his fault that Peter is where he is. He's not to blame for giving Hale's killer what he deserves. What a mess. Charlotte Morris had better come back, put everything into its right place, but he has a sneaking feeling she won't be returning. He watches as the two children who had been playing football, two girls around Maisie's age, stop and walk towards her. The three of them stand in a huddle speaking. What are they talking about? Where are their parents? They are strange there, standing together in the middle of the green like three statues. Maisie points back to the village, then to him. Their eyes are on him for a second and then they are with each other, heads nodding enthusiastically.

*Duncan Peck is clueless. We will have our revenge on Duncan Peck.*

That's it. He starts to pace towards them, and when he does the two girls catch him approach, quickly hug Maisie goodbye then run back to the football posts, leaving her on her own.

'What were you talking about?' Peck asks as he nears, feeling a bit silly.

'Mrs Twine.'

'Who the hell is Mrs Twine?'

'My teacher. She has really big glasses. I wanted to know what she was teaching, and Jane and Louise told me they had been working on haikus. Jane and Louise don't have to go to school today because their mother needs help with the apple trees but she doesn't need them until this afternoon and they are going to write haikus before then even though Jane doesn't want to.'

'Right.'

'A haiku is a poem. It has five syllables then seven syllables then five syllables.'

'A poem,' Peck echoes. 'Good.' The other two girls are kicking the ball between them again, as if he isn't there. He scratches the back of his head and looks around him, towards the wall on the western hill.

'I told them Father and Mother have been bad and that you're taking care of me.' Maisie says this with the same matter-of-factness as she'd talked about Jane and Louise and their poems, but her stance changes, her feet planted more firmly in the dirt.

'Listen, Maisie,' he says. 'Your mother hasn't done anything wrong. Actually, she has, I suppose, but ...' he trails off with a cough. 'Your father has done something bad. I mean, he has and he hasn't. I know he did something, and that thing was bad. Very bad. But other people are under the impression he did something else, something nasty, which I don't think he did.'

'What do they say he did?'

She doesn't know, he realises. Charlotte never told her. Should he say it to her now, in the middle of the green? No, this is not the right place and he is not the right person. 'It doesn't matter,' he says, with a wave of the hand and what he thinks is a warm smile. From the girl's expression he realises it must've been closer to a grimace.

'But my father still needs to be punished?'

'Yes, I think so.'

This seems to make sense to Maisie, who beams. 'I liked it when you let him move his arms again. That was kind.'

'You think so?'

'Cutting rotten rope,' she says, counting the syllables on her fingers. 'He moves his sore hands again. A flower in bloom.'

She looks pleased with herself. Peck remembers the applause he received in the square, how the villagers had been happy with his intervention. He hadn't been expecting that, but there they were, the men and women clapping as he freed a father's wrists. The mercy, the forgiveness. What a sight. It was moments like that when he felt that everything could be well. This is a place with schools and fields of barley, with beekeepers and carpenters. There is so much potential. The spring air is crisp on his collar and a six-year-old girl is telling him a poem. Is this what love is? he wonders. Is it feeling like you are finally home?

He moves to ruffle Maisie's hair but she jumps back with a yelp, then screams and runs away. 'Maisie,' he calls. 'Where are you off to, Maisie?'

She has run to the stage and is trying to pull herself onto the elevated platform with the strength in her arms. She tries but fails, and is left dangling on the edge, unsure of whether to stay there or let go. She eventually decides on the latter, plops back on the earth, then turns back to Peck, who hasn't moved an inch. He points to the side of the stage. She nods, runs to the side and vanishes behind its boards. The knock of small boots on wooden steps sounds above the grass, and a moment later she reappears. There on the platform, a handful of feet above the ground, her body changes its composure. The skip across the green becomes a tentative step forwards. Her body is overtaken by something that could first be taken for nervousness but which Peck thinks is closer to recalibration, her legs and arms stiff as a chrysalis on a branch. She looks out at Peck as if he is one amongst a crowd of hundreds, and then she stops walking altogether. 'I am going to dance,' she declares. 'I need to practise.'

He gives her a thumbs up. The two girls have stopped kicking their ball and are watching what is happening with interest. Maisie looks to stage left and right, pauses, explodes. She jumps with arms spread out, then lands and tucks her knees to her chin, then bursts into the air again. She twirls herself in circles, screeching vowels. She laughs at her own sounds, then makes them louder still. Without stopping, she runs from one side of the stage to the other, then back again, then back again, then back again, then back with a leap in the middle. She is laughing hard. She is running around in circles.

'What on earth is she up to?' Grace is beside Peck. He hadn't heard her approach. Her arms are folded and she stands watching Maisie leap and twist.

'I don't know,' he says. 'Is this normal? Should I stop her?'

The two girls watching Maisie begin to run towards the stage. They have left their ball behind them and soon they are on the stairs to the elevated platform. Maisie doesn't pause, but when she catches sight of them her movements become less chaotic. The girls join her dancing and it looks like they are following the same routine. They step in time.

'She's had a hard few days,' says Grace. 'Poor thing. I saw you both in the square. Were you taking her to see him?'

'She wanted to. What was I going to say?'

'That's a difficult one,' she admits, and they both start clapping as Maisie and the other girls take a bow. 'It's a horrible thing, what's happened. Not her fault.' She reaches for Peck's hand, her little finger touching his own. He opens his fingers and slides them between her own. 'You've taken care of her since yesterday?' she asks.

'It sort of fell on me.'

'And you're staying at James's still?'

'I am.'

There is clearly something she wants to say but she takes her time saying it. 'Why don't the two of you stay with me, at least for a couple of nights?' Her thumb is making a circle on his knuckle. 'I've got the space. There's really no issue. You could even camp out in the living room downstairs, if you're worried about all that.'

'All what?'

'If you're not comfortable.'

With the performance over, the three girls gather in a close triangle, speaking things Peck can't hear. They look at him, and they look at the wall.

'You don't want me staying there,' he says.

'I wouldn't ask if I didn't.'

Something has been said between the girls that has made Maisie take a step backwards. She is shaking her head.

'I don't know, Grace. Someone needs to look after Hale's things. His plant.'

'His plant?'

'You know, his potted plant, and the rest of the place.'

Maisie is walking away from the girls, but as she nears the edge of the stage something is said that makes her turn around and walk back. She approaches the bigger of the two girls and with a lunge pushes her backwards a few steps.

Grace pulls her hand away from Peck's, who instantly misses the warmth of her fingers. 'Please don't make me feel like an idiot,' she whispers.

'We hardly know each other.'

She looks him in the eye. 'I've got the size of you.'

'And Maisie?'

'We can make sure she's taken care of after Charlotte is found.'

'Found?'

'Well.' There's a deep breath and the roots of it run far from Peck, to a house lived in as children and haunted as adults. Maisie is saying something to the pushed girl. The other girl pokes her with a pointed finger.

'Do you think you have the size of her?' Peck asks.

'What do you mean?'

'Do you think you know Maisie? Because I'm finding her very difficult to know.'

The two girls try to grab her, but she slips past them to the scaffolding assembled in the centre of the stage; the manacles hanging from poles, gathered in a rig the height of a man. Grace does not answer. Her thoughts are tumbling into empty rooms, to worn socks and dust-caked shoes, hands holding each other under dinner tables, cabinets and chests, chairs and drawers, husbands and children and holes in the ground, patience gathered, protections kept, promises left like spare keys on windowsills, the toiling sea.

'It's very kind of you to offer,' Peck says.

'Very kind,' she echoes, mocking the words.

'It is.'

Maisie has picked up a metal pole that had been leant against the pile of scaffolding. She holds it above her head, then brings it down with a swoop in front of one of the girls.

'Jesus Christ,' Peck shouts. 'Maisie, what are you doing?'

The pole has missed the two girls, but Maisie is lifting it above her head again. She screams and brings it down on the metal scaffold and the clang is loud enough to disturb some birds in the trees beyond the green. It's probably enough of a noise to attract some people, Peck thinks, deciding the last thing he wants to deal with is a crowd. The two girls have backed off, standing with hands raised. He runs towards the stage, his boots flicking up soil as he nears the front.

'Put it down,' he orders, but Maisie swings the bar like a clock struck three, this time aiming for one of her friends. She misses again, but only by an inch. Peck pulls himself up onto the stage and stands there with arms outstretched. He could reach for the bludgeon and snatch it from Maisie's grip but doesn't want to have his kneecaps smacked if he misjudges her reach. 'Maisie, come on now. Stop messing around.'

'I hate them,' she yells.

'We only told her the truth,' one of the girls says defensively to Peck. 'That's all.'

'I hate them,' Maisie yells again, and raises the pole, farther back than the other times she'd swung it. Her eyes are open wide and her teeth are clenched, but she has held the bar too far behind her head; it is too heavy and she loses balance, falling backwards with a yelp.

Peck stoops to pick the weapon up before she rights herself, which she does with a scowl and tensed fingers.

A couple of people have drifted onto the green to see the source of the clanging. The two girls have run down from the stage giggling, and Maisie is left to stand and cry into her hands. Peck waits there with her until her breathing calms, and he watches Grace as she walks away.

Miles to the east a beast with six arms and two legs stalks across the moor. Charlotte stands at the entrance of the cave and observes its path over the muddy ground, passing through a field of purple heather. The beast's back is broad and hairy and it moves slowly up the hill towards her. It has taken a long time to get here. There are two boots and two hands, and four hooves that dangle lifelessly. JM carries a freshly slaughtered pony foal across his shoulders. The wiry mane on its head is matted with blood, and as he passes Charlotte she notices the pony's long eyelashes, parted over kind eyes.

Later, JM drapes strips of flesh over a rack made of metal wire. A fire gurgles in the open. Charlotte leans against the side of the tor and observes him arrange the meat; his fingers pinching the corners of the thin segments until they have been neatly placed and begun to spit. The grey sky swathes the hills on the horizon, over a pair of birds that dart between species. They start as skylarks but they vanish as ravens. Charlotte is unsettled by the hesitation, as if she is failing to keep hold of the land. How much has the ground moved since last night? How much of it has changed? She could paint a map of the village and its vicinity, but the place she has found herself in is confused. The slope beneath her feet feels as if it is steepening towards the bog. The light has begun to flush behind the clouds, the dirt becoming dim.

JM, however, moves like a god in his garden. When he is done with the meat, he separates the pony hide against a flat rock, cutting the skin into sections that can be used for mats and patches. It is done with the finesse of routine. With his hands on his hips he first studies the spread in its entirety. Then, when he has made a decision, he stoops towards the hide and cuts with a knife in a straight line. These pieces are carried to another boulder, where they are spread out in the air. JM walks back and forth between the two boulders, and the dying sunlight makes his shadow even longer than it already is, covering the ground up to Charlotte's feet like a sheet blown from a hanging wire.

She coughs. JM turns to meet her attention. Leaving the pelt, he walks towards her with his left hand on his right shoulder, massaging the muscles as he turns the joint. When he speaks, he does so with an enthusiasm that's hard to trace to its source. 'I try to use everything I can,' he explains with a smile.

Charlotte examines the horizon, soaked in red. There is no one in sight. No anchors in this limbo-land. 'What about that?' she asks, nodding to what remains of the pony. From its shoulders to its hindquarters, the animal has been flipped over and split like a piece of fruit. Its body has been torn into pieces, legs pulled from their sockets and left in a vague, disordered pile. Its head has been tossed from the white tip of its spine. In amongst its ribcage is a soup, running down from the body over the ground. What has not been hung to cook swims in that pungent mess.

'That's for the bog,' states JM, wiping his brow, rolling his big shoulders forwards. 'I'll carry it away in a while, somewhere it won't attract animals.'

'I could help,' Charlotte says. JM looks suspicious at this. The fingers of his right hand start to fidget against the palm. 'I could help,' she presses. 'No problem. We're not going far, right?'

'Just to the bottom of the hill.'

'It'll be nice to stretch my legs. I've not walked more than a few feet all day.'

For a moment Charlotte thinks he is going to say no, and in doing so make explicit the power he is wielding. What then? Will she be forced to do as he says? But these questions do not need answers, because JM shrugs and says it is her choice if she wants to help. 'I just didn't want you to get blood on your clothes, my dear.'

The light has gone by the time Charlotte cradles the pony head and follows her father-in-law as he drags the animal remains on a tarpaulin sheet. The scope of the moor is invisible, and the spread of JM is barely perceptible as he hauls his load downhill. The sound of his movement is clear in its rustles, but it is not until the ground begins to level, when he raises his hand to stop them going any farther, when the noise of his heavy breathing fills the air, that Charlotte realises how far they have come.

There, just feet from the mire, it seems they are standing on the precipice of a shattered lake. She knows that the water rests amongst clumps of grass, but it is dark, the grass unseen, and without those knots to bind its surface the bog is a scatter. Once more it feels as if the ground has moved when she wasn't looking. The sprawl of it reminds her of baby Jacob's clothing, spread across the living-room floor; all the swaddlings that had wrapped his feet and arms. Her heart aches, but the image in her mind passes from the smallness of her little boy to the eyes of Maisie, sharp and seeking and staring up at her through the hole in the ceiling.

Charlotte's vision has adjusted enough to make out the tallness of JM beside the tarpaulin. 'Come and lift the other side,' he orders in a low voice, and a beckoning hand ushers her to an edge of the plastic. She throws the pony's head on the pile of limbs and then the two of them tip the side of the tarpaulin so that the remains slide into the bog, where they do not sink but are borne on the surface like an island.

'Jacob,' Charlotte says. 'Can I speak to you?'

'Of course.' His voice is heavier in the dark, unhinged from his mouth.

'I can't stay here,' she says. He does not respond at first, and Charlotte begins to doubt she spoke at all. 'I need to see my daughter.' The pony is slowly becoming submerged, its eyes impassive as they approach the waterline. 'You were always tender to Maisie,' she says. 'Never unkind.'

'She has a sweet nature.'

'Don't you want to see her again?'

JM clears his throat. 'What do you want from me, Charlotte?'

She fears he is living with the truth of the Tragedy. Him alone. She saw what she saw but sight is a stitched chimera and there is this awful thought on her, a sickening idea, that he alone is certain, that he alone remembers it to the letter, out here with no one to drag it into writing. Her temple throbs at the torment, that what happened on that night happens only in his memory; enacted in a room she can never enter, not even peek through the keyhole. 'I want to forgive you,' she says.

'I have nothing to be forgiven for.' His voice is quiet but firm.

'You had your hand on him. He was making those awful sounds and I found you right there with him, not a candle lit, touching his head. I don't know what the hell you did but I'd never heard him cry like that before. And I could smell it on you, Jacob. As soon as I got into the room I could smell it.'

'I told you, he was ill.'

'How long were you there? Why didn't you pick him up, or wake me and Pete? I need to know the details. I need to know what happened. He can't have just died.'

'He did.'

'No,' she insists, raising her voice. 'You were there with him. There's some responsibility in that. We put it on the wall. It exists. You taught me that.'

'Be satisfied then.'

She lets out a frustrated grunt and watches the pony sink farther into the bog, its mane fanned out across the famished ground.

JM cracks his knuckles and the sound of it goes right through her. 'You said James Hale was shot by this relative of his. What's he like?'

The pivot in conversation wrongfoots her. 'Why?'

'Does he have friends?'

'Brian seems fond of him, and you know how that goes.'

At this, JM moves away to begin rolling the sheet of tarpaulin. It is infuriating, this reaction, and Charlotte's temper throbs. With a piercing cry she paces over to where he kneels and pushes him, the enormity of him, and it catches him off balance. He barks and falls on his side into the mud, and when he stands his gaunt face is dirty and gnarled with anger. She thinks for a second that he could lash out at her, and what then? Only the crows would hear. 'Are you scared of going back?' she asks, resolute. 'Is that it? Are you scared of seeing his grave?'

He takes a few steps towards her, his body an enormous skeleton. 'I have nothing to fear,' he scowls. 'There is nothing in that village that scares me. Those buildings would not be standing if it weren't for my hands.' His expression is hard to place but there is something in the wideness of his eyes that troubles her. He is no longer looking at her as a father would. A wind blows across her hair. The bog has swallowed the remains of the pony, and now there is nothing, absolutely nothing, except for the two of them in the dark.

'You're a coward,' she announces, and with that said she turns and stomps back up the hill towards their shelter. Behind her, JM kneels on the ground and continues to roll up the tarpaulin. The night is quiet, then, except for the sound of the plastic sheet chattering.

---

The hide of the pony hangs in strips from one side of the cave that night, soaking up heat from a fresh campfire. Charlotte watches JM squat opposite her as she tears into a platter of meat. She takes a bite and closes her eyes to the taste of salted fat. There were no words between them as the fire was made and the food portioned. Nothing in the way of a concession. She pities this pride. It is a weakness. A real weakness. And it is exposed out here without the admiration of others, which was only ever a few inches from fear and that, she thinks, is a drink that turns to vinegar if left for too long. James Hale might have won the village's favour with charm and an eagerness to please, and the Tragedy might have fixed JM's fate, but even without these things his tide would have turned sooner or later. Her father-in-law's pride had not made him many friends.

She had thought he had been waiting for the day he could return. Perhaps she had been wrong. Perhaps, in this cramped shelter, he has found an existence that suits him, where he can eat and sleep, listen to his kingdom. He never was a big talker but he did always like to listen. No doubt that's what turned them against him, even before she pointed the finger, when the invitations to dinners stopped coming and were replaced with stares across parted curtains. Perhaps life had grown harsher, she considers. Less trusting. Perhaps JM is a victim in all this. She isn't so sure. He had been the one to first organise a gang of chasers, after all. He had been the one to encourage punishments that went beyond public embarrassment. Thinking about it, he was the one to tell them as children to share what they heard from private corners. It was all done with a smile, of course, but the message had been clear: police your own. He had been the one that had told her to write down what she felt about others. He had been the one to say that the wall was a beautiful thing; something they all had a responsibility to use as a canvas for what needed to be uttered.

Out of nowhere he offers a smile, as disarming as those he reserved for Maisie, when she would sit on his lap and he would explain the hopes of their paradise. Charlotte rolls her eyes, but appreciates the effort. All at once he is an old man again, vulnerable and alone in a world that is heartless. Perhaps she has been unfair. He has suffered and it is her doing. The thought is blanketed before it has time to stem, because there are more immediate adversaries. The nightmare she is in is of Duncan Peck's making. His selfishness has already done harm, and it will do more in time. But it needn't. If their home was a paradise once, Charlotte thinks, then surely it could be a paradise again. The rules have slumped in all the wrong places but maybe people with kind hearts could correct them.

It looks as if he is about to speak, but instead JM places his plate on the floor and feels out towards one side of the cave. Charlotte stops eating. She sees him pick up something thin and white; chalk, she realises, kept inside a long-emptied dog-food tin. She watches him shuffle towards a section of cave wall that is flatter than the rest. The firelight flickers his stooped shadow over smudges on the stone. He rests one arm on the surface, to hold his body weight as he scrawls something out with the other. 'To soothe,' he explains as he writes.

HUSH, CHARLOTTE MORRIS

When he is finished, JM dusts off his hands by rubbing them together. Charlotte pauses, then plucks a piece of meat from her plate. 'What's the point of it?' she asks between chews. 'What do you want from writing that?'

'It's a reminder,' he says. 'To calm yourself. You're getting carried away and there's no point picking fights unless you plan on going hungry.' He exhales sharply through his nostrils. His face reddens. 'You're pushing me too far, my dear, always talking about things that are behind us. I do you the kindness of inviting you in, and you drag an unholy tangle with you, lay it at my feet, expect me to pick at the knots for you. You want someone to blame, I understand, but I don't want to spend another second thinking about what's best left buried. There is no space for it in this territory. So hush, and be still.'

Charlotte weighs this up. 'A reminder,' she repeats. She looks over the words, reading them to herself. After a few seconds pass, she stands, shaking the dirt off her trousers. Under the gaze of JM, she walks towards the surface. When she reaches the rock she stops to look at the letters again, up close. She follows them one after another with her finger, and when she gets to CHARLOTTE, she rubs it away with her sleeve. Satisfied, she stands back, looking at the ghost of her name. It is a hole in the sentence. She nods to herself, then moves back to where she was sitting beside the fire. Without meeting JM's eyes, she lies down on the ground, her face turned towards the opposite wall.

# Nine

**SARAH TWINE NEEDS TO STOP WHAT SHE IS DOING BEFORE IT'S TOO LATE.** MARTIN MOAR IS NO SAINT I AM TELLING YOU. *ELLIE HATCHER WAS SLEEPING IN THE CALVARY CROSS WHEN SHE SHOULD HAVE BEEN STITCHING TROUSERS.*

ASIDE FROM PECK, ONLY a few other people stand in front of the wall. The day is early and the paint is still wet. He could read the larger words as soon as he climbed the hill, but his attention is on the smaller messages. There are the same notes he'd seen when he first arrived. Reminders for the Rosy Singers and a call for a lost cat called Pudding. He is happy to see that they have been joined by other scraps of paper, stuck to the wall with nails and glue. Victoria Bray is looking for someone to help her at the bakery. There is going to be a village dance in a few weeks' time and if couples would like to sign up they should contact Judy Rudd. Does anyone need an extra chair for their table? Since Luke Holloway passed, Julia would rather see it go to use. Peck reads these messages twice, three times, and feels comforted at the signs of life.

He moves a few steps back to take in the wall in its entirety. Some of the words against Charlotte can still be seen, but many are plastered over by the new posters. The sentences about Peter have been buried completely and Geoff Sharpe is a distant memory. He thinks about how deep these layers go, and whether they are ultimately all that there is.

---

In Brian's home a fist of sunlight illuminates the air. 'I'm not saying I don't like the girl, but what's being done about it all?' Peck asks, looking to Maisie on the floor of the living room. She is lying on her stomach. All her attention is focused on the diary in front of her, and she scribbles as if only those words exist.

'How do you mean?' Brian dips a freshly baked biscuit into his teacup.

'Well,' starts Peck. 'Her mother? What's happening with that?'

'How do you mean?'

'Have people been looking for her? And have there been any decisions made about Peter?'

The portly man bites the sopping half of his biscuit. He takes his time to chew and swallow before answering with an air of weariness. 'There's been no sign of

Charlotte,' he informs before leaning in to lower his voice. 'Odds are, she's fallen into a bog. It's a sad story but there you go. The way of the world. If we catch sight of her, or if she wanders back into the village, of course we'll make sure she atones for her infidelity. We remember those that have wronged us. People still want to see results, that's for sure, but we could soon have other fish to fry.' He leans back with a knowing look in his eye.

'Fish?' asks Peck.

'Precisely. Talk is that Simon Dew, who mans the boiler, has been siphoning hot water for his own bath. A bath, can you imagine? Anyway, I'm not saying anything is going to be done about it. But I'm not *not* saying things will happen, if you get me.' Brian winks and sips his tea. 'People are upset,' he muses. 'Very upset. Can you think about it? A bath all to himself, with the water he's responsible for heating. There's been nothing like it. I personally can't remember a person in this town ever being so' – he searches for the word – 'brazen. Brazen about abusing their position.'

Peck can feel the frustration building behind his face. What are the rules to this game they're playing? 'And what about the father, then?'

'Simon Dew's father? Long dead, I'm afraid.'

'Peter Morris,' Peck whispers. 'Come on now.'

With a snort Brian looks at Maisie on the floor. 'My girl,' he says. 'You look as thin as a rake. Why don't you snout around for more biscuits in my kitchen?' He waves the remains of his own in the air. 'They are ever so rich but we need our treats, don't you think?'

After a passing glance to Peck, she folds her diary closed, stands and walks out of the living room. Compared to the energy she had in her yesterday, she has been sullen with him today. It is a relief, in a way. Despite the scene she'd made with the other girls, the two of them had done a service in telling Maisie what people were saying about her parents, about her. At least the girl knows where things stand. It had been wrong of Charlotte to keep her shielded. Selfish, he thinks. But what had the girl to say about it? Nothing. After that anger on the green she'd fallen inside herself, as slippery as an orange pip.

'She's delightful,' Brian says when she has disappeared. 'So sad about her family.'

'What are we going to do about Peter Morris?'

'Ordinarily, James Hale would have taken care of things. Words were made, the man was found.' A cough. 'After a day or two, mind, but he was found all the same. And then it would be up to the law and order to carry out a fitting penalty. Now, a large part of it is the symbolism, of course, but it's an important role and one that has been vacant since the sad death of your cousin.'

'Can't you just make a decision yourself?'

'Me?' Brian's face wrinkles into an ugly smile, his beetroot lips curving. 'I keep far away from things like that. People around here know I'm a reliable ear to speak to in confidence and it would hardly be conducive to that relationship if I were on the business end of a metal pole, as it were.'

Here it is, Peck thinks. The distance Brian Goss keeps between his fists and his full kitchen. This record keeper, this administrator, this minister will not have his name stamped on the judgements that he sets on their way. Perhaps it is cowardice. No doubt it is cleverness, to stand one step below the chopping block. Peck wonders where Brian stores his fabled books; the accounts Hale believed were kept on every person. He wonders whether a fire could make short work of them all. Brian changes his tone, speaking to Peck as if he is a confidant. 'A lot of it is like cooking, you have to understand. It's more about the seasoning than the meat and veg. The smaller crimes can sort themselves out, but Peter Morris, given all the fuss, has found himself in a position of uncertainty. The chef is dead and, to put it bluntly, the meal has gone cold.'

'But he shot Hale,' Peck snaps. 'In cold blood. Only a few days ago.'

A hand is raised to stop any more protest and Brian's voice grows firmer. 'You may think that, but there has been little in the way of public agreement on the matter. The opinion is that James Hale's death was a tragedy that has been put to bed. It is a shame. I was fond of him. But we move on.' He rearranges his weight in the armchair. 'And that brings me to the next matter,' he says. 'I was going to wait for a calmer time to tell you this but here it goes: I would like you, Duncan Peck, to step into the boots your cousin left behind.'

'What's that?' he asks, as if he has been slapped.

'I'd like you to head up the chasers, at least for the foreseeable.' With this he digs into his pocket and pulls out something stringy and golden; the chain Hale used to wear, or at least one that looks a lot like it. He pinches the end between thumb and forefinger and lets it dangle.

'Me?'

'You're the right person for it, I can tell. There's an integrity to you, if you don't mind me saying.'

Peck feels a surge of pride, immediately followed by shame. Not long ago he was disgusted at himself, sickened by the part he'd played in the village's turn against Charlotte. He felt tainted by dry specks clinging under his fingernails. Now, told that he is valued, he can't help but feel a swell inside his chest; the same swell he'd had that morning as he read notes for lost cats and choirs. He is part of something, and at the same time he is queasy at the thought of it. Peter Morris; there is no getting away from the fact that he is being asked to bring that matter to a close.

'I need someone to help corral the volunteers – help them get up in the morning,' Brian says. 'James Hale did the job nicely, but he's gone. Someone needs the whip, as it were. You've settled into his house, you should settle into his position.'

'I've hardly lived here.'

'No, that's true. There will be some in the village unhappy about it. They'll come around, though.' His eyes sparkle, and it dawns on Peck that this must all be a great pleasure for Brian, manoeuvring his influence as if he is peeling an apple. He sways the necklace back and forth, drawing circles with it. 'A fresh start is just what this community of ours requires. I'm so glad that James Hale invited you; someone keen to please and who has respect for our way of life. I think you'll be agreeable. I think you'll be good.'

The last word is a bolt in a gate.

'I'm very flattered,' Peck says. 'But I thought perhaps I could try to learn carpentry. I always did like the idea of building things.' As soon as he says this he knows the idea has sunk somewhere into the carpet. Brian looks upward to the ceiling for a moment, then shakes his head. He lets the necklace fall into a clump on his lap.

'You'll be well fed. And that'll be a help for your new life with Grace Horn. She's a lovely thing. Hard-working. Sociable. Very much liked around here. We're all over the moon about her getting a second chance at things.' There is a threat in there, Peck thinks. Hard not to see it. He contemplates Brian for a moment. The man is a manipulator but why say no to a few extra meals? If he wants to build, this could be the place to do it, not with wood and nails but words and actions. 'Fantastic,' Brian carries on, assuming assent. 'So that's agreed. If things tip one way with Simon Dew, out of the unspoken into the spoken, as it were, I'd like you to be ready to take charge of the situation. You've got to keep pace here, you understand? Keeping the peace, but also the pace.' A laugh rises up, up to the painting of the shipwreck. Peck looks at the sailor bound in ropes, muscles straining against the coils that fasten him in place.

'And Peter Morris?'

'I'd rather you squared it sooner than later. He's taking up room in the stocks. If you like, I can arrange for a gathering on the green tomorrow morning. A few games, some hot drinks and fresh bread. It'll be an opportunity for you to put things back on track after a difficult few days.' He raises his eyebrows and tilts his head, waiting for a response.

'Fine,' Peck says. 'Fine.'

There is a loud clap as Brian smacks his stubby hands together, then he picks up the necklace and throws it for Peck to catch. 'Excellent. And in the meantime, you want to keep an ear out for Simon Dew. I don't think any kind words will help with people's feelings there, ha! I mean, a hot bath using our water. Can you imagine it? The brazenness of it.' He leans in, and Peck can feel his breath against his cheek. 'You're doing good here. A lot of good. It has not gone unnoticed. Your name is very much on people's lips.'

Just as he leans back into his armchair, Maisie comes into the room with biscuit crumbs down her top. She looks at the two men and counts syllables on her fingers. 'I have eaten them. All the biscuits you have baked. There is nothing left.'

There are slapped backs waiting for Peck in the tearoom. Word spreads quickly, and it seems everyone already knows about his new position. He is hardly seated before men and women come to his table with their best wishes. Two by two they shake his hand, speaking as if they have known him for years; watched him grow from a boy into the upstanding man he is today. 'You absolutely have to come on Sunday,' he is told by Victoria Bray. 'We'll cook you a meal of pork and potatoes.' She squeezes his forearm through his jacket. No one mentions James Hale. Peck thinks about the state of his cousin's bones, buried in the graveyard. It seems an age has passed since they were last together and he misses the sight of him. He would give his foot for another day in James's company and there is a wash of guilt at the thought he has profited from his death, but it is not his fault. He is not to blame for it, not at all, and if the people want him to mind the law and order it is because they trust his judgement. He has been brought into the bosom of the community, held up to the heartbeat.

Not that everyone is happy to see him. There are those in the tearoom that keep their distance. They sit apart, watching and cursing him under their breath, no doubt.

*Duncan Peck is hardly here and already puffed up with more hot air than an oven. Duncan Peck killed James Hale and took his place.*

He knows he should be cautious, but he is tipsy with attention. Maisie is less enthusiastic. She leans over the table writing into her diary, not even raising her head to see the people come and go from her side. If she wants to sulk, let her. Things are going to get better. Peck had left the city to take control of his life, to become more than a ghost in burning streets. The wall in all its enormity had put him in his shoes, the scrutiny of others had brought him into his skin, and now he is bound up with the village. This community is his own. He is a part of it and why shouldn't he enjoy the embrace? Absent-mindedly he runs his finger up and down the new necklace he wears, given to him by Brian Goss.

'I heard your stock has risen,' says Grace, plonking a teapot in front of him so full that some of the liquid splashes over the rim.

'Careful,' he tuts. 'You don't want to break anything.' It is the first time Maisie has looked up from her writing since they got to the tearoom, and when she does Grace flashes her a smile that dissolves into a frown for Peck. 'Sit for a moment,' he says, touching her hand. 'Please.'

She looks over the tearoom, anxious about the eyes of others. 'I should work.' But before turning away she leans in to whisper in his ear. 'I told you we need to keep our heads above water.'

'My head is well above,' he exclaims, spreading his arms. 'Look at me now!'

There are glances at them from all around. Grace pulls away to walk back to the counter and serve the people waiting in line. Peck shrugs and smiles to the room and there are laughs and whistles from a few of the other tables as Grace goes back to work.

*Grace Horn is stuck-up. Grace Horn thinks she is made from gold and glass.*

'What are you going to do to my father?' Maisie's eyes are on him. They could stab him full of holes. In all the excitement, Peck had pushed down the knowledge, the stinging thought that tomorrow morning he will be expected to punish Peter Morris in full view of the village. Is it in him to do that? There is the weight of the revolver in his pocket. He tries to channel the anger he felt, seeing Hale with his brains spilled on the moor. But he finds only shame under the judgement of this six-year-old girl.

'It'll be over soon,' he mutters, and she is not content with this but scrunches her face and goes back to her diary. The lines are only inches out of reach. If Peck moved his head across the table he would be able to see what she is writing. How many pages must she have filled? What is she writing about him? Surely she is writing about him. But he doesn't lean forwards. He only gazes at the tops of letters, becoming parts of shapes unseen. As if she could read what he was thinking, Maisie moves her forearm to the top of the page so that it blocks the diary from view. Peck turns his attention outside, then, through the window to the village square. He looks at Peter slumped motionless on the stocks, so thin now. There's not much to him beneath the clothes that hang like wet washing.

He looks to the wall, towering behind the houses on the opposite side of the square. Its top edge cuts against the sky and the flagging sun is close to falling behind its bulk. A razor shadow moves across the cobbles. He feels in his pocket for the dead tooth, holds it to the light. For the first time he notices it is not a uniform black. There are shades of yellow and grey, details he is unfamiliar with but which were, until quite recently, part of him. It is not a gemstone, or a pillow, or a door knocker. It is a dead tooth. He turns it one way then the other, taking in its particulars, its grooves, then places it on his saucer where it sits circled by a ring of painted roses.

Leaving the tooth behind him, he stands and walks the length of the tearoom, past the other customers, straight to the counter. 'Can I kiss you?' he asks. Grace's eyebrows are buoyed. She looks nervously to the other occupants of the tearoom, who are all watching expectantly. After a moment's hesitation, she presses her lips against Peck's and he touches the back of her head with his hand. He can hear the applause around them.

The clouds are thronging, bruised and thrilled at the prospect of speech. Charlotte has watched them gather overhead, the evening climbing into itself. She has not strayed from the cave today, has not had the energy to do so. Besides a meander for her dailies, she's made do with sitting on a rock and watching the land tighten, release, tighten again.

From her vantage point on the hill she can see JM in the distance. The only thing moving. He has hardly spoken a word to her today. In the morning he left her a plate of pony meat as he went for a walk. He came back in the afternoon with a long face, only to leave again, to get more water from the river in a canteen stitched from leather. What does he have on his mind? she wonders. Ever since last night he has been avoiding her eye. Don't think she hasn't noticed. There is something he is not telling her.

At this distance and with only the moorland around him, JM looks minuscule. Unimportant. 'HELLO, JACOB MORRIS.' She cups her hands to her mouth to make the shout travel farther, but he does not move his head. 'I CAN SEE YOU THERE,' she shouts, intending it as a friendly salute to break some of yesterday's tension.

He does not wave, nor make any sign that he has heard her. Charlotte lets her hands fall back to her sides. The moorland seems to go on forever in each and every direction. JM keeps trudging back. Nothing else is moving, not even a bird, but there are traces of colour in the heather and the gorse. Good signs, she thinks. Spring is here. Undeniable.

He must atone. It is the only way for the door to be thrown open, certainty restored, and if she needs to suffer at the hands of her neighbours to see it through then so be it. Let them fling what they want. The shame will pass, will pale in importance next to what she will be given by his admission. She can feel the fear of the village's petty violence lifting, because whatever humiliation they have planned will be worth the pain to witness him there, in front of the village, give up the act and cast away the doubt that has clouded the weather. The air she will breathe then. The fresh, weightless air. JM the listener, the shield, the father. No longer depriving her of the certainty she needs, burning away the misgivings that have grown on her memory. And when their bruises have healed, then they can put the past months to rest. No more unearthing. Things will settle back into sleepy order, JM breathing deep and slow in front of the fire, Maisie by her side as life ticks along. She hopes Peter will forgive her. It hasn't properly occurred to her that he might not, but the hope remains that they will slip without issue back into the days and nights when the world felt more secure.

It's a picture worth imagining, but a deeper part of her knows that JM's admission will snub out those embers. She wants to forgive him, but there will be no going back to the warmth of the past once the doubt of his crime has gone from her mind.

'I CAN SEE YOU, JACOB MORRIS,' she shouts. Still he does not acknowledge her. What is he planning? How he must hate her. How her presence must pain him. A sense of vertigo spirals over her then, at the thought that JM will stand above her as she lays dying, unmoved by the last breath of the woman responsible for casting him out. She tries to put the thought out of her mind, fantasising instead about how they can move forwards together, find Duncan Peck and have revenge for the shit he has stirred. And she can feel it, her rage turning into a single black gemstone. All that her family has endured, the weasel will pay for it. All that has been cast adrift because of James Hale's death will be bound back on their return. It is pleasurable to picture his face under her boot. It is calming to think of him in pain.

'JACOB MORRIS,' she shouts. 'JACOB MORRIS. JACOB MORRIS.'

Her face has turned red at the effort but, finally, he stops in his tracks and looks to her.

By the time midnight rolls around Peck is drunk. He sits hunched over Hale's table, looking past half-closed eyelids at his cousin's potted plant. Maisie is curled on the camper bed, faint snores coming out of her mouth. Peck stands and shuffles across the living room to where the girl is sleeping. After a day full of conversations, things are now speechless. If only there was less uttered in the world, he thinks, then perhaps there would be understanding between people. Peck turns to the window in time to see a flash of white, followed by thunder. The rain is falling now, hard against the window, and he imagines ghosts batted about by the wind.

Maisie's hands are once again gripped together. On the floor, below where she lies, is her diary. He picks it up and considers the buckle that locks it shut. Before he knows what he is doing he has loosened the small leather tongue. What has the girl been hiding away about him? What has she been thinking? The handwriting is a mess but there are words that he reads without trying, phrases that pass into his head as soon as he grazes against them. Cutting rotten rope. A flower in bloom. It is enough for him to turn the page. He flicks through, finding words and drawings, but there is nothing of his name. There are only bad dreams.

Through the entrance of the cave, Charlotte watches lightning fork across the sky as she lies under her blanket. She closes her eyes and listens to the thunder roll through the moorland. She thinks about how many aches there are amongst the storm clouds. The rain falling over the tor, the wind and the rumble, all of them foreign languages. A thousand tongues wagging. And the hills are moving, the ground is rolling around her.

'Do they wait for me?' a voice asks, JM's, but unfamiliar and barely heard above the storm. 'Do they wait for me to return?'

Sleep is on her before she can respond. She is not sure when she starts to dream, but when she does it is of a room. There is a hole in the wall. The slabs have been smoothed by countless hands. She can walk straight through, into a dark chamber, towards the heart that's beating.

She opens her eyes to a human shape against the entrance of the cave. A man stands, lit by a lightning flash. It is JM, stooped as he passes into the world. She does not shift from the ground as he makes his way, but watches him go. His footsteps are silent. Hushed. He is even more enormous without the daylight to hem him in. What is he doing? She watches him stretch his arms and he becomes larger still. Another flash. Another rumble. The rain has made him incandescent. His arms are spread wide and his head is angled to the heavens. He turns towards her but she is careful not to move from where she lies beneath the animal furs. His body is a standing stone. Another flash and he turns once more, towards the imprecise land. She does not stir but watches from her spot on the floor as the giant departs. Another flash. Another rumble. His body is almost out of view, moving down the hill towards the bogland. She closes her eyes and thinks of stones on the ground as the rain patters. She thinks of granite pillars, a man wrapped around the rock, lichen-specked. Beneath the skin is a heart that's beating. But it slows, and slows, and slows, and stops.

> Yesterday we found a dead fox in the garden. My mother did not want me to look at it but I did and it had a scary face. There was a fly in its mouth. I had a dream that the fox followed me. I woke up and my father came and held my hand and told me there was nothing to be scared of.

Dreams evaded, she raises herself and looks around. Lightning flashes. JM is nowhere to be seen. Hands scrabbling on the ground she feels for her belongings, which she scoops and pushes into her backpack as the sky rumbles above, then she throws her coat around her shoulders and picks the sleep from her eyes. It is cold when she sets out into the open, the rain an ablution, and she cannot see a thing in the dark.

> The fox chased me. It had a face like a person and sharp claws like a monster. It was very angry. I didn't know what it was saying. My father has gone and my mother told me he is doing work. I hope he comes back soon so he can hold my hand and stroke my hair.

His body appears in a flash, distant, at the base of the hill. She follows as if she is sleepwalking, trudging through mud so deep in places that she is convinced she will sink. She tries her hardest to keep track of him, a faint shape moving farther and farther from the shelter of the cave. He walks on the edge of her vision but she refuses to let him slip out of view.

> The fox sat at the dinner table and I didn't know what it was saying. It was talking to me. It was talking and talking. I wanted to run away from the fox but I couldn't move. My chair was stuck. The fox was sad. It started to cry. It wanted me to listen but I didn't know what it was saying.

# Ten

THERE ARE PEOPLE WAITING outside. Peck can see them through the window. But before he opens himself up to the morning, he closes his eyes and enjoys the light on his face, orange and throbbing. The sun has not shone like this for some time. Only when Maisie tugs at his arm does he surface, to the chair he is perched on, into the boots he has laced to the top. She is wearing a dress dotted with flowers and has combed her hair straight, ready for what's to come. He had been careful to fold the diary away before she woke. Clasp the little strap beneath its holding. No sign that the notebook had ever been opened.

Grief has tied strings to his skeleton and it would be the easiest thing to be pulled like a puppet towards the stage in the green. He wouldn't need to kill him, just break Peter enough for the men and women, for him, to be happy that something had been done; a bloody reminder that they are watched, listened to, and then rabbit pie with a mug of hot cocoa. It would be a good start. A job finished. An acknowledgement of the people's opinions, respectfully addressed. No doubt it's what his cousin would have done.

He closes his eyes again, blocking the sight of Maisie, not that she disappears, not now he has read her hidden thoughts. When he opens his eyes she is waiting, curious about his stillness at the table. She has every reason to hate him, he thinks. Shifting on the seat, he reaches to stroke her arm. She looks unimpressed but does not recoil. 'I will make this right,' he tells her, then feels in his pocket for the revolver and, in full view of the girl, places it on the surface of the table. It won't be coming with them, he wants her to know.

Soon they are outside, facing the men and women who have been anticipating their departure; the same gang, Peck realises, he had seen days ago, on stage with Hale as his cousin smashed the butcher Geoff Sharpe's leg with a metal pole. All the same chasers, except for Peter, of course, and they each give Maisie a pitying smile as she emerges from the doorway with her diary tucked underarm. After Martin Moar explains that the group had wanted to greet their new captain in person, said with a palpable whiff of suspicion, they begin to make their way through the village, passing eyes behind net curtains, walking with blunt weapons between the cheers of a gathering throng. As they cut through the square, Maisie grows visibly nervous and Peck tries to shield her from stares.

On the green there is already the smell of wild herbs and meat cooking above coals, sharp and heady, and it is having its effect with a clatter of laughter building in volume. There is the sound of drums. Flasks have been carried out, a stand assembled close to the pig pen. Grace Horn is pouring out water into cocoa powder for those who want it. On the edges, men, women and children are being urged onwards. Dominic Martin's hat has blown from his head and a group stands laughing as he fumbles for it on the ground. Victoria Bray lifts the hem of her skirt as she is helped over a puddle by Jim Dowry. Geoff Sharpe is supported by a bandaged Gerrard. Simon Dew is whistling to himself as he rolls up his sleeves. Sally Lester is handed a piece of buttered bread.

There are children around Peck, speaking to Maisie as she clings to his hand. 'When are you coming back to school?' a girl asks. 'Is your father going to be set on fire?' asks a boy, to which Peck responds by shoving him in the mud before pushing farther towards the stage. Eventually, room is made for the gang of chasers to climb the stairs to the raised platform, and Peck tells Maisie to wait by the edge and not move an inch unless he tells her to. She nods and looks apprehensive of what comes next, as Peter Morris is carried in a wheelbarrow through the jeering crowd, which giggles and spits as the prisoner is brought forward. Peck thinks to himself that this is a lot more energy than they ever showed during the whole time Peter was sat in the stocks. He remembers the applause that came when he cut the rope binding Peter's hands, and assures himself that people can get excited about mercy as much as cruelty, as long as a show is made of it.

When he breaches the stage, he looks to the wall in the west. Martin Moar had told him on the way that nothing new was up there. Too much attention on the gathering and Peter Morris's punishment, which has been a long time coming. The enormity of the wall remains, though, looming like a disembodied mouth, a pair of red lips flapping with speech. The presence of the chasers on the stage has sent a ripple of excitement through the villagers, pressing forwards to fill the space. Even the burdened, with their weights of drawers and cupboards, move closer and in their number Peck recognises Thomas Rample, who not long ago had come to Grace's tearoom pleading for help. There is still a nightstand bound to his neck, but he strains against it to watch Peter Morris as he is guided up the steps amongst a crash of hoots. There are cheers when he is tied to the structure of manacles, but the biggest noise comes as Brian Goss follows in his wake, buoyant in freshly polished shoes. Peck notices that the gang of chasers has stood respectfully in an ordered line and so he slips into place, keeping his head upright and eyes forward.

'Normally, I would let the captain of the chasers get things underway,' Brian bellows, loud enough for everyone in front of him to hear. 'But, as you all know, this is his first day on the job.' There is some laughter and there are some whispers. Peck can feel their attention on him. In the corner of his eye, he can see Maisie on the side of the stage.

'I wanted to do you all the kindness of a proper introduction,' Brian continues. 'Duncan Peck has not been here for much time, but a great deal has happened since his arrival and it has shown him for the upstanding citizen he is. Many of you have been impressed by the way he has acted, as have I.' At this Brian turns and beams in his direction. Peck senses Brian wants to use him. He suspects there have been conversations behind closed doors, and they have landed on Peck's freshness, his relative distance from the squabbles and the potential for this to be put to good purpose. Yesterday's giddiness has given way to understanding. All the same, he smiles back at Brian, who continues talking. 'So please speak to him today. Please take him aside and say hello if you've not done so already. Shake him by the hand.'

He beckons Peck forward, and when they are standing side by side he reaches out to grab his hand, or more accurately to clasp it between both of his own in view of the village, to which there is a prompt, dutiful applause. There are those who do not meet Peck's eye as he looks out on the gathering. He catches Grace, but she is talking to her neighbour, glancing at him only for a second before carrying on with whatever she is saying. It is not until Brian coughs that Peck realises he is expected to speak, and so he clears his throat, readies himself. Nudges are made and concentration is paid. Soon, the commotion has ceased. 'Thank you,' Peck says.

'Louder,' someone yells.

'Thank you,' he tries again.

Brian takes this as his cue to move to the side of the stage, where he stands beside Maisie with a firm hand on her shoulder. In the ensuing quiet, a muffled noise can be heard; the moans of Peter Morris as he sobs against his cloth gag. It is a pitiful sound, like a dying dog, and before saying anything else Peck turns to observe the prisoner, whose head is drooping downward. Maisie is looking at him too, her face scrunched with emotion at the sight of her father strung up. She does not run to him, though. She does not slip under Brian's hand and try to free her father, but stands exactly where Peck had told her to and something about this scares him. The stillness, in spite of the horror.

'Come on then,' someone yells.

Peck looks back to the crowd, basking in the light, waiting for something to happen. He breathes in and reaches for his voice. 'There will be a golden age,' he begins.

She had not been walking long before the sun rose, and when it did it had set the world aflame. It had ignited the night's rain, turning hills of wet grass into burning slopes, as beautiful as they were unreal to Charlotte, who had stopped and caught her breath by a wooden kissing gate.

Since then she has been journeying without confidence, grasping a path beside a low barrier made of piled stones. JM has been out of view for what seems like an hour, outstripping her with his long stride. The last she saw of him was in this direction but there is a tightness of breath at the thought that she might be mistaken. The daylight has given shape to the land around her but there is still nothing she recognises on the horizon. She considers returning the way she came, where she may well find her father-in-law slicing pony hide against a bloody boulder. It is not clear that she could return, even if she wanted to, given the darkness when she set off and the difficulty she is having in piecing the moorland together.

'Stop following me.'

The low voice is JM's, sat with his back against the barrier, nestled in a ditch where he is sheltered from the wind. Crouched on a rock, his water pouch in one hand, a strip of dried meat in the other. He has stopped for a break, it seems. Charlotte is frozen to the spot, speechless until her father-in-law takes a bite.

'Where are you going?' she asks.

He chews. 'Go back. I don't want you with me.'

'Are you going home?'

He blows air through his nose. 'James Hale is dead and the people miss me.' He swallows his mouthful and looks to the side, along the barrier that runs the length of the valley.

'You left me behind,' she notes.

He doesn't meet her eye. He wraps what remains of the dried meat in a dirty blue handkerchief and fastens his flask, then places both inside his backpack. There is shame in the swiftness of his movements, she thinks. He stands and feeds his arms through the straps of his bag. And then he is away, walking farther along the stone barrier. She follows, mind darting over images, uncontrollable in its flight through open windows. It has been torture, having the past brought back to her like this, but there is vindication at the end of this journey, she thinks, and so she puts one foot in front of the other and catches up.

He does not acknowledge her, but neither does he try to elude her. As they trek in silence the day settles into itself, and with it the thought that she will be face to face with her neighbours. In a few hours she will be back at the business end of their scrutiny. She will find herself once more with Duncan Peck, who won't last a week before he is kicked out or kicked apart. Maisie will soon be in her arms. Peter will be brought back to her and it will be time to have another child, finally time, so the past can be carried away and she can wrap her baby's clothes around a new laughing thing, loving them both, the living and the dead.

JM heads down a hill towards an overgrown road, following it as it winds between dense hedgerows. Soon they are by a brook to collect water, and then they are crossing the open ground again, the moor's anatomy laid bare. It is a warm day. The first truly warm day of the year. Both of them arch their head at intervals towards the sun as it glows; a great and good thing, Charlotte thinks, beyond doubt, beyond contest. It distracts her from the thought that JM does not want her there. The ground sparkles as they walk, as they pass the remnants of cairns, circles and standing stones. They move westwards, careful not to stray too low towards the mires. The sky may be cloudless but the bogs are deep, deeper from weeks of rain. Charlotte's foot is sunk by a misplaced step and for a moment she thinks JM will keep moving without her, but to her relief he stops and she is lifted before the rest of her follows. A pair of ponies is seen in a valley amongst the boulders, their heads touching tenderly. One nudges the other, its partner lies on the rocks unmoving.

He has not mentioned guilt, nor remorse, and although she knows articulation is not always easy it would ease her mind to hear him say it: that she was right to lay the blame at his door. The sunlight makes his tension clear, just as it makes the land visible. She wants to believe he has every reason to be tense. Close to a year has gone by, after all. But the way he keeps glancing at her, looking elsewhere as soon as he is spotted; it is making her suspicious. If she turns her back on him, what will he do?

As they pass a fallen tree she catches JM mouthing something to himself. Is he praying? Or is he practising the things he will say, when they make it to the village? For a split-second his face is a snarl, teeth bared. But then the expression disappears, coming and going for no clear reason. It's unnerving, but she does not mention it. 'Are you excited about seeing Maisie again?'

she asks, trying to find a stable point of conversation. 'She's grown since you last saw her.'

He looks at her as if she is a stranger, then seems to pull himself back into civility. 'Yes,' he says. 'My dear granddaughter.' There is no elaboration. Clearly he does not want to talk, but within a few minutes she can feel his eyes flashing white in the corner of her vision.

As they walk a dirt path that cuts through a level stretch of land, Charlotte swears she can hear humming. It is not coming from JM, though, rather the air itself. The sound is a single, drawn-out note, not unpleasing to the ears. After a few seconds it stops entirely. She looks around for its source and that is when she sees the shape, not far from them: a child hovering above the flat land, face pallid, arms stretched rigidly outwards. Charlotte can only stare wide-eyed, and when he notices she has stopped walking JM stops too, following her gaze until he settles on the apparition. He takes a few steps towards it, away from the path, then laughs a loud clap before turning and carrying on in the direction they are headed. 'God knows how that got there,' he calls without looking back at her, and only then can she see it for what it is: a child's coat wrapped around the top of a stone cross, its hood hung from the uppermost point.

The coat fidgets in the wind. The stony face below the hood has no mouth, no eyes, but there is expression in the mossy grooves that run across the granite. It's a sign that they must be getting close to other people, which should be a relief, but as they continue walking she cannot shake the image of a stone child from her mind, strange in the sunlight. As the ground curves upwards, as the path becomes fainter, she thinks about the face beneath the hood, features filed down to nothing. She thinks about the arms, reaching outwards to be held. It disturbs her, the thought of its sightless eyes pleading at her not to walk away.

After reaching the highpoint of the hill, the wall finally enters her sight again. The landmark is a ballast for her vision after days of unanchored land. She can't help but feel her attention drawn to its right angles. She makes an effort to look away, back towards the limbo-land that seems to stretch forever, the thin soil clad close to granite. She tries to look away, down to the stone cross, but her gaze drifts back to the shape of the wall. She cannot see the writing. That detail will come, but for now she can see its body. And the presence of it changes something in JM's composure, she notices. His tension is getting tighter, as if he is a coiled spring.

They walk a little farther along the ridge of the hill. 'Are you scared?' she asks.

He avoids the question. 'This is the closest I've been to it for a long time.'

'Does it look different?'

'No.'

She is keen to press on but he drops his backpack by a rock. A final pause before the homecoming. 'Why do you keep looking at me?' she probes, keeping her voice calm, picking up a stone to scrape the mud from her boot.

'I'm not.'

'You are.'

The way he glowers at her then. It squeezes her insides. But instead of walking on she takes off her backpack as well, settling it like his beside a rock. She rolls her shoulders and stretches her arms, and when JM crouches to open his bag Charlotte spies long coils of rope within, enough to tie a person's arms and legs. After a brief rummage, he pulls out two dried strips of pony meat, stands and offers one up. She accepts, and they chew on the rubbery flesh.

'Are you going to atone?' She can feel her pulse quicken as she asks the question. He doesn't answer, only lets out a long breath. She knows he is bigger than her, and she would not be able to stop him from pinning her down, even binding her legs with rope and leaving her there on the hillside, should he wish. 'Are you going to admit what you did?' It is taking all of her self-control to speak without her voice breaking. She pictures the stone child and tries to banish it from her mind. Please let him say it. Everything will be done with when he says it. JM lets his right arm fall by his side and she notices that his hand is clenched.

'It's time to put the past behind me.'

'So you admit it?' she asks, heart thwacking. 'You did something to him? I need to know.'

A crow sails overhead; the only thing in the sky except for the sun. He is about to speak, but cannot bring himself to utter whatever is on his mind. His head falls forward and she watches him shake it as he stares at the ground. When he looks up again, the expression on his face is adamant enough to snap the sticks that have propped her up. 'I have nothing to face up to.'

'I want to forgive you, Jacob.'

'I have nothing to be forgiven for.'

The howl that comes out of her is loud enough for JM to take a full step backward.

'Do you want me dead?' she screams. The question stumps him for a moment, but Charlotte doesn't wait for an answer. She picks up the stone she'd used to scrape her boot and flings it, hitting him straight in his mouth. 'Would it be simpler to put it behind you without me standing here?'

A wad of blood is spat on the soil. He starts towards her and she moves in the opposite direction. Before she knows it she is running across the dirt, trying not to lose her footing. A glance behind and she can see him closing on her, but she is lighter and younger and it is easier for her to weave between the granite boulders that fill the ground as it starts to curve downward.

'Come back,' he shouts. She leaps into the bracken as the hill plummets into steepness and she lets herself be thrown forward with each step, knowing that a foot wrong could send her toppling. She cannot see anything below her knees, so thick are the ferns, but she trusts in the ground not to disappear and runs with head pounding until, too late, his big hand is on her and she is being pulled backwards like a caught pigeon. 'What are you doing?' he barks. 'Where are you going?' JM's face is sweaty and red, but she does not let him hold her still; grasping his arm and twisting with enough power for them both to tumble, they fall through the bracken, downwards and out of control, jerking with each hit against the ground until they are bouncing on thin grass and something cracks against a stone, goes limp and rolls a little farther before coming to rest in a puddle.

---

Charlotte is on her back in the water, looking up at the blue sky as she gasps from the agony of a broken wrist. The crow is circling and she screams at it. The bird seems to listen, and she lifts herself on her elbows to watch it land on a small boulder close by, smattered with blood. There is the sound of insects buzzing. She examines the angle of her hand, the suggestion of bone beneath the skin. With an effort she gets to her feet, cradles her forearm, and hears JM calling. He is a few feet away, buried up to his chest in a bog.

'Help me,' he cries, reaching out. She walks a couple of steps, wincing at the pain from her wrist, but stays on the firm soil. His face is bloodied, his nose broken. 'Please,' he begs.

The crow tilts its head at her. The sun is bright in the sky. Charlotte stands and waits for JM to say more. There is panic in his eyes as he realises what is happening. 'No,' he says, desperation filling the word, but then something in him peels away. 'I cursed God. The sounds he was making. I thought I was able.' He looks at her imploringly. 'I didn't kill him. I swear on Peter. On Maisie. I tried to help him but I wasn't able. I should have done better but I did not kill him, I'm telling you. There's nothing I did to him. Charlotte, believe me. Get me out of here. Help me. Don't let me die.'

The ground is up to his neck, one arm already below the waterline, the other outstretched towards her. Charlotte searches for the truth in his face, keeps searching for it right up until the moment his mouth disappears below the earth, and then she turns around and slowly hobbles back up the hill.

'It's a beautiful day,' Peck tells the villagers as he cuts their bindings. The burdened have been commanded to approach the stage. Amongst a ripple of mistrust they have been given room to file forwards, one at a time, to the raised platform. In front of the crowd, Peck uses his penknife to cut the ropes that are coiled around a young man's shoulders, shaking beneath the weight of a leather armchair.

Soon the piece of furniture has fallen to the ground, coming to rest on its four wooden legs. Peck helps the man to rise to his feet. People are unsure how they should react, but they take their cue from the freed man, who embraces his liberator and cries fat tears of happiness. Slowly, applause spreads across the audience. 'The sun is out and spring is in the air,' Peck shouts, holding the young man's arm aloft, to the delight of some and the unmistakable booing of others.

'Stop this,' Brian snips in his ear. After some time considering Peck's commands with curiosity, it seems he has had enough and has rushed from the side of the stage. 'Scott Doyle still had eight days to wear his shame.'

'Trust me,' Peck says back, sprightly with adrenaline, then pulls away to gesture to the next person in line. There is an attempt made by Brian to grab his arm, but the portly man does not have the strength to keep him in place and ends up holding only air. The sight of this struggle has made the audience rowdy. Such open misbehaviour. There are shouts for Peck to get off the stage, but there are also cheers when he cuts the next knot of rope, this time holding an ornate cabinet against the back of a young woman with a scabbed lip. As soon as it crashes to the floorboards, she runs to the man Scott Doyle and clasps her arms around him, burying her head against his neck.

'It is spring and, whatever else it is, spring is hopeful,' Peck shouts, holding the remains of the rope above his head with both hands. 'What is more hopeful than this? What is more inspiring? The sun is out. Not a cloud in the sky.' There is delight at this, and for the first time it is loud enough to drown the cries of protest.

'There will be hard days to come, make no mistake, but they will be worth it for what we are building here,' Peck tells the people, and the emotion is welling up inside him. They see it too. The energy of the villagers transforms in front of him. Bodies are pressed closer together, hands held aloft. Above them the sun shines and it makes him feel as one with them. 'There will be a golden age,' he shouts. 'I promise you. Deep down I know it. Things are only just beginning. So let us be newborn. Let us remember today that it is in us to forgive.'

The rapture grows louder with each unburdening. He can feel the atmosphere branch outwards, stemming into new territory as furniture is untethered, as the chairs and tables and desks and cabinets and hat racks and clocks and drawers and bookcases are dropped in the centre of the stage, piled one on top of the other into a pyramid of faces and legs. Only when it is complete does Peck look at what is around him. All the other chasers have retreated to the side of the platform, where they are grouped around Brian, listening intently to what he has to say. Many of the unburdened villagers have returned to the crowd, to join their families. But others have been drawn towards Brian too, pleading expressions on their faces. How much longer will they let this display of mercy go on?

'I want to thank Brian Goss,' Peck says. 'For giving me an opportunity to show how much your acceptance means.'

Brian stares at him blankly from the edge of the stage. When the audience cheers, he is compelled to step into view. This is the crucial moment, Peck thinks. Before Brian can say a word, Peck offers him a hand to shake. The man in the polished shoes stands dumbfounded, looking to the offering, then back to the other chasers who are watching with arms crossed. Only after looking at the expectant faces of the crowd does he take Peck's hand, gripping it as before between both of his own. A seal of approval. 'Very clever,' he says in Peck's ear. 'Very clever.'

It is as if there has been a catharsis. The amassed villagers are elated, Brian's support for the impromptu unburdening giving them licence to celebrate. The smell of cooked food is comforting, and some have already peeled off to fill their bellies. There is laughter and mugs of hot cocoa clinked. There are slapped backs and warm embraces. Under the sun, there is a great public relaxing and conversations flow like rivers burst from banks. With a final squeeze of Peck's hand, Brian walks away, back to the group that had circled him, and they follow in his wake as he makes his way from the platform. Soon it is only Duncan Peck and the manacled Peter Morris on stage. In the midst of the excitement, the villagers seem to have forgotten about the very reason they had gathered. Peck scans for Maisie but, like a punch in the gut, he realises he cannot find her. 'Maisie Morris,' he cries. 'Where are you?'

The villagers that are still listening exchange looks. They strain their necks to see where Peck is pointing, towards the edge of the stage. 'Maisie,' he calls once more, and to his relief she appears, having hidden under the stairs in all the tumult. 'Come here,' he says, and is taken aback by the affection in his own voice. She holds his hand, looking nervously to her father as he slumps in the scaffolding. Peter lifts his head, watching the two of them like a saint amidst his own martyrdom.

'Do you love your father?' Peck asks, loud enough for the people to hear.

She nods her head. The diary is in her hand. An ache of guilt passes through him at the sight of it, though not enough for him to admit that he has read her nightmares. 'Tell them,' he says, beckoning with his hand for her to step forwards. And the crowd quietens, even those that have spread over the green, as Maisie Morris readies herself to speak. When she does, it is loud and clear, and she counts the syllables with her fingers.

'My father loves me, under the morning sunshine, as my mother leaves.'

The villagers wait for her to say more, and when she only turns away and resumes her place by Peck's side, there is feeble clapping. He touches her shoulder and can feel the muscles tighten beneath his palm. A few soft pats and then he is raising his hands above his head, approaching Peter Morris like a charmer to a snake. 'This man wronged me,' he shouts. 'But I forgive him.'

There is renewed anticipation in the remaining audience; they watch as, one manacle at a time, Peck loosens the clasps that bind Peter to the scaffolding. Eventually the prisoner falls forwards onto his fore-arms, totally unbound for the first time in days, and space is given for Maisie to help him stand on his feet. Peter is shaky, deathly pale. The skin has worn away around his ankles, where he has fought against the stocks. With his daughter's help, though, he keeps himself upright and the sight of it brings applause. There are heckles too but they are lost in the noise of the festivities, which at this point have diffused far beyond the stage to each pocket of the green, to the stalls with their pastry and bread, to the tea and treats. Everywhere, people are enjoying themselves in the warm daylight. And Peck looks out over the scene with a sense of pride. Deep down we really are fond of each other, he tells himself, and searches for Grace but cannot find her.

Behind him, Peter is embracing his daughter. He is crying into her hair, and when he catches Peck watching he looks up, red and bleary. He is about to say some-thing, but starts to weep and collapses violently onto the floor. Peck moves to help him but Peter pushes his hands away. 'Get away from me,' he screeches, and with a struggle brings himself back upright. Maisie holds his hand, and they head towards the stairs to hobble into the gathering.

No one is paying Peck attention now, and so he walks from the pile of furniture on the rope-strewn stage to join the people. There are gracious smiles waiting for him, but the villagers he passes are involved in their own conversations. For a while he lingers close to Victoria Bray and Thomas Rample, free from his nightstand, but aside from a cursory nod and toothy grin they continue their discussion without bringing him in. And so he walks, looking for Grace, whom he finds busy at work behind a tea stall. Feeling bold, he pushes past the line and surprises her with a kiss on the cheek. Her face spasms and the expression she gives him is lukewarm at best. 'I'm swamped right now,' she explains, and goes back to serving hot drinks. Perhaps at night, when things have calmed, he will pay her a visit and they can talk the day over. For now he leaves her to the work, and strolls on with hands in trouser pockets until he sees Brian Goss, encircled by a group of people. The administrator has them enraptured but before Peck can get close they have turned to him, all at once, and it stops him in his tracks. Observed, he offers a smile and Brian reciprocates.

'That seemed to go well,' Peck says.

'Yes,' comes the chilly response. 'It did.'

No one else in the circle says a word. There is a cough and someone nudges the ground with the tip of their shoe.

'See you soon,' Peck tells them with a small wave, and moves away, far away, somewhere he doesn't have to think about people speaking about him behind his back.

*Duncan Peck has lost his marbles. Duncan Peck has overstepped himself.*

Let them mutter, he decides, knowing that there were those who had been heartened by his words, his sincerity. His actions will have sent a message and there will be plenty of days to see it through. He wants change, after all. He wants to help things grow, even if it takes a struggle. He walks outside of the green, leaving the crowds behind as he saunters beside a field of barley, wispy and yellow, more yellow than it had been the last time he saw it.

He touches a stem with his fingers, plucks it and mindlessly picks at the grain, thinking about where the next field can be planted, and in which direction the village should grow. It won't be long until the sheep need shearing, which will mean new clothes stitched and given. He presses a barley grain between his thumb and forefinger, rolling it back and forth as he returns to the village, past the chicken coops and Grace's home, past the school with its outdoor toilet pot and The Calvary Cross with its mead drinkers, gathering around benches and basking in the sun. He passes the bric-a-brac shop with its lengths of rope, the butcher's and the tearoom, all of it in sight of the wall on the hill. He walks to the home of James Hale, now his own, and before he opens the door he thinks to himself how lucky he is. Just as his mother used to always say, there is goodness and kindness in the first signs of spring.

Inside, there are two things waiting for him. Charlotte Morris and a gunshot. The sound of the latter runs him through and his first thought is whether anyone else will hear. If it reaches the square, will it be caught in the commotion? That question is buried by pain, as Peck slumps to the floor clutching his chest, blood running through his fingers like he has squeezed a ripe tomato. He sees Charlotte sitting at the dinner table, one hand supported in a sling made of rope, wrapped around her neck, the other hand holding the revolver. The sound of her panicked breathing fills the room. 'This is your fault,' she tells him.

Her clothes are torn and there are deep cuts across her brow, Peck notices. The colour has gone from her face and her eyes are spilt milk. There is a warm sensation against his ankles, and he realises it is his own blood soaking into his socks. 'I let your husband go,' he struggles to say.

She drops the gun onto the floor with a thump and cradles her forehead in her good hand. Her shoulders are shaking. 'You've been nothing but trouble,' she says, her voice unsteady. 'Nothing good.' She looks like she is about to be sick and despite the agony he feels sorry for her.

The sun is coming through the window and Peck wishes he had fallen closer to where the light lands, instead of in the shade with Hale's welcome mat prickly against his back. Collecting his strength, he begins to crawl across the floorboards, but does not make it very far, drawing only a short red line towards the table. Facedown, he hears Charlotte stand and walk around him to the door, which she opens, walks through, and closes gently behind her.

Alone, Peck rests the side of his head against the floor and listens to what he can. There are distant birds. There is a thrum inside his own head. He listens for voices. He imagines Charlotte standing in the street, waiting for Peter and Maisie to walk down the road towards her. As soon as the girl spots her, she will run from her father's side, rushing as fast as she can.

# Epilogue

*SIMON DEW HAS BEEN KEEPING HOT WATER FOR HIMSELF.* SIMON DEW ONLY CARES ABOUT HIMSELF. WE PUT A LOT OF TRUST IN SIMON DEW AND HE HAS LET US DOWN.

THE SWELLING HAS ALMOST completely gone. After a fortnight spent inside with a balloon for a forearm, Charlotte delights in the fresh air. The sunlight makes her feel at home in her body once more, although the wooden splint still itches her wrist and she'd like nothing more than to pick up a twig and scratch the skin raw. It is as if Maisie can read her mind, because the girl distracts her by taking her good hand and leading Charlotte away from the wall, partway down the hill to a nook in the earth laden with hoary bones. 'Look.' Maisie has one foot on a stone, and points at the skeleton in the dirt.

'A pig,' Charlotte tells her, and bends to look at the perfect circle of the animal's eye socket. 'It was a pig,' she corrects herself, repositioning her sling. It must have broken free from the pen, some weeks ago by the look of it. One less pig to feed them. Maisie seems disappointed at the answer and runs away down the hill with her arms spread outwards. Her first week back at school has seen her coming home each evening with questions about animals. The kitchen has been full of facts about all manner of beasts, many of them no doubt consigned to mythology. Do Mother and Father know what tigers eat? Do they know the names of birds?

They walk to the graveyard overlooking the Blackbrook, where Maisie chases bees as Charlotte lays a fistful of wildflowers in front of Jacob Morris Jnr's headstone, before doing the same at the grave of James Hale. She doesn't say anything, only pictures his face, which is already proving hard to remember. It takes some concentration and the effort upsets her. On the way out, they pass DUNCAN PECK, chiselled into a small slab of granite on the edge of the field. Poor soul. Suicide. When Brian Goss heard about it they say he wept a tear in private. What a shame. There had been no argument that the newest captain of the chasers had lost his mind and taken his own life, which some said was foreseeable given his performance on the green. There was less certainty about what to make of Charlotte Morris's timely return. Brian had played no small part in quashing talk, making it clear the matter had come to a natural, if tragic, close. She had spent two days in the stocks and that was taken as atonement. Despite the fretting and fuming behind closed doors, not to mention the acid lingering in the eyes of her neighbours, it was eventually accepted that Charlotte Morris had been punished enough.

In truth, she does feel guilt. A great deal of it. She had her revenge, and for that is satisfied, but how much of it Duncan Peck deserved she does not know. If things had not ended so violently with JM. If the gun had not been there waiting for her. If he had not been alone when he opened the door ... The day could have ended differently. All she is sure of is that the anger she had felt so strongly has gone. It is as though a knot has been undone in her stomach. Life seems lucid once more. Still, there is guilt. On her second night at home she decided to admit to Peter what had happened. Beside her in bed he fell quiet, told her seriously that he never heard her say any of it, and has not mentioned it since.

She has not uttered a thing to him about JM. As far as the village knows Charlotte found her own shelter during her exile. She knows she should tell Peter, but how will he look at her then? The two of them have hardly been able to keep their hands off each other since they were reunited. Strange, what a scare can do. It's as if they have been living on a cloud and she does not want to say anything that will bring them down to earth. Each night she thinks about JM in the bog, but this too will fade, she tells herself. In a month it will be like a dream. Perhaps when she has more strength, perhaps then she will take a trip to the place her father-in-law fell, to make some kind of mark on the ground.

They walk towards the square, where her husband is talking with the other chasers as ropes are tied around Simon Dew and a wooden chest of drawers. After Duncan Peck was found dead, it had been decided that Martin Moar would take his place as captain. Given all the personal upheaval in Martin's life, it was felt a substantial task would be just the thing to perk him up. What a good idea. He had taken to it, and as soon as Peter was fit and able he had pleaded with Martin for a place in the gang. Despite being publicly pardoned on that first warm day of the year, there were still misgivings about Charlotte's husband, a great deal of them, just as there were about her. She knew this. They both had work to do in making friends, which was something they had neglected for too long. For the time being, though, tongues were bitten, and so Peter was allowed back into the chasers on a provisional basis, on the condition that he gave priority to his job as a roofer. It is good weather now but no one is sure how long it will last. The last thing people want is leaky ceilings under April showers.

In the tearoom they have two slices of apple pie between the three of them, served by Grace Horn who has a spare fork at the ready in the pocket of her apron. 'When you have time we should spend a morning together,' Charlotte tells her with a warm smile, and for a second Grace falters, unsure of how she should respond.

'I'd very much like that.'

When she is standing back behind the counter, Charlotte catches her staring into the distance, into nothing, when she thinks no one is watching.

After lunch is finished they head home for the afternoon, enjoying the last hours of Sunday before the week starts again. They sit and they play cards. They read and they chop carrots. Peter grasps her hand as they eat dinner, squeezing it under the table, and it makes her feel like a seventeen-year-old.

'Did you know that foxes are born blind?' Maisie asks.

'Are they?' Charlotte responds automatically.

'They scream like people,' Peter adds, rubbing his foot against Charlotte's leg.

When the night comes it is quiet, and Charlotte puts Maisie down while Peter washes himself. She wants to make this work. More than anything she wants this life of theirs to keep on, just as it has been today. She wants them to thrive, on and on, never-ending. In no time her daughter is asleep, and Charlotte kisses her forehead, wishing her only sweet, sweet dreams.

Acknowledgements

Thank you to:

Harriet Moore.
Alexa von Hirschberg. Allegra Le Fanu.
Lauren Whybrow. Katherine Ailes. Greg Heinimann.
Ros Ellis. Rachel Wilkie. Emilie Chambeyron.
The Society of Authors.
Jonny Greenwood.
My parents. My brothers. My sister. My friends.
Lydia.